TRIGGERED

TRIGGERED

A QUAKE RUNNER: ALEX KAYNE THRILLER

KEVIN TUMLINSON

happy**pants**books

CHAPTER ONE

I COULD BE IN PARIS.

As Alex Kayne clung to the suspended rails of the drop ceiling, covered in dust and fiberglass from insulation, hands and arms itching and aching from the pressure of holding herself steady so that she wouldn't fall into the room below, she reminded herself that she had a *purpose.*

But I could be in Paris.

She was on the run, sure. She could technically drop out and be anywhere in the world, that was true. She could disappear from the face of the Earth, in every practical sense, and so cleanly that the FBI and the NSA and the CIA wouldn't even remember she existed.

She could do that, and never have to crawl around in the ceiling of an office building again. Never have to sweat and train and keep a constant eye on every exit. Never have to pick up and travel at an instant's notice, living without roots, without family, without much of a life.

But she had a *purpose.*

And that meant she had a job to do.

Sweat beaded on her forehead, as much from the heat rising from the offices below as from the strain of keeping herself immobile. She felt the bead crawl along her face until it finally dripped from her chin, creating a tiny, damp circle on the dusty roof tile below her.

It may have been below freezing outside, in the blustery Winter that had come over Colorado Springs. But here, in the Palentine offices, things were toasty warm, even at night.

And heat rises, Alex thought.

It was certainly going to rise for Dan Trager, Palentine's CEO.

This was Alex's final incursion into the Palentine building. She'd been in these offices three times now: First on a guided tour; second while posing as an employee. She'd located what she was after, on that second trip.

This third one was just the cleanup.

The thin gap she'd created in the ceiling tiles was her only source of light at the moment, but it was more than plenty. In fact, things seemed so bright up here, she half worried that someone might spot her. But no one had come through this suite of offices since the security guard had last made his rounds. According to Alex's timetable, the guard wouldn't be back for another 35 minutes. Plenty of time.

She inhaled and exhaled, then meticulously and precisely moved her left hand, releasing the painful grip on the rail and nudging the loose ceiling tile over a bit more, widening the gap. She then double checked the line clipped to her climbing vest. The other end was attached to a piton wedged into the cross section of two I-beams above her. The connection seemed a bit janky for her tastes, but she'd tested it throughly, and had been mostly suspended from it for the past couple of hours. So far it was holding fine.

She'd been up here long enough that certain biological

urges had come and gone. Alex always marveled at this. Where did the pee *go?*

It was a mystery. And maybe a kidney stone.

The things she'd endure for a client.

She shifted her weight, moving her feet forward as she rolled her upper body up and back. She gripped the line above for stability and balance, and to keep her full weight off of the suspended ceiling. When her feet cleared the edge of the gap, she started feeding more line from the spool at her waist, and lowered herself into the room.

Slow. Steady. Inch by inch until she was clear of the ceiling tiles.

Once she was past the edge of the ceiling she let the line play out a bit faster, gliding downward at a quick but controlled pace, until she touched down on the floor.

She checked her smartwatch. She'd burned through nearly ten minutes of her half-hour window. She needed to move quickly.

She unclipped from the line and hastily made her way to the bank of lateral files that dominated one wall of the suite.

There were a lot of files. A lot of paper.

Physical, paper files.

Her kryptonite.

She could use QuIEK—pronounced "quake," which stood for Quantum Integrated Encryption Key—to crack any digital "lock" on the planet, and gain access to even the most sophisticated security and computer systems. It could let her peek into Palentine's servers as if she were in a sort of "God mode." Even the server admins didn't have the level of access she had—all the way down to the core machine code, if necessary.

The same was true for the servers of the FBI and the rest of the US law enforcement alphabet. Kind of the biggest reason she was on the run, when it came down to it. The government tended to get antsy about people who could access all of their digital secrets on a whim, if she cared to.

QuIEK could get her any digital information she wanted or needed, from anywhere on the planet, any time she wanted it.

But it couldn't get her a *physical file*.

Stymied by manilla folders and filing tabs. So humiliating.

The records here, however, were old. Really old. Some dated back to a time in Colorado's history when mining stakes were up for grabs by whoever got to them first.

Palentine Investments had managed to get its hands on thousands of these sorts of documents, each outlining claims for a number of properties throughout the US. One of those properties belonged to the estate of Eugene Harlan—the grandfather of Chris Harlan. Alex's current client.

Alex rifled through the drawers until she found the file she was after. Old. Stained by coffee and dirt from grubby hands. This file had been locked in a personal safe for decades, until Eugene Harlan had passed away, leaving everything in his estate to his only living relative.

Or attempting to.

Palentine Investments had sent a goon squad in the middle of the night to take the folder, and to force Chris to sign for and accept a paltry sum as "payment."

He'd had very little choice at the time. His signature—shaky, from fear and outrage as two large men with guns ensured he made it—had effectively given Palentine full claim to his grandfather's land, and all the mineral rights that went with it.

Eugene Harlan hadn't known that he owned one of the most valuable pieces of property in the United States.

Neither had Chris Harlan, when he'd started looking into his new piece of property. He'd visited what he remembered to be a rocky, weed-covered patch of ground that his grandfather had used mostly for hunting, only to discover that Palentine had illegally staked its own claim to the place. Eugene Harlan hadn't been in good health for several years and hadn't been out to see his property in quite some time. So he'd never known that Palentine had turned it into a cesium mine.

He hadn't known that his property was worth *billions*.

Cesium was big business.

More valuable than gold or practically any other metal on Earth, cesium was a key component in technological development. For decades now, the US and China had been in an arms race of sorts, trying to gain a monopoly over the rare metal, and thus establish technological dominance.

People had died in this fight. Chris Harlan would have been one of them, if he hadn't signed away ownership. By most counts, he'd gotten off easy.

And because of the forced signature, he had no legal recourse for reclaiming what was stolen from him.

But he did have Alex Kayne.

She'd come across a file on Chris and his dilemma in the FBI's database, and had noted right away that there was nothing being done. The FBI's hands were effectively tied. Chris was left to file pathetic and anemic lawsuits, which were swept away almost as quickly as his attorney could draft them. Palentine had billions, while Chris had just a paltry life savings.

Money had run out. The payment that Palentine had given him had barely covered the first round of attorneys, and they'd called it quits almost the instant they met with resistance from Palentine's own high-powered lawyers. Chris's pro bono lawyers were about to give up on him as well.

It was a lost cause.

Hopeless.

Alex found what she was looking for and slipped the folder

into the streamlined pack on her back, zipping it closed. She then used QuIEK to set up a bridge.

In her earlier, second incursion into the Palentine offices, she'd planted a half dozen bots—little microcomputers that were part of a vast virtual network she referred to as "Smokescreen." These were built with off-the-shelf components, and she'd gotten quite good at camouflaging them to look like innocuous things.

In many cases, in cafes and hotels and small businesses across the US, her little devices were disguised as just one more indecipherable component in an array of electrical utility boxes and wires and doohickeys. Who would notice one more metal nodule jutting from a wall filled with them? Each with labels such as "WARNING! Electrical hazard. Do not open." It was like having city regulators telling people to leave her gear alone, on her behalf.

For good measure, she sometimes affixed stickers with official seals, such as state or local government, warning that tampering with the device was a crime.

It held up pretty well. Few of the devices were ever discovered or taken down. And Alex was continuously adding new ones to the array, as she traveled, ever expanding the network.

Smokescreen helped her to keep law enforcement looking anywhere but where she was.

In the case of Palentine, Smokescreen would help her bring down Trager, and bring some justice for the Harlan family.

She had disguised the devices here as motion sensors, which hid the micro cameras and microphones that Alex had built into each. She'd kept all of this offline until now. But as she finished up and prepared to make her exit, she used her phone to switch on the local network. Smokescreen would link to the building's WiFi, and QuIEK would hack the system's security.

She was invisible now, as far as technology was concerned. But in addition, all of Palentine's files would be copied and mirrored to a virtual, cloud-based server off-site, along with a series of incriminating video and audio recordings.

Palentine's digital security was about to snitch on them.

All of this would be sent to Agent Eric Symon, of the FBI. Or, rather, it would be sent to someone in the FBI, and they'd be informed that Agent Symon had headed the discovery and provided some evidence. Local FBI would swarm on this place, and Agent Symon would get the credit for bringing down another bad guy.

Once Alex was well clear of the place, of course.

She'd given the FBI more than enough to work with. It should be a slam dunk.

The tricky part was making it look like a whistleblower within Palentine was responsible for the whole thing. It was the only way to get the FBI involved without making it look like they'd violated the company's security themselves.

There were plenty of candidates for the role of whistleblower, however. Palentine's shady business practices made for a plethora of enemies, inside and out. Alex had chosen someone who had enough shade in his own history to make him deserving of closer government scrutiny. All files were sent using the IP address of his computer. It wouldn't take much to track him down. Even when he denied having anything to do with it, he'd likely end up cutting a deal to protect himself, and turn whistleblower anyway.

Alex figured this place had about a week to live, and she intended to be several states away when the expiration date came due.

With the Harlan file safely tucked away, and her work finished, she clipped herself to the line once again and started her rise toward the opening in the ceiling. She was nearly there when she heard the noise.

She instantly knew what it meant.

Before she could react, however, the piton was wrenched free of the I-beam, and Alex found herself falling onto the desk below her, the force of her impact sending the computer and everything else on the desktop flying outward in a loud racket.

She lay there for a moment, a bit stunned. Blinking. Body aching.

There would be bruises.

"Hey!" she heard a man shout.

The guard.

"Stay right there!" he shouted again.

Alex hoisted herself up, springing to her feet as she leapt to the floor, even as every muscle her in back and shoulders yelled at her for being insensitive. She ducked, keeping hidden behind the wall of the cubicle she'd fallen into.

"Hey!" the guard shouted again.

Alex moved, scurrying on all fours to crouch behind the large copier in the middle of the room. There was a support column there, and it helped provide a bit more cover. She peered over the copier to see the guard, weapon drawn, as he moved cautiously toward the desk where he'd last seen her.

A dictionary of swear words went through Alex's mind as she thought about what her next move had to be. She shifted her position, crawled around the copier, and waited, crouched and ready.

When the guard spun around the wall of the cubicle he quickly scanned the scene, gun thrust forward.

Alex moved.

She leaped upward, springing onto the desk opposite of where the guard stood, and without wasting the momentum she jumped, raising her legs so that she slammed into the guard's chest, feet first.

For the second time, she landed in a heavy, rib-bruising heap on the desk. The guard was thrown backward, slamming into one of the file cabinets along the wall.

Alex recovered and ran for him, grabbing his gun hand by the wrist. The weapon fired, sending a round into one of the distant walls. Alex thanked God that no one was left in the building. No one but the two of them.

She brought the man's arm down hard against her knee, hitting him at the elbow.

He cried out in pain, and the gun fell to the floor. Alex kicked it away as she spun, twisting the man's arm, using her weight and momentum to force him forward. His body had no choice but to follow that line of momentum.

He rolled forward, landing hard and flat on his back.

Alex leapt onto his chest, slamming the palm of her hand into his nose.

Stunned, the guard made a strange, groaning noise.

"Really sorry about this," Alex said, and she pressed the man's carotid artery, cutting off oxygen to his brain. He was so stunned, he made no move to fight back, and in a moment Alex heard a soft grunt.

He was out.

She released him, checked his pulse and breathing, and then shifted him into a sitting position. She used computer power cables to tie his hands and feet.

She really had to hustle now.

First, she climbed onto the desk and replaced the ceiling panel. She then wiped down the desk to remove footprints. She straightened things up a bit, putting things back to rights on the desk.

There would still be some evidence of the tussle, but that

was fine. What she wanted was to skew the details a bit, so law enforcement would focus more on the assault of the guard than on her incursion into the offices.

With her climbing rig now on the floor at her feet, there was nothing left in the crawlspace above to indicate how she'd gotten in here. The guard had come in after her fall, and he might have a difficult time explaining what had happened.

She stooped and gathered the line and the piton from the floor, rolling it up and carrying it with her as she sprinted out of the office.

She found the stairwell and raced down as quickly as she could. When she got to the ground floor she burst out of the emergency exit, into the brutally cold Colorado Springs evening.

An alarm sounded.

Good, she thought.

She was worried about the guard, and she wanted to make sure someone found him quickly. But she also wanted to make sure no one found *her* quickly.

She raced away from the scene, straight to the rental car she'd stashed nearby. She'd take this to the van she'd bought earlier that day, and leave the car in the parking lot with a note and some cash for the rental company's trouble.

Before she got moving, however, she took out her phone and used QuIEK to access her Smokescreen network, particularly the array within the Palentine offices. She bridged into the building's security system and deleted all footage from the evening. An inelegant solution, but it would help mask her exit.

She finished up and zipped away in the rental, winding through the eerily empty streets of Colorado Springs at night. When she parked next to the van, she transferred over and was on the road in minutes. She hadn't heard or seen any sign of police in her route. Doubtless they were descending on Palentine even now, but she was miles away, and giving no reason for anyone to find her driving suspicious.

The job was done.

She'd get the property deed to Chris before leaving town, along with everything he'd need to re-stake his claim. When that was done, she'd be on to the next town, the next client.

She pulled the van into a gas station and sent a text to Agent Symon.

She couldn't resist.

Merry Christmas, she wrote. *Your present is on its way.*

A few seconds later, Symon replied, *Turning yourself in, finally?*

She smiled and shook her head. She had no doubt that Symon would arrest her, if he got the chance. It was who he was. She also knew that despite this, he also knew who *she* was. He'd do his job, but he knew her purpose. He also knew she wasn't going to make it easy on him. He'd have to chase her. And if he ever managed to catch up to her... well, she'd cross that bridge when she reached it.

Not just yet, she replied. She included a winking emoji, just for effect.

A moment later she was back on the road, bound for the next job.

CHAPTER TWO

Agent Eric Symon never bothered getting worked up over the text messages. It had been this way for months now.

Alex Kayne, fugitive at large, would send him some cryptic text message at any time of the day or night, and a short while later he'd get a package in the mail or an email or a phone call—some case would fall into his lap. Evidence would be neatly arranged. Bad guys would be smartly implicated. Innocent victims would be given justice.

A message from Alex Kayne invariably led to the takedown of someone pretty awful.

It didn't always lead to comfortable conversations with his superiors, however.

One of those uncomfortable conversations had just wrapped up, in fact.

FBI headquarters in D.C. was always an interesting place to visit, but at times Symon would be happy to go without. It seemed that ever since the events surrounding the arrest of his old boss, former FBI Director Matthew Crispen, Symon's face time with his new bosses in D.C. was all but pleasant. And now, with a high profile fugitive keeping him on speed dial, conversations could get even more tense.

He was being kept on the case, in pursuit of Alex Kayne, because after two years of her being in the wind, Symon was the only agent to have made the sort of headway he'd made with her. Like most agents, he'd "almost got her" a few times now. Unlike any previous agents, she actually stayed in touch with Symon. And... more than stayed in touch.

Somehow, Symon had become her "pet agent," to use the term his supervisors had repeated more often than he liked. Kayne would do all the footwork to take down some bad guy, and she'd call Symon to bat cleanup.

It wasn't that unusual an arrangement, at the heart of it. Plenty of agents in the Bureau had confidential informants or assets who might be criminals themselves, but were working with the FBI to help bring down worse threats.

The primary difference was that those agents had some influence and leverage over their CIs. Symon couldn't say the same for his relationship with Alex Kayne.

The bump in closed cases on his docket did have its advantages, though. It was giving him great numbers on paper. Sort of a perk of being in contact with Kayne.

But it wasn't exactly endearing him to his superiors. It made them skeptical and paranoid, and maybe that was rightly so.

Symon might personally think that Alex Kayne was innocent of espionage, but she was still a fugitive at large, and—only Symon knew this next part—she was still in possession of technology that made her a threat to national security.

Global security, he reminded himself.

There was no computer or digital technology on the planet that was safe from QuIEK.

The world was lucky that Alex Kayne had been given a

strong moral and ethical upbringing. It was the only thing between her and supervillain status.

As it was, his superiors didn't like the situation at all. They wanted her brought in. They wanted her held in custody and held accountable. Above all, they wanted QuIEK unlocked, and safely in the hands of the US.

He hadn't actually given them the full story.

He hadn't revealed that QuIEK was *already* unlocked. That, in fact, it was the tool that allowed Alex Kayne to move about freely in the world, despite being on every government agency's most-wanted list. While most of the world thought that QuIEK was dead-locked on an encrypted hard drive—a level of encryption that would take the combined effort of every computer on Earth a billion years to crack—Symon knew that Kayne actually had the software unlocked and running out in the wild.

Which, in turn, kept *Kayne* running, out in the wild.

Small and lightweight enough to run on her phone, QuIEK was Alex Kayne's superpower. And her secret.

Symon's secret, as well.

He wasn't sure why he hadn't shared it with anyone else.

Maybe it was because he *liked* Alex Kayne? Because he thought she'd been framed?

Could be. He had some level of sympathy for her, at any rate. He'd studied her enough to know her character, that she had a strong moral center even if her actual morals might be a bit "flexible." He wasn't telling his superiors about QuIEK, but he also wasn't telling them that he was investigating the cases surrounding Alex Kayne from both sides.

He was looking for anything that might prove her innocence.

That might be the reason he was keeping her secret for her.

Though, admittedly, he wasn't prone to favoritism or

special favors. Symon would arrest Kayne the first chance he got, because that was the job. Regardless of how he felt, he would do his job.

That was something Symon and Kayne had in common—they both stuck it out until the job was done. It was how Symon had *almost* caught her a few times now. Even when Kayne knew she was about to be cornered, she couldn't leave her clients in the lurch.

That's what made this so hard.

Symon believed her when she said she was innocent. He felt he knew her by now. He knew she was the real deal, somehow framed for espionage, forced to run or face life in a deep, dark hole somewhere. But his job was to bring her in. And he would.

Of course, maybe he kept QuIEK a secret simply because it was *dangerous*.

That made a lot more sense, in Symon's view.

QuIEK was the most advanced technology on the planet. Whoever controlled it could control the world. But Alex Kayne had controlled it, exclusively, for two years now, and hadn't used it for much more than getting some free hotel rooms and rental cars. Oh, and cracking into the computer and security systems of bad guys, not to mention the FBI's database.

Illegal stuff, for sure. But Kayne did it with a purpose in mind. She did it to bring justice to people who needed it most.

Symon had seen it for months now. He knew Alex Kayne was legit. Wanted, yes. Guilty, maybe.

One of the good guys?

Definitely.

So that could be why he kept the secret. And it was a doozy. A career-ender, if it ever came out. Maybe even a freedom-ender. He could be in a cell right next door to Kayne, some day, if things went just wrong.

He'd deal with that if it happened. For now, though, his gut was telling him that Kayne was innocent, and that QuIEK was safer in her hands than anyone else's. Whether that was his call or not, he was making it.

He left the D.C. offices, returning to the tiny apartment he was temporarily subletting.

This wasn't home. No place was home these days. Symon moved around so much that he had decided to give up his apartment and take a page out of Alex Kayne's book. He lived wherever he needed to live, in whatever accommodations he could find, for as long as it was necessary. And then he moved on.

He'd only been doing this for a few months now, but at times it felt exhausting.

Kayne had been doing it for the past *two years and counting*.

He could hardly believe it.

Part of him figured he was doing this so that he could get into her shoes. *Know your target, learn to think like them, and they're easier to track.*

That could be it. It was certainly right out of the fugitive-hunting playbook. But he also thought there was some part of him that...

Well, that *envied* Alex Kayne, in a way.

He'd never met anyone who was as autonomous and free to move about in the world as Kayne was. She could be literally anywhere. QuIEK opened up possibilities that most people could only dream of. She was the most *free* fugitive in history.

And yet, she stuck close to shore. She tempted fate, constantly. Several times now, the FBI had caught up with her, only to lose her at the last minute. They'd track her down again, somewhere else in the country, and promptly lose her again, just like that.

And repeat.

It was frustrating for the FBI, but Symon thought it might be sort of energizing for Kayne. Each time they'd come close, Kayne had regrouped, picked up new tricks, and disappeared even more. She was learning from every encounter, and getting better.

That was supposed to be the FBI's job.

It was counter to everything Symon knew about fugitives. Usually, the mistakes piled up and the person on the run inevitably collapsed under the weight of trying to stay off the grid and off the radar.

Kayne just kept going. Kept learning. Kept getting *better* at it.

It was maddening. It was brilliant.

Symon opened the little fridge and found some leftover pizza and a bottle of sparkling water. Not much, but it would have to do. He was leaving in the morning, on to wherever the current leads took him. No point in buying groceries, when he'd be on a flight out of town in the morning.

His phone rang.

"Agent Symon," he answered.

"Agent Symon, this is Director Liz Ludlum."

Symon froze.

He knew what this call was about.

He'd been avoiding making a decision.

He'd known this call was coming, but he still didn't have an answer.

"Director Ludlum," he said.

"I know it's late, but I got word you were in D.C. I happen to be here right now. Do you have some time? Care to grab a bite to eat, so we can chat?"

He looked at the cold pizza and sighed. "Perfect timing," he said. "Name the place."

. . .

THE PLACE TURNED out to be *Vial Grande*, which Symon learned was one of the most expensive and hippest new restaurants in D.C.

"Being backed by a billionaire has its privileges," Director Ludlum said, rolling her eyes and smiling as they were guided to their table. "One of them was getting last-minute reservations in this place. When I asked Ethan Patterson what he recommended, he told me he'd have his people arrange something. I wasn't expecting it to be... this. I hope you don't mind. It's a bit much. I'm usually a fish and chips kind of girl."

Symon exhaled and shrugged. "It's not the usual perk of the FBI. We don't even get discounts at Chili's."

Ludlum laughed, and Symon was relieved. After years of working in federal law enforcement, and the past few years under severe scrutiny and suspicion over Director Crispen's fall from grace, Symon knew that not everyone appreciated a sense of humor. He was still erring on the side of caution with Ludlum. Optimistic caution, at least, but he was trying to tread lightly.

He had looked into Ludlum when she'd first reached out, trying to recruit him to join Historic Crimes. Her background was impressive.

An African American woman, she'd gone into medicine to follow in the footsteps of her grandfather—a small-town doctor who had still made house calls well into his eighties. He'd left Ludlum his medical practice when he died.

He'd clearly been a big influence in Ludlum's life. She took on his practice, moving home from the big city for a time, struggling to keep the doors open. There wasn't much call for a concierge doctor in Alabama these days, however, and eventually Ludlum was forced to close it down.

She had other interests she wanted to pursue. One of those was law enforcement.

Leveraging her medical background, she returned to University to study forensics, eventually graduating at the top of her class. This led to her first job with the police in Mobile, Alabama, followed just a couple of years later by a move to New York and a role with the NYPD.

She worked forensics for various Burroughs until she'd risen (quickly, Symon thought) to the role of Lead Forensic Specialist. From there, she'd been recruited into the FBI—specifically as Head of Forensics for the newly minted Historic Crimes task force.

Recruited, Symon had noted, by none other than Agent Roland Denzel himself.

That was where Symon felt a bit of a hangup.

Denzel and his partner, Dr. Dan Kotler, had been instrumental in bringing down Director Crispen. And though Symon had never met either Denzel or Kotler, he'd gotten to know them very well, studying their case records, taking note of their involvement in a number of high-profile events. They certainly got around—they'd even played a role in recovering the Senate members who had been abducted by a terrorist organization.

Their names got a lot of mention, in the halls of the FBI.

Symon wasn't a fan.

He was willing to admit that he had some biased opinions about both men, stemming from his own hellish experience. It was because of Agent Roland Denzel and Dr. Dan Kotler that Symon had been forced to spend a couple of years rebuilding his reputation from scratch. The two of them had brought a lot of grief and headache into his life.

Symon had been Crispen's golden boy, in the eyes of the FBI. Any tarnish on Crispen had been considered tarnish on Symon, as well. So even after Symon learned that Crispen was dirty, and that he deserved the takedown, he still had to suffer through the scrutiny and suspicion and the constant derailment of his life and plans. All because of Agent Denzel and Dr. Kotler.

So yeah... not a fan.

Symon had come to grips with it, eventually. What choice did he have? He could be the FBI's whipping boy and continue his career, or he could go try to find work elsewhere.

There wasn't much call for tracking down fugitives in the private sector. And what little work there was didn't exactly appeal to him. Was he going to become a skip tracer? A bounty hunter? Maybe just a PI?

He couldn't see himself in any of those roles. He was law enforcement. It was something he'd dreamt of his whole life. Backing off of it wasn't an option.

Not without a fight.

So it came down to proving to the FBI that he wasn't tainted by Crispen's betrayal. Symon was determined to show that he was his own man, and a good and loyal Agent. He had worked hard to prove that to the FBI and was finally making some headway.

The prospect of walking away from that, after all the work and sweat and discomfort he'd endured, wasn't entirely attractive. It almost felt like giving up, leaving the job unfinished. That wasn't how he operated.

And there were other hangups.

Ludlum worked closely with both Denzel and Kotler. In fact, it was rumored that she and Kotler were an item. Symon wasn't sure how that worked out with Ludlum taking over as the Director of Historic Crimes, just as the department's previous Director was murdered. More than that, the taskforce itself had just recently been minted as a brand new branch of

US Federal Law Enforcement, with all the autonomy and resources that came with it.

Now that, Symon had to admit, was intriguing.

A whole new agency, with an oversight committee that included some big names in Washington, as well as billionaire technologist, Ethan Patterson.

The guy who, according to everything Symon had read, was going to get everyone on Earth *off* of Earth, some day.

The space race would now be a privately owned rush to the stars, it seemed.

There were also the cases. From what Symon had seen and read, Historic Crimes ended up with a caseload that could be described best as "unique." Somehow, this tiny task force that started as an extension of the White-Collar Crimes division had taken on some of the highest profile cases in the Bureau's history. And their close rate was phenomenal.

That could explain why the unit somehow managed to make phoenix-like comebacks, even after crashing and burning multiple times. If there was one thing the Bureau liked, it was closed cases.

All of those things made Historic Crimes an odd but interesting prospect. It was something new in the world, and something with some real potential for *helping* the world. Symon was being asked to essentially transfer his job to a new agency, which was unusual in every way he could think of. But it could mean some interesting new perks.

Fine dining in high-priced restaurants, for example—that certainly wasn't something the FBI would have popped for.

But it might also mean a fresh start.

That was one thing that did appeal to Symon. After years of fighting to re-establish himself in the eyes of the FBI, despite the fact that he had nothing at all to do with Crispen's traitorous acts, the offer to start off with more street cred and no cloud of suspicion hanging over him did have its appeal.

He'd just gotten on some solid footing with the FBI again, though. Was he ready to walk away from that, after years of working so hard for it?

Their waiter offered a chair to Ludlum, who smiled and sat, seeming a bit uncomfortable and out of place among the finery of *Vial Grande.*

Symon took his own seat, glancing around at the other patrons in the room. All were enjoying candlelit dinners, and most were dressed in clothes that would have cost him a year's salary just for down payment.

He felt a bit awkward, but was encouraged by the fact that Liz Ludlum seemed to feel the same.

"I'll have to let Ethan know that most federal agencies don't have the budget for places like this," she smiled.

Symon laughed lightly. "I'm trying to imagine what sort of response I'd get if I turned over the receipt for this place. Accounting would probably take out a hit on me."

Ludlum laughed at this, nodding. "Until about six months ago, it would have been the same for me. Most of the time, Dani and I..." she hesitated.

Symon saw something pass over her features. Sadness. Regret.

There was a slight glisten in her eyes as she continued. "Director Danielle Brown," she said, her voice firm. She shook her head and forced a smile. "Dani. She was my boss, and my friend."

"I read about her murder," Symon said, gently. "I'm very sorry."

Ludlum nodded and dabbed at her eyes with her napkin. "It's still a bit fresh. But let's not talk about it. I wanted to connect with you, to see if you'd had time to consider our offer." She smiled at him as she replaced the napkin on her lap.

The waiter returned with a bottle of wine, to which Ludlum nodded. She took the glass once it was poured.

Symon hesitated, but nodded as well.

"So, Agent Symon," she said, "have you given it any thought?"

Symon took his own glass and sipped, then placed it back on the table. "I have," he said. "I'm... still not sure. I'm sorry."

Ludlum shook her head. "Nothing to be sorry about. I'm literally asking you to leave the career you've spent your life building and join a fledgling agency that may not even be around in a year." Her smile was radiant, and ironically self-aware. "I'd really be concerned if you were willing to just jump without hesitation."

Symon chuckled. "Well, you certainly have your elevator pitch perfected."

Ludlum blinked, then laughed, shaking her head. "Yeah. It's something I'm still working on. The thing is, all of this is very new to me. It's something I'm not yet entirely comfortable with. I've led teams of scientists for the past few years. They're easy. Give them the facts, give them the objective, and they take care of the rest. But this?" She shook her head and sipped her wine. "I'm learning as I go."

"Should be about the same for law enforcement," Symon said, shrugging. "Facts. Objectives. Rules. We shouldn't be so dissimilar from scientists, I think."

Ludlum considered this, nodding. "I think that's a good perspective."

Symon sipped the wine and placed the glass back on the table. He thought for a moment. "I've looked over the materials you sent, and I've done some digging of my own. Until about six months ago, Historic Crimes looked like an on-again, off-again kind of thing. Just a task force under the FBI's White Collar Crimes. But somehow it..." He paused, huffing, shaking his head. "It just keeps coming back?"

"Like a bad penny," Ludlum smiled. "Some of that is due to Dan."

"The former Director?" Symon asked.

Ludlum's eyes widened and brightened. "No, sorry! Dan *Kotler*. Dr. Kotler. He's... well, he's an archaeologist. It's a bit hard to explain."

"I know about him," Symon said, trying to keep his tone even. "He was part of bringing down Director Crispen."

There was more edge to his voice than he'd intended.

Ludlum studied him and nodded. "That's right. I forgot you were part of Crispen's inner circle. It must have been hard, when he was taken down. I wasn't part of the FBI yet, when it happened, but I've gotten the full story. It was... kind of part of the DNA of Historic Crimes. Where it all started."

Symon sipped his wine again and wished for something stronger. "It was hard," he nodded. "I spent a couple of years having to prove I had nothing to do with what he was into. And I didn't, by the way," Symon added hastily. "Just in case it's still a question. I had no idea what Crispen was into or what he was doing. In all the years I worked with him, I'd never seen any hint that he would be wiling to work with terrorists. But he... he kind of groomed me. He was the one who brought me into the FBI. Kind of a mentor, really. I rose in the ranks a little too fast for some people's comfort, so when Crispen went down, I looked pretty dirty."

Ludlum was watching him. "But you aren't?"

Symon met her gaze. He shook his head. "I'm not."

She nodded.

"Director, I fought hard to get back to where I am. I had to take on a lot of garbage cases. I was still hunting down fugitives, but they were mostly handing me cold cases. *Ice* cold. It was primarily paperwork, and a lot of it. They tried to bury me under a mountain of it."

"But you dug your way out," Ludlum said.

He nodded. "94% close rate," he said. "I decided that if these weren't the cases I wanted, then the best way to be rid of them was to solve them. So I did. I put everything I had into it. Off hours included. If I was awake, I was hunting. And I got the bad guys. A lot of them. And it got noticed. Eventually I was back on higher profile cases. Which really just makes sense because..."

He hesitated.

He'd gotten a little too comfortable, which he tended to do. Symon knew that people saw him as having an ego, sometimes. He'd been called arrogant, and he'd often been accused of bragging.

But that wasn't really it. He wasn't bragging. He just *knew*. He knew he was good at what he did.

It wasn't arrogance, it was *awareness*.

Maybe there was a thin line between the two. But most people, including his superiors, saw it as arrogance anyway.

"Because," Ludlum said, "you are the best damned hunter in the Bureau."

Symon blinked. Then laughed. "Well... yes. It sounds less braggy, when you say it."

Ludlum returned his smile, laughing a little herself, which Symon found encouraging.

"Which is why we want you to join us at Historic Crimes," Ludlum said. "A lot of what we do involves hunting down bad guys who are really good at staying hidden. We have people on our team who are very good at solving puzzles and figuring things out with little to nothing to go on. What we need is someone who can get to the bad guys faster. Someone like you."

Symon shook his head, laughing.

"You disagree?" Ludlum asked.

He looked at her. She looked young. Very attractive. Not like anyone he'd seen in charge of something as big as what Historic Crime was shaping up to be. But she was also clearly and obviously very smart.

She reminded him of the biggest reason why he was hesitating. Of the *person* who was his biggest reason to hedge.

"There's a fugitive," he started, then huffed, laughed again. He shook his head, not quite knowing where to go with what he'd been planning to say.

"Alex Kayne," Ludlum said.

Symon looked up at her, surprised. "You know the case?"

"I've read up on it," she nodded. "Brilliant female inventor on the run? Evading even the FBI's best headhunters for two years? It's the stuff of thriller novels."

Symon nodded. "I'd read them. Maybe it would help me catch her."

"You're having trouble?"

Symon laughed again. "Actually... I've gotten closer to her in the past two months than anyone else has in two *years*. Literally had my hands on her. And she did what she does."

"What does she do?" Ludlum asked.

He sighed. "Escape. Run. Actually, what she does is think ten steps ahead of anyone on her trail, and one of those steps is to think twenty more steps ahead. She's absolutely brilliant."

Ludlum was smiling at him when he looked up. "You sound like a fan," she said.

Symon smirked and shrugged. "I am. A little. I'm also really annoyed by her. She has a habit of sending me leads on cases, so I can bring down whichever bad guy she's hunting at the moment. Only they aren't really leads—they're the *entire case*, wrapped up in a bow. If she weren't a fugitive, she'd be the best damned agent on the planet."

He shook his head. "And she keeps getting away. So... I keep chasing her. It's only been two months. Wait, no," he corrected. "Technically I've been hunting her for about nine months total. But two months ago, I had her. And then, she was gone."

"And you feel like you can't leave the FBI until you've gotten her?" Ludlum asked.

He paused, studying Ludlum, deciding if he could or could not safely say what he was about to say.

He decided he could.

"I am the only one in the Bureau who has any shot at getting to her," he said. "I *know* her. Not just her profile—that workup is just about pure fiction. It's written based on a string of bad assumptions. The Bureau wants her for espionage, but... well, I believe she's innocent of that."

"Didn't she collude with the Russians?" Ludlum asked. "Trying to sell that software she invented? What was it? Quick?"

"*Quake*," Symon corrected, smiling. "Q-u-I-E-K. It stands for Quantum Integrated Encryption Key. But I feel like the name mostly means that someone really wanted to call it 'quake,' or something equally memorable. It's essentially an advanced artificial intelligence software, and probably the most advanced code-breaking software on the planet. An evolutionary leap for digital security, in the right hands."

"And the ultimate weapon in the wrong hands," Ludlum said.

Symon nodded. "Which is why she locked it up tight before she went on the run. At least, that's what I believe."

"So you think she wasn't working with the Russians, but

she encrypted the software so that no one could have it because, what, the world was safer if QuIEK didn't exist?"

Symon shrugged. "Look at her pattern of behavior since encrypting that software. For two years she's run around the country helping people who would otherwise fall through the cracks in our legal system. I have a list of her... well, *clients*, for lack of a better word. They're all people who had cold cases on file with the FBI. They all suffered, with no sign of ever getting justice. Kayne helps them, and I think it's because she relates to them. She's taken down corporations and individuals that were bullying or taking advantage of people, circumventing the law if not outright breaking it. Hundreds of people, by now. Even though it puts her at risk of being caught and going to prison, even though she's nearly been caught a dozen times, she just keeps doing it. When I caught up to her in Orlando, she was helping a girl to get back her stolen prosthetic arm. It was the kind of case that the FBI put on a shelf, and maybe we'd get to it, eventually. Alex Kayne solved it in just a couple of weeks."

"And now Abbey Cooper has her arm back," Ludlum said.

Symon blinked. "You know the case?"

"I know all the cases," Ludlum replied. "We've been studying Alex Kayne for the past few months."

Symon thought about this, realization dawning.

"You're not just trying to recruit *me*," he said. "You're trying to recruit Kayne."

"You said you believe she's innocent," Ludlum said. "Why?"

Symon shook his head. "Gut instinct. That's it. The evidence says she's guilty."

"And you're determined to arrest her, because that's your job," Ludlum nodded. "That's admirable. It's why we want you on the team. Part of the why, anyway."

"But the rest is that I have a link to Alex Kayne?"

"No," Ludlum said firmly. "I want to make it clear, we were looking to recruit you before we even knew about her. Your link to Alex Kayne is the bonus, not the prize. We want you because of the very reason you're hesitating to join up. You have a job to do, and you won't let anything, not even your own gut instinct, keep you from doing it. You're going to do what's right, and trust that others will do the same. That's why we want you."

He laughed at that. "Not to sound cynical, but I don't think any of that at all."

She frowned. "No, ok. Let me rephrase that. You're going to do what's right, and then *continue* to do what's right, even if no one else does. You'll bring in Alex Kayne, and then you'll keep working to provide any evidence you can find that proves her innocence."

Symon once again studied Ludlum. He just wasn't sure. Not about what to say, nor what he thought of her. Or what he thought about Historic Crimes.

"You're asking me to leave the FBI," he said. "This job... it's what I wanted all my life. It's a hard ask."

Ludlum shook her head. "It doesn't have to be all or nothing," she said. "We're an interdepartmental agency. A cooperative agency, built from agents that come from every branch of law enforcement. You can retain your position with the FBI, if you like. It would mean some adjustments to how you work and who you report to, but you'd still be part of the Bureau. We have agents doing just that. Because we're new, that's just how it has to be. But we're also recruiting full-fledged agents to the team. That's a slightly different process, and one that may be a bit different from what you're used to. But it's an option."

"What about Agent Denzel?" Symon asked.

He wasn't even sure why. It was just a question that was clinging to his brain.

Ludlum sighed. "He's still deciding. I made him an offer—

well, let's just say I'm trying to bring him into a leadership position. He's been hesitant. Kind of like you." She smiled.

Symon smiled back, chuckling.

He knew what she was doing. Giving him common ground with Denzel. Giving him a path that would let him maintain his career, while taking it in a new direction.

He appreciated it. But still wasn't quite sure.

Their food arrived, and the two ate, continuing to chat. They meandered from work to current events to personal takes on movies and books and other mundane things. Until, finally, Symon dropped his napkin on his plate and sipped from the fresh cup of coffee that had been brought to him moments before.

"Ok," he said. "So—I just need to hear it plain. Am I being recruited so that you can get to Alex Kayne? Even in part?"

"You weren't," Ludlum shook her head. "Like I said, we had you on our short list of agents we wanted to recruit, before we even knew Alex Kayne existed."

"And now?" Symon asked.

"Now," Ludlum replied, leaning back slightly and holding her own cup of coffee in both hands. She sipped, and was watching him over the rim, then placed it back on the table. "She's definitely someone we're interested in."

"Why?" Symon asked. "A fugitive? Maybe a traitor? How could you ever trust her?"

"How can you?" Ludlum asked.

Symon blinked.

Ludlum shook her head and held up a hand. "No, I know. You *don't*. Not exactly. But the thing is, Historic Crimes has kind of a... *complicated* history. And not all of it is above board. There are forces at work, behind the scenes, that have agendas on top of agendas. And the thing is, one of our founding members has a tendency to... I don't know. Color outside the lines?" She laughed, shaking her head. "He's pretty amazing, though. And somehow, I see a bit of him in Alex Kayne."

"You're talking about Dan Kotler," Symon said.

She nodded. "I am. But I think your gut instinct is right. I've read everything the FBI has on Kayne. Especially your reports. And my *own* gut is telling me that nobody goes on the run, as hard and fast as she has, never stopping and never resting, while the whole time risking it all to help the helpless. That's something rare. And weird."

She sighed, leaning forward. "Basically, Eric, I want you to be a part of my new agency because you are the best there is. And because of you, I discovered Alex Kayne. And I want her, too. Because she's also the best there is."

Symon considered this and shook his head. "I... think I still need time."

She studied him, then nodded. "Ok," she said. "Take it. But can I get an answer in the next two weeks? Is that enough time?"

He thought, and nodded. "It is," he said. "But listen, Alex Kayne... I'm not exactly her handler or anything. If you're looking to recruit her, I think things are going to be a little messy. The Bureau isn't the only agency after her. The CIA, the NSA, even a few foreign agencies—she's a big deal."

"I know," Liz smiled, picking up her coffee cup again and taking a sip. "That's why I think she's a perfect fit."

CHAPTER THREE

This was not a perfect fit.

Something was wrong.

Swimsuits hadn't been a part of Alex's wardrobe much, for the past two years. In fact, this was only the second one she'd bought, in all that time, and apparently all of her measurements had changed somewhat. She'd even gone down a cup size.

Must be all the running.

She switched the suit out for another, and after peering critically at herself in the mirror, she decided that this one was better. A one-piece suit, but still a touch sexy and flattering, with the little diamond-shaped divot displaying a hint of cleavage.

She smiled at herself in the mirror.

Practicing, mostly. But some of it was genuine.

Because all of this seemed so *normal.*

It was kind of a treat, to be able to shop for a swimsuit at a touristy resort. It seemed like something purely *aesthetic.* And innocuous. No real purpose to it, but no harm, either.

So much of what she did these days was all about *utility.*

Everything had to have a function, and preferably multiple functions. Plans had to be meticulously thought out, followed by thinking through all of the ways to ruin those plans, then meticulously planning for the contingencies.

In a life on the run, from the best fugitive hunters on the planet, even wardrobe choices had to be stringently considered.

The Alex Kayne of two years ago could afford to be casual in her shopping. But these days, everything had to be part of a strategy.

Of course, the woman in the mirror looked nothing like the Alex Kayne from two years ago. She'd undergone dozens of transformations, since then. The way she looked, the way she behaved in public, the way she did something as simple as consume a meal—all calculated. All measured. All done with escape plans and contingency plans and contingencies for her escape plans firmly in place and top of mind.

No wonder she looked different.

Her current hair color an auburn shade, skewing a bit toward red, and it was textured and arranged in a stylish cut. Just the right look for a woman of means taking a little vacation.

Her cover story.

She was a little pale, but that was tough to help. She didn't want to risk an artificial tan—turning orange didn't mesh well with trying to blend in on the run.

What seemed more like a stark change to her looks, though, was how *trim and fit* she was.

She'd always been a little thin. She'd kept herself in shape, through college and into her career, as a matter of habit and necessity. Hours spent hunched over a computer, trying to crack the code to develop the most profound piece of encryption software in history, could take its toll on a girl's figure. So she had eaten well, exercised regularly, and kept in good shape.

Just not *this* good of a shape.

She hadn't realized how toned and muscular she'd become. Her arms had lost some of their softness, as had her legs. Her neck and face still looked essentially the same, but maybe that was cognitive bias. She saw her face every day. It was just that her body wasn't the body she remembered.

She was... well... kind of *cut*.

It was the result of all the running and climbing and training she did, she knew. Necessary. *Vital*. She had a rock climber's body. An athlete's body. A *fighter's* body.

She was as strong as she looked.

Being fit was good, but she reminded herself that it could also be a liability. It was easier to blend in when you looked like everyone else. Or what everyone else expected you to look like. Being "striking" as a fugitive wasn't exactly an asset.

But it was what it was, and she couldn't help feeling a little thrill over how she looked. A small pleasure, taken in a life that was otherwise full of chaos and stress and constant anxiety. It was worth the moment, to take it in.

She would wear the suit out, she decided. At the counter she passed her phone over the touchless pay system, using QuIEK to foot the bill. It was a little unethical, but the funds were coming from Palentine Investments' former CEO. She had fewer qualms about siphoning money from the corrupt, who seemed to have no trouble with piling injustice and suffering onto innocent people. Turnabout, she figured. Karmic balance.

Taking money from the corrupt was sort of like a fee, Alex decided. Payment for services rendered, after having gone to all the trouble of bringing these people down and taking care of her client. Payment for setting things right.

And since these people were the reason things had gone wrong in the first place, it was only fair to expect them to pay for the cleanup.

Of course, the biggest chunk of the money had ultimately gone to her client, Chris Harlan.

Alex had masked the transactions, hiding their origins and laundering them through a variety of channels so that no one could ever claim that Chris had anything to do with Palentine's downfall—or the CEO's coming financial troubles. From the outside, it would look like Chris had suddenly come into some inheritance that had previously been overlooked. And as part of that inheritance, he received the file showing that he was the owner of a very lucrative cesium mine.

Balance was restored.

Suitably attired, and attempting to mask her slight feeling of self-consciousness and vulnerability about wearing a swimsuit in public, Alex moved out toward the beach. She took at seat at one of the tables in the shade of two palm trees—a reserved spot, just a few feet from the Tiki-themed bar. Island music was playing, and there was a real feeling of the tropics all around.

Though this particular beach was actually on Lake Michigan.

It was a bit incongruous, being surrounded by the tropics with the Chicago skyline within sight. But the locale was tourist-heavy, which provided a bit of urban camouflage. Alex could meet the client here without worrying much about anyone taking notice.

Still, just to err on the side of caution, she had multiple escape routes mapped out. If anything went wrong, she could be in the wind within seconds.

In fact, this particular table had been chosen because of its proximity to a dozen resources.

Alex liked resources.

Just as she'd arranged, she placed her smart watch on the edge of the table, and waited.

She knew what the client looked liked. She'd studied him for weeks, vetting him to make sure he was legit, but also getting a feel for his life, getting to know the full story.

She had to be cautious with this one.

It was the first time she'd taken on a cop as a client.

Though to be fair, Kenneth Hebert—pronounced "A-bear" in the French-Acadian tradition—was no longer a cop. After ten years on the Force, he'd been drummed out and even spent some time in jail, on charges of theft and extortion.

According to his case file, Hebert was accused of planting evidence in the homes and vehicles of wealthy locals, then demanding payment in the form of cash or valuables, under the threat that he would arrest them if they didn't comply.

It was shocking and preposterous, considering Hebert's long and distinguished career. It seemed impossible, particularly to anyone who had known or served with him. Hebert was as straight-laced as they came. He'd never do something like this.

But there was evidence.

When the charges were leveled, a warrant had been issued and Hebert's car had been searched, as was his home and a storage unit rented in his name. Nothing was found in the home or the storage unit, but the car turned up some damning evidence.

In the trunk, hidden in the rim of the spare tire, under a carpeted mat, investigators found a stash of nearly $90,000 in cash and a collection of expensive jewelry and other items that some accusers claimed Hebert had taken.

Hebert was adamant that he'd had no idea how the cash or the items had gotten into the trunk his car, but it didn't look good. Hebert was arrested and tried.

In consideration of his career in law enforcement, the

District Attorney offered a deal: Two years inside, followed by five years probation, contingent on Hebert pleading guilty.

Hebert's attorney urged him to take the deal. The evidence was strong, the case was pretty airtight. The victims were all wealthy, credible members of society. Hebert was just a Police Detective with a lot of outstanding debt and a car full of evidence.

Hebert had taken the deal.

But as he started serving his time, he had a change of heart. He couldn't stomach being thought of as a thief, he'd said, when he'd served his whole career putting bad guys away.

Worse, as a result of his arrest, many of the cases he'd helped to close were being re-examined. Real criminals were being set free. It was as if all the good he'd done while on the Force was being unraveled. It haunted him.

Hebert recanted, swearing his innocence and publicly retracting his plea. He asked for a new trial.

Before the case could be reopened, however, Hebert had served his time.

Two years inside. A rough two years, to be sure, surrounded by criminals he'd helped to put away, constantly having to watch his back, spending much of his time in isolation, for his own protection.

All the while he wrote letters, passed on by his court-appointed attorney, asking the judge to hear him out, pleading with friends on the Force to help him.

But time ran out. He served the time. He was now free—a term that didn't mean much for someone who couldn't leave Chicago, and couldn't find much work in the city, either.

Almost daily, Hebert had to endure scrutiny, ridicule, and flat-out hostility, and he had no real means of escape. He was making a living with a series of part-time jobs, constantly juggling schedules, with no benefits and no time off.

A hard life. Maybe even harder than what he'd experienced on the inside. Especially hard, Alex thought, if he really was innocent.

This wasn't the sort of case Alex generally took on, but she'd come across something in the FBI's database that was tangentially tied to Hebert's file, and it had immediately gotten her attention.

About a year prior to being arrested himself, Hebert had been the arresting officer and a key witness on a felony case. The defendant was Jason Hawthorn—the son of Anthony Hawthorn, a wealthy business owner who had recently become a Congressman. With his wealth and resources, Hawthorn had won his seat with little loss of momentum.

There had even been talk of running for President some day.

Hawthorn was that kind of big deal.

When Hebert was charged and arrested, Hawthorn had been among his accusers. He had given the DA evidence that Hebert had attempted to extort money from Jason.

The evidence had been flimsy and circumstantial at best, by Alex's estimate, but coming from a wealthy and respected Congressman, it had been enough for the DA to push for a conviction.

That was bad news for Hebert, but his troubles went deeper.

With Hebert going to jail, the cases being re-examined included Jason Hawthorn.

Given the alleged extortion, and the nature of the charges against Jason, the Hawthorns got an appeal, and eventually the verdict was overturned.

Hawthorn's son was exonerated as the Federal case fell to pieces, and Hebert was blamed. This exacerbated the hostility toward him. No one liked a dirty cop, but they especially hated cops that let bad people go free.

The case against Hebert seemed a little pat, to Alex's thinking. As did the end result.

The lynchpin in Jason Hawthorn's case turned out to be a dirty cop, brought down by his own greed? All while a Congressman moved up the ladder of government and got a significant boost in approval ratings upon the exoneration of his son.

It seemed to Alex that somebody was playing dirty, but it wasn't Kenneth Hebert.

The pile of circumstantial evidence should have been the first clue. Evidence in his car—but nothing in his financial records, nothing in his home, nothing in the storage unit. Hebert supposedly had ninety-grand in cash stashed in a spare tire, but he was so mired in debt that he lived in a low-rent house in a shady neighborhood. He bought clothes from second-hand stores and shopped at discount grocery marts.

There had been nearly a quarter of a million dollars worth of watches and jewelry stashed in the car, but Hebert wore a used Timex with a cracked face, bought from a pawn shop.

Things just weren't adding up.

Or, things *were* adding up, they were just adding up a little too neatly.

Alex was watching the crowds, taking note of people moving through the maze of lounge chairs, dropping towels and personal possessions to save their spots as they took a dip in the pool or walked along the edge of the lake.

Tourists being tourists. Chicago folks, used to long and tough winters, out enjoying some sunshine.

Hebert was easy to spot. Maybe a little too easy.

He'd done as Alex asked, wearing shorts and a pair of sandals, with a short sleeved Hawaiian-print shirt. Despite this, he looked about as out of place as anyone could, among tourists and vacationers.

He was heavy, maybe pushing 300 pounds. And he was pale. His legs practically glowed in reflected sunlight. His hair was a bit long, though he did have this combed into a part, flyaways partially under the control of some sort of hair product, Alex assumed. His beard was long and untrimmed, however.

Frankly, Herbert looked like a homeless guy who had wandered into the resort. Which was a little too attention-getting for Alex's taste.

She broke protocol.

Usually the rule was she would let the client look around and spot the watch on the table, and then she'd meet their gaze so they'd know it really was her. They'd wander over, and things would seem just casual enough that no one would pay any attention. It was just two people meeting, maybe for the first time. Nothing to write home about.

This time, however, Alex felt she couldn't risk having one of the resort's staff intersect Hebert.

"Kenneth!" she shouted, waving him over.

He glanced around, perhaps as nervous about exposure, in his way, as Alex was herself. He'd been a public enemy and a pariah for some time now. Being called out could be unpleasant.

Hebert moved toward her, and at her gesture he took a seat across the table.

They were in a fairly private spot, far enough from the blaring island music that they wouldn't have to shout to hear each other, but close enough that the music would help cover their conversation. Alex had also picked a spot that would make it difficult for someone to walk up from behind. There was a rail running along the deck where she was seated, and the deck itself was raised enough that anyone attempting to come from that direction would become noticeable, fast.

Of course, Alex could be over the rail and off like a flash, if she had to be. There were at least three escape routes in that direction.

She flagged a waiter, and when he arrived, she ordered a drink and some appetizers.

The waiter turned to Hebert.

"I... can't..."

"It's on me," she said, locking eyes with him. "Don't worry, Kenneth. Get anything you need. It's covered."

She said this last in a gentle tone, trying to let him know it was ok. She was here for him. This wasn't some elaborate trick. She wasn't going to add to his suffering.

He shifted his eyes from hers, but grumbled an order for a burger and chips, and a beer.

The waiter left, and Alex reached out and retrieved her watch, fastening it to her wrist. "Thanks for meeting me here," she said. "I try to keep things as public as possible."

"Are you..." Hebert started, but stopped. He shook his head. "Listen, I really appreciate you reaching out, and it's been good to have someone listen to me and... and *believe* me. But I can't see how you can help me. Things are what they are."

"Sometimes," Alex said, nodding. "And sometimes they aren't. I don't think anything about this case is exactly what it seems to be. I've looked into you, Kenneth. I've seen your service record. Distinguished. Honors. Recommendations from up and down the chain. You never had so much as an unofficial reprimand in your file, and then this? So yeah, I believe you're innocent. And I believe you when you say it was Anthony Hawthorn who set this up. I'm going to make this right."

Hebert was shaking his head, as if all of this was too good to be true. "How? I just don't see it. Who... who was it you said you work for again?"

"I'm sort of an independent contractor," Alex said. "I've done some work with the FBI, which is how I found your case. I have full access to their database."

None of this was a lie, exactly, though it was a slight bending of the truth. With QuIEK, Alex did have full access to the FBI database, as well as all digital systems for every agency and government and business in the world.

QuIEK was her own personal digital skeleton key, unlocking anything she needed to help people like Kenneth Hebert.

And she really had "worked" with the FBI. Mostly, she'd given Agent Eric Symon and his team everything they needed to officially bring down bad guys, as a result of working with one of her clients. And people who did work without pay could at least call themselves "independent contractors," couldn't they?

She might be stretching things a little, but the real story was too complicated and raised too many follow-up questions.

"So you're what, a private investigator?" Hebert asked.

"Not really," Alex replied. "I'm a freelancer. I find cases where people have been victimized or suffered some kind of injustice, but the FBI and law enforcement have run into a dead end. Or, sometimes, they have nothing to work with. I'm pretty good at working with nothing."

He was studying her now, and Alex could see a glimmer of the cop he was. He was skeptical, doubting her story and her motives, questioning not only his good fortune but her veracity.

That was good. Doubt could keep you alert and keep you alive.

But she needed him to trust her for everything that was coming next.

"Look," Alex said, leaning forward. She was about to speak, but the waiter returned with their drinks and food. She leaned back, and once everything was in place and the waiter had moved on, she leaned in again. "I know you are going to have a hard time trusting me or anyone else. But you really have nothing left to lose here, right? If what you say is true, this guy took *everything* from you. He gets to go to Washington, to travel freely, to live however he wants, while you're stuck here, scraping by. All because you did your job, and he didn't like it. That's the sort of thing I can't just ignore."

"He's rich," Hebert said. "Powerful. He has a lot of friends here. If I start making waves, he can make things worse for me. It's tough now. It can be worse."

She nodded. He was right. Things could always get worse.

"I'll keep you out of it," she said. "There are ways. You'll lay low, and I'll make sure this is worked out without implicating you."

He laughed and shook his head. He picked up the beer, turning it up, taking a long swig. When he put it back on the table, he shook his head belched under his breath. "Haven't been able to afford beer," he said. He then motioned toward the surrounding resort. "Or time off. Place like this? I had to miss a shift just to meet you here. Lay low?" He shook his head, laughing. "That's a luxury I don't have. Can't afford to lay low and pay rent."

"You'll find you've had a financial windfall," Alex said. "A new employer has advanced you some funds. Enough that you can leave all the jobs you have."

Hebert said, skeptical. "New employer? Who?"

"Me," she smiled. "As of right now, you're working for Quake Industries. Head of Security."

He barked at this. "Security," he said, taking another swig

of beer. "Nobody's going to hire me for security. I can barely get a job bagging groceries."

"Full time, with benefits, and an advance on salary," Alex said. "Starting today."

He stared at her and became wary. "What's the catch? What are you asking me to do?"

"I want you to babysit my client, keep him out of sight, make sure he's reporting to his parole officer and that he's getting cleaned up and fed."

Hebert made an expression. "Who's the client?" he asked.

She smiled and shook her head. "*You*, Kenneth. You're my client. Your job right now is to go home. Stop by and get some groceries on the way. Don't overdo it on the beer. I want you to stay in your apartment and don't call attention to yourself. Take a breather. Get some sleep."

He was watching her, and she could see a play of emotions passing over his features. Mixed emotions that he clearly wasn't sure how to deal with. Something stirred, rose, then fell back. He was a man who had been so badly beaten by life. He was afraid to hope.

"I can't accept charity," he said.

"The hell you can't," Alex replied. "But this isn't charity, anyway. I'm serious about hiring you. I'm going to pay you to keep yourself safe. It's the only way this is going to work."

"What, exactly?" Hebert asked.

She picked up one of his chips and popped it in her mouth, then finished her own drink as she got to her feet. "I'm about to bring down a US Congressman. So sit tight, Kenneth. You're hired. Go do your job. Take care of yourself, and I'll take care of the rest."

CHAPTER FOUR

THERE WAS NO ONE, single way to start a job like this, but Alex tended to favor certain approaches.

First, she started a deep dive into Anthony Hawthorn. What she found was both colorful and revealing.

Hawthorn had moved to Chicago four decades earlier and had started working in the financial district. Over the years, he'd made several lucrative investments, diversifying and growing his portfolio, and expanding his wealth. He eventually parlayed that wealth into a business of his own: Hawthorn Industries.

The business got its start in textiles, but it quickly diversified into all sorts of revenue streams. It didn't take long for textiles to become just a small part of a much larger business.

Primarily, the company shifted its focus to providing support and resources to corporate office environments. The textile business became a vendor and supplier for Hawthorn's larger furniture business, which manufactured office chairs and cubicle walls, as well as higher-end furnishings for executives.

That line of business led to expansion into office supplies, including paper and other consumables, and then into office equipment, from copiers to phone systems to desktop computers.

As Alex dug deeper, she discovered that Hawthorn had leveraged the office supply business to branch into government contracts, where he further diversified. The office equipment side of the business got an upgrade, and before long Hawthorn Industries was supplying various support technologies to the military—GPS systems, handheld devices, communications systems, and an entire catalog of additional tech that grew more expansive and encompassing each year.

The real money started flowing when military contracts were on the table.

So did Hawthorn's contacts.

With each new foray, and each expansion, Hawthorn became more deeply connected to some powerful people in Washington. People with lots of influence. The benefits from these relationships snowballed for Hawthorn Industries, which continued to gain more government and military contracts, and more money.

A *lot* more money.

This was good for the bottom line of Hawthorn Industries and its investors, but it also paved the way for stepping up Anthony Hawthorn's own entry into politics.

Starting locally, in the early days of the business, Hawthorn ran for City Council, where he served for a handful of years. It was apparently just the appetizer he needed, because from there he made a bid for Mayor.

He lacked the support needed to win that office, at the time. It didn't seem to matter much, though, because soon after his loss he was back at it, running for a state office, which he *did* win.

Though from what Alex could uncover, the election results were a little suspect.

News stories from that time were rampant with allegations of poll tampering and ballot stuffing. There were even hints that people were being intimidated by local mafia.

Hawthorn's PR team had efficiently and impressively rebuffed all of these claims, and Hawthorn went on to serve a significant role in state government.

When it came to allegations of corruption, Anthony Hawthorn seemed to be Teflon.

As Alex kept digging, she came across archives of news stories alleging that Hawthorn had ties to local organized crime, though nothing ever seemed to pan out. The stories themselves were buried in the archives, difficult for even Alex to find, as if someone had gone out of their way to take them off the record. As it was, if she wasn't able to use QuIEK to dip into the backup servers for the Chicago Tribune and local news affiliates, she'd have missed these allegations altogether.

Nevertheless, despite hints of being a mafia puppet, Hawthorn's career in state government was actually close to admirable. He was directly responsible for several initiatives that led to school system reform I'm the state, as well as a number of community cleanup programs. These initiatives made him popular among state residents and voters, especially Chicagoans.

Hawthorn served nearly ten years in state government, with multiple reelections. And eventually he started his run for Congress.

Hawthorn's money and connections increased as he went, but so did his contributions to both local and state charities. His record for creating jobs made him popular among voters, as did his history as a man who had more or less brought himself up by his own bootstraps.

All that goodwill seemingly overpowered and even eradicated any memory anyone might have about insidious allegations and potential mafia ties. Hawthorn was publicly known for all the good he'd done. And so it was almost a shoo-in for him to win his Congressional seat.

That was the official stuff. The public stuff. Alex now turned her attention, and QuIEK, toward the darker side of Hawthorn's history.

Digging into Chicago PD's database, she found that Hawthorn was not always the sparkling-clean citizen he appeared to be. A lot of his record had been locked away, scrubbed pretty clean as he made his rise to political power. Alex was able to reopen all of those locked files and see the real story.

Multiple DUI's, for a start. It seemed Anthony Hawthorn liked his brandy a little too much. On one occasion, he liked it so much that he ran head-on into the back of a parked SUV.

That one had landed him and the SUV's driver in the hospital for weeks.

There were no charges on file from the SUV owner. But as Alex snooped, she found that all of the woman's medical bills had been covered, above and beyond insurance, and there was a very large deposit to her savings account, shortly after the accident.

An off-the-books settlement, Alex figured.

She kept digging, finding that Hawthorn's colorful past went deeper than drinking and driving. In the DA's database she found several long-forgotten files building a case against him for everything from monopolistic business practices to extortion. There were more hints of a connection to local mafia. And there was at least one suspicious disappearance—a local business rival who went missing, early in Hawthorn's career—

that somehow went cold after a sizable donation was made to the then-mayor's political campaign.

Threads. Lots of threads. Plenty that might cause Hawthorn some political heartburn, if it ever got out. But nothing that Alex thought she could use to not only hang Hawthorn but get Hebert back into good graces.

Alex needed more than what QuIEK could dig up remotely. She needed a hands-on, insider's access to Hawthorn's world.

She was sitting in a coffee shop in downtown Chicago, sipping from a latte as she scanned local and Federal databases. If she'd been anyone else, this would be a fairly low-key remote working scenario. However, Alex had to keep her mind on both her research into Hawthorn and on the surrounding environment. She scanned the faces of the other patrons, glanced frequently toward the exits, forced herself to do the checks again and again.

The FBI had snuck up on her before.

Seeing no signs of impending capture or pursuit, she turned back to her work. It was time to take a new tack.

Surprisingly, the FBI had very little on Anthony Hawthorn, beyond the hints of mafia involvement. But they did have plenty on his son, Jason.

Hawthorn the younger had certainly followed in his father's footsteps. As a grand start, he'd had his first DUI when he was just 14 years old—an incident that was not only sealed in his juvenile record, it had been erased from the Chicago PD database altogether. Alex had found it when scanning through digitized backups of paper records from the DA. Someone had really wanted to keep Jason out of hot water, and they'd done a damn good job of it.

It was hardly the only instance. Jason had a pretty spotted history, with multiple arrests by the time he turned 21, and more beyond. He'd been implicated in all sorts of shady business, including drug dealing and illegal gambling. And like dominoes, every time Jason set one up, the charges got knocked down. On the local level, at least.

The FBI wasn't quite as prone to bribery and corruption—something Alex was glad to see.

For about two years, the FBI had been building a case against Jason Hawthorn. He had graduated beyond the arguably petty crimes of his youth, escalating into full-blown drug smuggling. From small-time dealer at parties and raves, Jason had become one of the biggest importers in Chicago. And when he'd graduated from drugs to weapons—including weapons that were finding themselves in the hands of gangs and organized crime—Jason started to get the FBI's full attention.

It quickly became obvious that Jason wasn't the brains of the operation. If anything, he was just the face man. The guy people came to when they wanted things they shouldn't have.

This may have been due to his father. Jason's familial connection to a prominent businessman turned high-ranking politician made him a valuable asset to the right sort of people.

The FBI agreed.

Alex scanned through reports and debriefings, reading up on everything that agents had discovered or speculated over during their investigation into Jason Hawthorn. It became obvious that the FBI had a plan in progress.

Their case against Jason Hawthorn was turning into an operation to use him to bring down whoever was really behind the drug and weapons trafficking. They wanted the source, not the face man. And to that end, Alex determined, they were far more interested in the weapons than the drugs.

This seemed to be a relatively new business for Jason, however, and whoever was running it must have caught wind that things were heating up for the younger Hawthorn. Jason's involvement in the supply chain seemed to dry up suddenly—or to at least reduce to a trickle.

This was due largely to the fact that Jason went and got himself arrested, on multiple counts of possession of narcotics, with intent to distribute.

This was where Kenneth Hebert came into the story.

Detective Hebert had also been building a case against Jason Hawthorn, parallel to the FBI's efforts. He's spent months tracking drug deals, working his way through local dealers to find their source. And to Hebert's thinking, that source was Jason Hawthorn.

When Hebert had his evidence—a shipment of drugs in a large enough quantity to put Jason away for a very long time—he did his job. He got a warrant, organized a raid, and brought down a supply chain that was dumping narcotics onto the streets in frightening amounts.

Hebert had been a hero, stemming the tide for a bit. He had no idea that he was disrupting a larger FBI operation in the works. Or that he'd pay a high price for being good at his job.

Alex looked into all the files surrounding Jason's arrest, from both the FBI and Chicago PD. She also started looking at bank records for key players, including the DA, the Police Commissioner, the Mayor...

She was seeing the pattern.

Anthony Hawthorn had gotten better and smarter about his bribes, but ultimately he still had to move money from one place to another. And though this particular money started in offshore accounts, buried under dozens of different shell corporations, Alex could see that Hawthorn had initiated the transfers using his home computer and a VPN.

A virtual private network—a VPN—was a way to mask a user's online activity by shunting it through a server or multiple servers in some other part of the world. Essentially, it was like a shell game. The user could be in one location while their internet activity appeared to be coming from a different location. This allowed the user to appear to be accessing a file or website from one part of the world while they safely operated in another.

To anyone looking, it would be impossible to pinpoint where the user really was.

Alex used a VPN herself, as part of her Smokescreen network. It was one of the ways she kept the FBI guessing as to where she was and what she was up to. For the most part, activity on these systems was untraceable.

Unless you had QuIEK.

And, she had to be honest, unless you also knew the beginning and end points of the transactions. Even QuIEK couldn't peel back time and show her where a user interaction originated from, if there was no through-line to trace. But since she *knew* that money was appearing in certain accounts, and she *suspected* that Anthony Hawthorn was the one moving it, she could use basic math to add two and two and come up with *twelve million dollars.*

That was the total figure, transferred to half a dozen state and local officials, that led to Jason Hawthorn's felony case getting a softer touch.

Anthony Hawthorn had bribed nearly every local official who had any sway over whether Jason faced hard time. To Alex's relief, however, not everyone in the DA's office seemed to have been persuaded by dollar signs. Despite a few roadblocks and diversions, Jason still went to trial, and he still went to prison. Albeit on a much lighter sentence. Practically a slap on the wrist.

The FBI, seeing that the asset they were grooming was now a liability, dropped their case. They would track down the source of the weapons some other way. Jason Hawthorn would serve time for possession with intent to distribute, and Anthony Hawthorn would have a political black eye, just as he was starting to make his bid for Congress.

Except...

Jason did go to prison, but was only in for the better part of six months before his case fell to pieces—thanks to the arrest and conviction of a "corrupt cop."

With the implications of Hebert being labeled an extortionist, planting evidence and demanding payment, Hebert lost credibility. But it got worse, fast, when evidence conveniently appeared in the trunk of Hebert's car. That, coupled with a handful of corrupt officials who could suddenly afford bigger homes, meant that Jason Hawthorn went free, and Kenneth Hebert got the worst end of a plea deal.

Alex sat back, shaking her head, inhaling and blowing out a breath in astonishment and frustration.

There were so many twists and turns and loops in this, it would give John Grisham a stomach ache. As she looked over her compiled list, she saw immediately that there was very little chance she could leak this information to Agent Symon, or anyone else, and have any real hope that it would hold up. Or that it would result in anything useful.

Some of the most damning evidence was only available because Alex happened to have a cheat code to digital data. There was practically no chance she could put this in front of anyone in law enforcement and make any actual headway. The case would fall apart before anyone could even crack their knuckles and roll up their sleeves to start building it.

It was enough to convince Alex, however. Enough to give her the gist of what had gone down here, and to prove to her that her gut was right about Kenneth Hebert.

He really was innocent. This really was an injustice. She really did have to do something about it.

Now, the trouble was, she had to figure out *what* to do about it.

She looked around the coffee shop, once again taking in every face, making note of anyone who might be looking her way.

She'd been here too long.

As a general rule, these days, she tried to keep out of public places for too long at a stretch. She didn't want to lock herself in her room 24/7—she needed to stay acclimated and alert, to keep in touch with the world so she could blend into it as necessary. She couldn't afford to become agoraphobic.

But since her run-in with Agent Symon and his team in Orlando, months earlier, she'd been forced to amp up her paranoia. Someone had recognized her in Orlando, and that chance encounter had led to the FBI literally getting their hands on her. It was only her OCD-level preparedness that had kept her from being arrested.

She didn't want a repeat of that kind of dumb luck.

Alex at least felt pretty strongly that she was a lot less recognizable at the moment. She'd kept the auburn hair, but had it slicked back over her head in a severe style. Short as it was, the effect was a pronounced framing of her face, but otherwise her hair could be far shorter for all anyone would know.

She'd also dressed in a stylish black top and pants, both of which hugged her figure. Her shoes were heels, which were infinitely impractical except that they could come off in an instant if she needed to run, and the soles of her feet were protected by a thin layer of skin-tone latex that would give her traction for sprinting and climbing, if she needed it.

It was a little weird feeling, but she'd gotten accustomed to it. And she could slip on running shoes from her bag in a hurry, if she needed to.

Basically, all of her fashion choices came down to their utilitarian use, these days.

She took another sip of the latte and shook her head.

This was her life.

This had *been* her life, going on three years now. It was such a habit by this time, she almost didn't notice it anymore.

Almost.

She'd done this long enough to know, you never get used to being on the run. You never reach a point where you can simply *relax*. Even in moments where you let your guard down, there's a sense that, inevitably, *they will find you*. You will be caught. You will go to prison. It will all be over for you.

But you can only be so paranoid.

In Orlando, Alex had slipped. A few times, actually. It had given Agent Eric Symon and his team a chance to literally put their hands on her, and she'd nearly been caught a number of times before she'd managed to resolve the case for her client and get moving again. She'd had some luck, but the thing that saved her was preparation.

She lived and died by preparation. By thinking twelve steps ahead.

But even she couldn't plan for everything.

There was a chirp from her phone.

That was rare. No one had the number, so she couldn't get direct text messages. Instead, she used an app that relayed texts to and from her phone after they'd passed through dozens of modules in her Smokescreen network. Enough to make any of the Federal law enforcement agencies dizzy, if they were trying to track her.

She peered at the phone and blinked.

Agent Eric Symon.

Rare indeed was the day he reached out to *her*. It usually went exclusively the other way. She thought maybe he avoided contacting her as a sort of message: *We are not friends. Don't trust me. I will arrest you.*

Alex could live with those ground rules. It was just the way it had to be. She was the fugitive, he was the FBI agent chasing her.

Their relationship wasn't about friendship as much as it was about connection. This was a lonely life. Alex was often isolated from everyone, even her clients. Having a connection to Agent Symon meant she at least had someone to relate to. And it helped that he could sometimes lend a hand with bringing justice for her clients.

Symon might not be her friend, he might even be her enemy, but the two of them were united under a similar cause. At least, that was how Alex chose to see it. She and Eric Symon both worked to bring justice for those who needed it most. It was the one thing they had in common. And it was enough, for Alex. It had to be.

But he *never* called.

She felt her pulse quicken, and immediately shoved her laptop into her bag, then slung the bag over her shoulder. She turned slightly in her chair and slid her feet out of her heels, feeling the tacky grip of the latex on the linoleum floor. She was prepared to sprint if need be. She had multiple exits out of this place, already planned and prepared, beyond just the front and back doors.

She checked the message.

We need to talk, Symon had written. *Have you ever heard of Historic Crimes?*

CHAPTER FIVE

"I don't get it," Mayher said.

Agent Julia Mayher had joined Agent Symon from Boston, where she'd been working an assignment. She and Symon now sat in a hotel bar in Pittsburgh, where Symon had gotten a lead on Alex Kayne.

The lead had, of course, turned out to be fruitless. Like pretty much all leads, when it came to Kayne. But they did find one of her Smokescreen devices in this very hotel, disguised as an electrical junction box in the utility room.

They'd long ago learned that there was nothing useful to mine from these little microcomputers. They were really not much more than relays, running a basic operating system and a VPN. Kayne would connect to one from wherever she happened to be, and it would make it appear she was in Pittsburgh, or Scranton, or Poughkeepsie.

She never was.

And the modules didn't provide any way to detect where she was *actually* hiding. The tech team had even tried keeping the relays active and monitoring them for incoming data streams, but Kayne always seemed to know this was happening. The relay would fall out of rotation and go dark. Or it would provide some tantalizing lead that turned out to be a rabbit trail. Nothing ever led them to Kayne herself.

At any rate, these relays didn't provide anything useful at all, except maybe some insight into Kayne's psychology—which, again, wasn't much. In fact, Symon doubted whether anyone else, besides him, considered the implications of these things at all.

Kayne was a master at using misdirection. She planned ahead, meticulously. But she also used data and information as tools. More than that, she *weaponized* information.

Symon had determined that if they relied solely on digital means to try to track Kayne down, they were playing entirely in her field. She controlled that game at a level that the FBI and every other agency on the planet couldn't hope to match.

They would never catch Alex Kayne with technology, because technology was Kayne's domain.

Symon and Mayher were seated at the hotel bar, and Symon had just laid out Director Ludlum's offer. He'd also told Mayher about Ludlum wanting to bring Kayne into the circle.

"She's a *criminal*," Mayher said, incredulous.

"A fugitive," Symon corrected.

Mayher rolled her eyes. "Ok, an *alleged* criminal. But she's definitely wanted by the FBI and pretty much every other agency out there. What is Ludlum's game, here?"

Symon was swirling a tiny straw around in his Manhattan. He lifted the glass and took a sip. "I think Ludlum has kind of a unique perspective on this sort of thing. Her boyfriend is Dr. Dan Kotler."

Mayher blinked. "The archaeologist? The guy who took down..."

She hesitated.

"Who took down Director Crispen," Symon nodded.

Mayher said nothing for a moment, then shook her head. "Ok, so, what does that have to do with wanting to recruit a fugitive?"

"Ludlum doesn't think Kayne is guilty. She thinks she's been framed. And as a way to... I don't know... to *redeem* Kayne, Ludlum wants to arrange a deal. Kayne works as an agent, on a short leash, and in exchange she doesn't go to prison."

"Sweet deal for Kayne," Mayher said, a slight edge to her tone.

"Very," Symon nodded. "Sweet deal for us, too."

Mayher studied him, shaking her head. "Us? You said she offered *you* a job. How am I included in that?"

"Ludlum doesn't want me because of my winning personality," Symon replied. "She wants me for my skills and resources. You're one of those resources." He sipped his drink again and gave a quick shake of his head. "If you want to be, I mean."

Mayher considered this "So... you've made your decision?"

Symon shook his head again. "No. Not yet. I wanted to run it by you first. And by..."

He stopped, staring ahead, not meeting Mayher's eyes.

"And by Kayne," Mayher said.

Symon sighed. "Yeah. Look, I don't think Kayne is a deal breaker for Ludlum. But I do think she's sweetening the pot a little. Ludlum is smart. She sees the potential in this. I think she wants to set things right for Kayne, but I think she also wants to build a team that can serve the angels."

"What about the software? QuIEK?" Mayher shook her head. "The government isn't going to let her keep that locked up. Not after all this time and all the resources that have been put into play trying to unlock it."

Symon measured his next words. Mayher didn't know that

QuIEK was not actually locked onto the servers of Populus—Alex Kayne's old company. Instead, Symon believed that the government was busy trying to crack the world's biggest red herring.

Kayne was playing three-card monte with law enforcement. The government had put its money on the card they thought would get them QuIEK, while all the while Alex Kayne was out actively using the software out in the world. She had moved the queen, and when that fact came out it was going to cause things to heat up.

"Any deal Ludlum cuts with Kayne will probably involve QuIEK," Symon said. "She turns that over to the government, and maybe she gets to stay out of prison. She'd be on a leash, but she'd be free. More or less."

Mayher huffed. "Ok. Well, what do you know about Ludlum? She was FBI, right?"

"She headed Forensics for Historic Crimes, when Agent Roland Denzel was in charge."

"And he's not anymore?"

"Hasn't been for a long while," Symon replied. "Ludlum has been courting him to be her number two, though."

Mayher was studying him. "How do you feel about Denzel being a part of this? Maybe even being someone you report to?"

It was a fair question, if a bit complicated. Symon wasn't sure *how* he felt.

He shrugged. "Part of the deal. If I do this, Denzel and I will have to interact. I can't fault the guy for doing his job and bringing Crispen down. The Director was corrupt. It was his own fault, not Denzel's."

Mayher shook her head and sipped her own drink. "How very pragmatic of you," she said. "But you went through hell for years after that. You gotta have some kind of grudge."

Symon scowled. "We're adults and we're Federal Agents," he said. "We'll deal."

Mayher nodded. "If you say so. And, what... you're trying to recruit *me*, now?"

"I'm asking if you're interested," Symon replied.

"And what about Ludlum? Is she interested? In me?"

"She knows I'm here, and that we're having this conversation. She's looked at your personnel file. She thinks you'd be a good addition to the team."

Mayher shook her head. "Historic Crimes," she said, then laughed. "What kind of name is that for an agency?"

"Something new," Symon replied. "It's weird. But coming together, I think. Ludlum tells me it's interagency and interdepartmental. Like a governing body over a wide team of assets. We'd still be FBI, but we'd report to this new agency." He chuckled. "To be honest, I still haven't made up my mind about any of this, which is the other reason I wanted to talk to you. I just don't know the right move to make yet. But... I think I wouldn't want to make it without you."

Mayher's eyes widened. "Agent Symon, did you just push all responsibility for this decision onto my shoulders?"

Symon laughed. "Not quite. But your opinion does carry some weight in this. I'm telling you that it will influence my decision."

Mayher rolled her eyes. "Ok, fine. I need to do some vetting, though. Check out Ludlum and Historic Crimes. See what I'm getting into."

Symon nodded and picked up his phone from the bar. He made a few swipes and taps, and Mayher heard a chime from her own phone. "Everything I'm allowed to give you," Symon said. "Ludlum wanted to make sure you had plenty of material to start with. She's apparently had some personal experience looking into the background and history of Historic Crimes."

Mayher looked over what was there and shook her head. "Ok, then. This is real."

"Very real," Symon replied. He paused, inhaled and exhaled. "Julia, I'm serious. If this happens, I want you to be a part of it with me. You're a good agent. We work well together. I want you on my team. And honestly, it's a deal breaker. So if you say no, or if Ludlum says no, then it's no from me, too."

Mayher picked up her drink for another sip, shaking her head. She hesitated, then said, "I'll do my due diligence, for my part. I can't control whether Ludlum wants me in or not."

"Do what you need to do," Symon replied. "I'll handle the rest. Also... I think it might go without saying, but don't mention this to anyone in the trees above us. I don't think anyone in the FBI knows about this offer, and I'd rather keep it that way."

Mayher nodded. "No problem," she said.

There was a chime, and Agent Symon looked at his phone. He huffed and nodded. "Ok," he said. "Now that I've talked you through this, it's time to have a conversation with Alex Kayne."

"That was her?" Mayher asked.

Symon held up the phone to show her Kayne's message.

Ok, color me intrigued. Get on a laptop and go to this IP address: 10.12.19.72. *Password, SWORDFISH.* 9 PM *your time.*

"Swordfish?" Mayher said, looking up and grinning. "Like from the Marx Brother's movie? Isn't that the password used in every spy movie ever?"

"What can I say?" Symon shrugged. "Kayne likes her tropes."

CHAPTER SIX

AFTER HER TALK with Agent Symon, Alex leaned back, stunned.

An offer to come in from the cold. A chance to legitimize the work she was doing, and to stop the chase.

No more running. No more hiding. No more endless planning, mapping out escape routes and contingencies and contingencies for her escape routes.

She could live a normal life.

It seemed too good to be true.

Which meant it probably *was* too good to be true.

She had come across "Historic Crimes" during a few of her forays into the FBI's database and had seen it as a curiosity. There were odd things happening with that task force—stuff that Alex found intriguing, but usually didn't have time to dig into.

She'd never bothered to look closely at it.

And now it was becoming its own full-fledged branch of law enforcement—sort of. It was still an interdepartmental, inter-agency organization. It would just have its own, autonomous systems, with oversight from a board composed of government officials and private citizens.

Bizarre.

Even more bizarre that the new Director wanted *Alex* to be a part of it.

Was it a trap?

Could be, she figured. She'd known Agent Symon for a few months now, but had dug so deep into his history that she could tell him what he'd had for breakfast on this day six years ago. She knew that he'd arrest her the instant he had the opportunity, and he'd use any subterfuge or ruse necessary to lure her out into the open.

It was something Alex kind of liked about him.

But she also knew that Symon wasn't stupid. He had to know that Alex would dig into this, to determine how real this was, and what it would mean.

And she would.

She just couldn't do it *right now*. Not while she was in the middle of a case and still trying to get a grip on how she was going to bring justice for Kenneth Hebert.

Alex made some notes in a document in the cloud. She'd look into Director Liz Ludlum and Historic Crimes. And, just as she promised Agent Symon, she'd give an answer, in a couple of weeks.

She shook her head.

Come in from the cold.

Standing from the little desk, tucked into one corner of the single-room Airbnb, Alex stretched. It had been a day of sitting, hunched over her computer, not getting much exercise. Too much coffee. She was wide awake. She glanced back at her laptop. She could probably put in some more time, do some more research. Either do some more digging in Kenneth Hebert's case or start looking into Historic Crimes.

Or she could go for a walk.

That sounded better. A chance to let her muscles unspool, to let her blood flow, to let all of these new thoughts play out.

But first, she started cleaning up the little apartment.

She had hung blankets all around, as a way to both disguise her environment and to dampen sound from the outside. Both could have been clues the FBI could use to track her current location. Ambient noise could be like fingerprints, depending on where you were. Podunk little towns in flyover states usually weren't a problem, but cities—like Chicago—could have "tells." A local church bell, a train whistle, the sound of a band playing at a local restaurant—any of these could be a dead giveaway.

So could the decor of the Airbnb or hotel room she was in. All it would take was a screen grab, and the FBI could run the image against publicly available listings online.

There was a time and place to drop clues for the hunters to find her. But that sort of thing needed to be tightly controlled and coordinated so that the exposure worked as part of a plan.

It was a lot to consider. A lot of thought and work and effort and energy. It was exhausting.

It was exactly the sort of thing she could stop worrying about, all the time, if this offer to join Historic Crimes turned out to be legit.

She finished pulling down the blankets, folding them neatly and storing them in the top of the little closet. She tidied up a bit more, then took a breath, pulled on a wig and a ball cap, and left.

She'd walk the city for a bit, thinking about Liz Ludlum's offer. Later, she'd dig in and find out everything she could about Ludlum and Historic Crimes. For now, she needed the exercise, needed to clear her head and get her brain off of any single set of tracks of thinking she might have lapsed into. She needed distraction, needed to let her mind wander, so that new, good ideas could have a shot at emerging.

It would never do to keep her mind locked on only one way of thinking. Nearly three years on the road had taught her that.

So for tonight, she was a city wanderer, out for some fresh nighttime air and a little exercise. No real agenda. No place she needed to be.

Tomorrow morning, however, Alex had plans.

It was time to visit Congressman Anthony Hawthorn.

HAWTHORN WAS HOME BETWEEN SESSIONS, which made things a lot easier.

And *what a home.*

As mansions went, it was one of the most mansiony she'd ever seen. If Alex were pressed to put a term to it, she'd have to go with "palatial."

Located well off of the beaten path, outside of Chicago proper, the house was just one of several buildings that were part of a sprawling estate. Trees grew in groves all around, providing privacy but also obfuscating the home from the approach of any vehicles. The residents—or their security team —would know if someone was approaching miles ahead of their arrival.

The house itself was epic in proportions. It resembled a modernized British Abbey, with white stone that rose in towers, and a roof of gleaming copper. Seated on a rise in the land-scape, it overlooked a number of outbuildings. Ostentatious indeed, for a Congressman. Business was clearly good for Hawthorn Industries.

Even when Alex had been counted among the rich and wealthy in the tech industry, she'd never been comfortable with this kind of display. She had her indulgences, for sure—a very nice and very expensive apartment that overlooked San Francisco, a Tesla, fine clothes. She wasn't averse to nice things, she just wasn't into advertising her assets.

Showing off everything you have just tells everyone where to hit you and make it hurt.

Her Papa Kayne's voice always popped up when she needed a wisdom refresher.

And he was right. Alex took note of exactly where she could hit Hawthorn and make it hurt, if it came to it. He'd given her some hints at his tender spots.

As she pulled the rented BMW up to the front of Hawthorn's home, she was greeted by a valet—one of several people Hawthorn employed to keep his estate in order. More outward signs of wealth, but also a hint at some of Hawthorn's psychology. He kept himself insulated, with plenty of layers between him and outsiders.

She handed over the keys to the rental car, and was escorted into the house, then led to a sitting room where she was offered refreshments and told to wait. She graciously accepted a sparkling water.

Today, Alex was dressed in a smart-looking women's pant suit. Her hair was longer, thanks to extensions, but it was slicked back and tied in a tight, all-business bun. She was wearing only a touch of makeup—enough to even out her complexion, with a dark shade of lipstick making her lips seem fuller than they were.

Makeup tricks—picked up from YouTube—had become one of Alex's favorite ways to completely change her appearance. She'd never been much for makeup before, but seeing artists expertly shift their features into a whole new look was enough to convince her. The transformations could be extreme.

In this case, however, subtle did the trick.

All of this added up to give her a severe, all-business look, which was exactly what she was going for.

As she waited in the sitting room, sipping sparkling water, Alex scanned the shelves and furnishings. Hawthorn may have been ostentatious in the size and display of his home, but he was austere in his choice of decor. Everything was tasteful and comforting. Nothing seemed garish or gaudy. Hawthorn had taste.

Or his decorators did.

It was several minutes before Alex heard the click of a door open from one side of the sitting room. That space had been simply a blank wall, to the casual observer, but it opened outward as a butler stepped into the room, holding the door for Congressman Hawthorn as he made his entrance.

More hints at Hawthorn's psychology. He came in from an unexpected direction, instead of through the door. His entrance was camouflaged. He had someone introduce him, so he could appear elevated. He watched instead of speaking, taking in the other person's demeanor, their expressions, their body language.

He observed and calculated, and he used his wealth to control others.

The butler introduced the two of them, and then left through the same door, clicking it back into place until it disappeared as a seamless part of the wall, once again.

"Miss Royal," Hawthorn said, giving her a nod, using the assumed name Alex had given. "I was intrigued by your email." He motioned for her to take a seat across from him, at two plush antique chairs. There was a small, ornate coffee table between them.

Alex smiled and took her seat. "Thank you, Congressman. I had hoped you would be."

"Call me Anthony," Hawthorn smiled.

Alex nodded. "Anthony," she said. "You may call me Regina."

Hawthorn chuckled. "Regina Royal," he said, shaking his head. "Your parents must have had a sense of humor. Doesn't Regina mean 'queen?'"

Alex smiled, nodding, feigning being impressed by his knowledge. "Yes, it does! And yes, they did. Or... it might be more accurate to say they had *aspirations*. My mother, in particular, had grand plans for my life."

Hawthorn nodded. "Parents often do. My own father pushed me to make the grades I'd need to enter into Princeton. And I did," he said, his tone jubilant. "Full scholarship, though I did have to work my way through."

"In finance," Alex said, nodding.

Hawthorn looked amused. "You've done your research."

"I always do my research, Congressman... I mean, *Anthony*. That's why I'm here."

Hawthorn studied her for a moment, then suddenly stood. "Would you care for a refresh of your..." he indicated her drink.

"Sparkling water," she nodded. "Please."

Hawthorn took the glass and walked to a small wet bar. As he busied himself with pouring her another sparkling water and himself something amber and dark, Alex took her phone out of her hip pocket. She used QuIEK to run a pre-programmed scan, finding and linking to any security devices in the room.

The home's security system was a closed circuit, except for cellular and landlines that could call for emergency services as needed. These were outgoing only, however. Any attempt at an incoming call automatically flagged the security team, which mean she couldn't crack her way in via QuIEK without alerting someone to her presence.

It was only at this moment, in physical proximity to the

system, that Alex had been able to get in. QuIEK went to work scouring any evidence of her visit and ghosting the live systems. To anyone watching, the feed would continue uninterrupted. To the digital storage systems, there would be a gap.

QuIEK was also building a bridge, creating a way for Alex to return, virtually, to the scene of Hawthorn's crimes, without detection. Later, when she wasn't in the villain's layer, she could get back in and take a peek at whatever she needed.

She slipped the phone back into her pocket just as Hawthorn returned with their drinks.

"Alright, Miss Royal. I'm listening. You said you have information that could help me with some of my political strategy?"

Alex smiled. "Actually, I said I have a *new* strategy for you. One that will put you in the White House."

Hawthorn nodded and sipped his drink, his features inscrutable. "Yes, I saw your pitch. You know, I have an entire team of very smart people working toward the same goal. What intrigued me about your email, however, was the information you included about Senator Solaira."

Alex nodded. "She's probably the biggest roadblock to you. Her base overlaps yours significantly and... well, at the risk of being offensive, she's more popular than you are."

"Yes," Hawthorn frowned. "So I'm told."

"But like most things, that could change. Very quickly."

She was watching Hawthorn closely. She knew from her research that, like public examples of his wealth, Hawthorn valued political power. Which meant he valued *approval ratings*—the currency of the power candidate.

Senator Isabella Solaira was miles ahead of him in that particular race and therefore represented a weakness that Alex could exploit.

She'd done a bit of research into the Senator, and had

uncovered some choice bits of history that could lead to black eyes and point drops, if any of it ever went public.

Alex had no intention of letting it go public, though. Everything she'd sent to Hawthorn could be excised or mitigated, using QuIEK. Even if it leaked, at best it could dinger Solaira by a few points at the polls. But it made for a perfect lure to get Hawthorn in and get this meeting.

Over the next hour, Alex gave Hawthorn tiny tastes of everything he ever wanted. She shared a couple of the dark details of Solaira's past, and promised she could provide more, including verifiable proof that could be leaked to the press through third parties, keeping any of it from being traced back to Hawthorn.

She outlined a strategy for keeping suspicion off of Hawthorn even as he benefited from the political windfall. She also implied that she had the pull to get him into some very important meetings with potential backers—the kind of financial support and public endorsements that would grade the path to the Oval Office.

She could see that Hawthorn was listening closely, intrigued. But also skeptical. Maybe even suspicious.

That was fine.

Alex wasn't actually trying to sell him on hiring her. It would be handy if she were given direct access to his inner circle. But that was Plan A. She had contingencies mapped out that would let her keep working this, even if Plan A failed.

As they talked, QuIEK was silently creating the bridge between Hawthorn's internal network and the outgoing cellular line used by his security system. It was building a back door that would let Alex get in any time she wanted. That was the real objective of this meeting, and as long as she got that far, she could regroup and pick a new direction any time, as needed.

They wrapped up their conversation, and Hawthorn told her he'd let her know. "But I like your approach," he said. "You've given me a lot to consider."

Alex said that was good news, that she hoped they could work together, and then she was led out by Hawthorn's butler.

This had gone well. No matter what happened next, she felt good about the progress.

The valet was retrieving her car when Jason Hawthorn arrived.

He pulled up in a metallic green Porsche 911 GT3 RS. A car, Alex knew, that cost nearly $200,000.

She thought back to Kenneth Hebert, dressed in second-hand clothes, living in a run down duplex, working multiple jobs just to keep himself in food and shelter. Hebert's life was so limited, he could barely leave his house. Jason Hawthorn, in contrast, operated as if he owned this city.

Which, in a lot of respects, he did.

It was like seeing a metaphorical slap to Hebert's face glide to a stop in front of her.

Like his father, Jason Hawthorn liked to show off his wealth. Perhaps even more so. Cars, clothes, money spent at clubs and resorts. Father and son relied on many of the same trappings.

Unlike Anthony Hawthorn, however, Jason was all flash, very little bang. While the father used his wealth to amass more and more power, the son seemed willing to fake it and call in Daddy if things went wrong. Power by proxy was still power, though, as Alex knew.

Jason stepped out of the car just as Alex's BMW arrived. He tossed the keys to the valet, who fumbled a bit to catch them. Jason laughed derisively and then walked toward the front door.

He stopped when he saw Alex, his expression shifting to something between a leer and a smirk.

"Hell-o," he said.

Alex felt her douchebag-creep senses tingling and fought the urge to roll her eyes and gag.

"Hi," she smiled, instead. She held out her hand, "I'm Regina Royal. I was... conducting some business with your father."

He nodded, taking her hand, looking her up and down. "Jason Hawthorn," he said.

"Very nice to meet you," she smiled.

She was pouring some winsomeness into it. She knew Jason was a philanderer, notching his bedpost with conquests ranging from club bimbos to fashion models. It was the thing he kept on display, for the world to see. The place where he'd hurt most, if he took a hit.

Or a kick.

Alex seriously wanted to kick him.

"Nice," he said, a brief pause and a smile as he again scanned her up and down, appreciatively. "To meet you, too," he added with a grin.

"I hope we get another chance," she replied. "I have to make another meeting, but I'm hoping your father and I get an opportunity to work together."

"Dad? How about working with me?" Jason grinned.

She smiled. "Maybe," she said, her tone softer, seductive. She dug into her purse and handed him one of the same business cards she'd given to his father. "In case you... ever need to reach me."

He took the card, laughed and nodded, then went inside.

Alex kept the smile on her face until she was safely in the BMW and rolling away.

Then it was all she could do to keep from vomiting.

The things she did for her clients.

But it was a good sign. Having both Hawthorn men at least mildly intrigued by her played into Plan A, and might make things a lot easier.

Of course, it could make things worse, too.

That just seemed to be how these things worked.

When she was off of the Hawthorn property, she drove the rental back to the lot, tossed the keys into the return box, and caught the first of many Ubers back to home.

She'd study everything she could find on Hawthorn's network, now that she had full access. She'd look for anything she could use to redeem Kenneth Hebert.

And, hopefully, to bring down the Hawthorns.

CHAPTER SEVEN

"HAD A GOOD CHAT WITH YOUR GIRLFRIEND?" Mayher smirked.

It was morning, and Mayher joined him just as he was sitting down for a continental breakfast.

Symon frowned. "You know I'm your *boss*, right?"

Mayher smiled, shaking her head and taking the seat across from him. She ordered coffee when the waiter appeared. "Well, if you'd like to get a little more close and personal, I may have a lead on her."

Symon arched his eyebrows, his eyes widening. "What do you have?"

Mayher hesitated, studying him. "This doesn't... *bother* you? Weren't you just offering her a chance to clear her slate? Go legit?"

Symon shrugged. "Until that happens, she's still a fugitive and we're still FBI agents. Our job is to bring her in. That's the gig. Besides, if we have her in custody it'll be easier to persuade her to join our side."

Mayher shook her head. "Ok. Well, we got a call from the

branch office in Colorado Springs. There was some activity there recently that fit Kayne's profile. The CEO of Palentine Investments was just brought down by a company whistleblower."

Symon frowned. "One second." He took out his phone and checked email, shaking his head. "Dan Trager?"

Mayher gave him a look. "How did you know?"

"Kayne," he said, holding up his phone. "This email isn't *from* her, but it has her fingerprints all over it. I got an email from the Director in Colorado Springs, thanking me for providing them with my case files and leads on Trager."

"You had case files on this?" Mayher asked.

"Once Alex Kayne set them up and forwarded them on my behalf, yeah," Symon said.

Mayher stared at him, wide-eyed, and whistled. "That's..."

"Dangerous in every way? Yeah, I know," Symon said. "Thank God she seems to be playing for our side. So far."

"So she set this up and gave you all the credit?" Mayher asked.

"Gave *us* the credit," Symon said. "Just like the last few cases. Just like Orlando. We're establishing quite a track record, by remote control."

Mayher was shaking her head. "I'm thinking *control* might not be the right word."

Symon said nothing. He had to agree. Whatever the situation was with Alex Kayne, he certainly had no *control* over it. In fact, in a lot of ways, it was the other way around. Kayne had QuIEK, and that gave her the power to manipulate things however she felt was necessary.

Things. And people. Including him.

His gut was still telling him she was innocent, and that she was doing all of this out of a sense of purpose—he still believed she was one of the good guys.

His training, however, was telling him that this wasn't good. She needed to be stopped.

It was a challenging incongruity to live with.

"Well," Mayher said, "she slipped up this time. Got into a fight with the security guard, and he was able to positively identify her. Security cameras in the place were glitched out while she was there, but we lucked out and picked her up on a traffic cam. We were able to track her to Illinois."

"Illinois?" Symon replied. "From Colorado? How'd we swing that?"

"She drove in a van and never switched vehicles. It took some time, but video forensics was able to trace her in hops. They were able to follow her out of Colorado Springs, and from there they picked up her general direction. She stuck to highways the whole time, so there were plenty of stops and plenty of cameras to check."

"Diabolical," Symon said, smiling.

"Us, or her?" Mayher asked.

Symon shrugged. "Both. Hard to believe she slipped on something like this, though. She's usually pretty good at thinking twenty steps ahead."

Mayher shrugged. "Everybody slips up, eventually."

Symon knew this was the common wisdom, and it was practically scripture when it came to hunting fugitives. He believed it, too. He'd cracked hundreds of cases thanks to keeping this one fact in mind.

Fugitives always slipped up, eventually.

But Kayne was different. Always had been. She was a four-dimensional thinker in a two dimensional world. For her to make a mistake like this... it had to mean something.

Maybe she wanted them to find her?

She'd done that sort of thing before, though usually going to the other way. She would drop red herrings and bread crumbs leading to false trails. If she wanted the FBI to be in one place, while she was in another, she was certainly capable of pulling it off. She'd done that in Orlando, and in a couple of other locations since.

Maybe more disconcerting, Kayne had proven that she thought of Symon and his team as a *resource*. It was reasonable to assume that she might flip the script, from time to time, and draw them to wherever she was headed, if she needed them to be there. It fit her MO.

Then again, for all her smarts and strategic thinking, Alex Kayne *was* still human. Even with QuIEK giving her an edge, she could still make mistakes. That was how Symon had found her the first time, after all. She'd gotten a little too relaxed, hadn't covered her tracks as well as she usually did. An FBI agent on vacation with her family had recognized Kayne and reported the sighting.

It had been a lucky break for the FBI, but it was the result of Kayne screwing up. Textbook.

Being on the run was exhausting. No friends or family to turn to. Limited resources. Constant pressure. No matter who it was, people eventually *did* make mistakes. Even four-dimensional thinkers with seemingly unlimited backup plans.

Mayher brought out her laptop, and together she and Symon ran through the collection of footage that forensics had compiled. There was an animated map above the clips, showing a red line that marked Kayne's progress across the country. Just as Mayher had said, Kayne had kept to the highways and main roads, making rather predictable stops along the way. They had clear shots of her at a variety of gas stations, traffic lights, and restaurants.

"She's finally screwed up," Mayher smiled.

"Yeah," Symon said, scrubbing through footage, stopping to see Kayne's face, verifying that it really was her. "Maybe."

Mayher eyed him. "You don't think so?"

"I think Kayne has been pretty good at this game so far, and this feels like a rookie move. So... I'm skeptical." He shook his head. "Skeptical or not, though, it's a lead. And we'll follow it. Do we know where she landed, in Illinois?"

Mayher sighed. "Our best bet is Chicago, so far. Major metropolitan area. Lots of places to hide in plain sight. Seems to fit her MO."

"Ok," Symon said, nodding. "I agree. We'll start there. Get in touch with the locals and tell them we're coming in. Set us up with a home base and resources. And get them watching for signs."

"Signs like what, exactly?" Mayher asked.

"Start watching local CEOs, government officials, that sort of thing. Anyone in power who suddenly starts having a really bad day. If Alex Kayne is in town, *someone's* going to have a bad day."

Mayher nodded, then got to work, making phone calls and sending emails.

Symon left her to it, making his way back to his room. He'd be packed in minutes, and could probably have flights booked for the two of them within the hour. They'd be in Chicago by the afternoon.

What they'd find, when they set down in Chicago, was anyone's guess. Symon couldn't pretend to know Alex Kayne very well, but he knew how she thought. He knew that she operated with a purpose—always some sort of mission to bring justice for an innocent victim.

It was admirable.

It muddied the waters a bit, too. Some profilers in Kayne's case had noted these tendencies, and their current theory was that it was all driven by guilt. Kayne was attempting to make up for her crimes by doing good deeds, they said.

That wasn't it.

Symon had worked up his own profile on Kayne, based not only on her files and history but also on his personal interactions with her. The emails, the occasional phone calls, the text messages. He had some unique insight into her that other profilers lacked.

But there was something else.

The pattern of where she went and what she did said a lot. Symon had worked this out months ago. Kayne wasn't trying to find absolution. If Symon was right, she never took any credit for the work she did. And if something went sideways—if it looked like she could get caught if she stuck around—she kept at the work all the same. She risked capture to *ensure* that the clients got justice.

No, Kayne wasn't after absolution. She was trying to find a purpose. A *reason*. She was giving meaning to her existence.

Knowing that was critical, and it changed Symon's approach. And it was paying off. He'd made more progress toward apprehending Alex Kayne than any other Agent to date, and it was solely due to this understanding of her and her motives. He *knew* her, as much as anyone could know her. That was the difference between his profile and the profiles used to date.

Alex Kayne went after bad guys to help good guys, and that was simply the reality of who she was.

So if Kayne was in Chicago, it meant that she was there to help someone. It meant she was planning to bring someone to justice. The *who* and *what* and specifics would have to be determined, but knowing Kayne the way he did meant Symon knew where to look, and where not to.

Bag packed, flights arranged, and hotel rooms reserved, Symon went back down to meet up with Mayher.

Next stop, Chicago.

CHAPTER EIGHT

ALEX WATCHED FROM HER AIRBNB, using her laptop to tap first into Hawthorn's home security system and then into various cameras along his route, as he was driven by a chauffeur to his local Chicago offices. It seemed to be a business as usual sort of day for the Congressman. She could see by his digital calendar that he was due back in Washington in three days, and while he was here in town, he had stacks of appointments.

A busy man.

Some of those appointments were intriguing, though. Local government officials wanted face time, as did state officials. But there were also local business owners—some of whom would, presumably, have very little legitimate business to conduct with a Congressman.

One of these business owners was Salvatore Russo.

Officially, Russo was the sole proprietor of Russo Waste Management—a local garbage pickup serving the largest percentage of Chicago and outlying suburbs. It was a family business, handed down to a short list of family members every few years, until Salvatore took the helm in the late

80s. From that point on, Salvatore had been in charge, and RWM had been one of Chicago's leading waste disposal services.

It was also a front for the Chicago Outfit—the local mafia.

According to the FBI's files, Russo was a *Capo*, running his more illicit business under camouflage, using Russo Waste Management as a front for everything from money laundering to the "disposal" of unwanted merchandise.

Such as evidence that might be used against someone.

Or sometimes the *someone* themselves.

None of this could currently be proven, of course, but there were a few "strong hints."

The FBI had files on RWM going back to the early 1960s, and a number of the Russo family line had graced the inside of a prison cell from time to time over the past seven decades. Somehow, though, they always managed to find a loophole, or the right evidence would appear—or disappear—and their convictions would be overturned.

This had been the case for Salvatore Russo only six years earlier. Just about the time Hawthorn was starting to make serious progress in his political career, Russo got a reprieve on a 30-year sentence. Evidence that had been rock solid during Russo's trial and been re-examined and thrown out on the grounds that there was no clear chain of custody. The entire case unspooled quickly, and Russo was back at his desk within a week.

The implications were pretty clear—Hawthorn had aided Russo, and in return certain roadblocks to Hawthorn's foothold in government were softened and removed. Bribes changed hands, opponents were intimidated, officials were coerced. Certain vocal nuisances either became silent or disappeared entirely.

Alex dug in, but finding digital records to back up these

implications was nearly impossible. The mafia tended to be distrustful of computers.

Hawthorn wasn't, however. And so Kayne was at least able to trace a few questionable financial transactions. For instance, Hawthorn Industries seemed to spend a great deal on garbage disposal—Russo Waste Management had a very lucrative, long-term contract with them.

This was all interesting, but Alex could see right away why the FBI hadn't made much progress in taking Russo down. There just wasn't enough here. At best, they could nail him for a handful of petty crimes that might put him away for a few months, maybe even a year or two. The sort of convictions that would leave Russo serving softball sentences in cushy environments. Hard time wasn't even on the radar.

What the FBI needed was something solid. Something that tied Russo directly to a significant felony. Evidence that would be very difficult to dispute.

Alex had access to the cameras in Hawthorn's offices, but the minute Russo arrived the place became a dead zone. Everything went dark.

It was likely a condition of Russo meeting the Congressman on his own turf. No cameras. No recordings. No evidence, and no witnesses.

It probably worked out for Hawthorn, as well. These were conversations he certainly wouldn't want on books.

Alex couldn't be sure, but her gut was telling her that she could find the best leads on Kenneth Hebert's case if she could just get into that room. She needed to know what went on between Hawthorn and Russo. It would be a start, at least. A lead in this case that otherwise had a bunch of dead ends.

She checked Hawthorn's calendar and saw he had another meeting with Russo in just two days, right before Hawthorn was to return to Washington.

That gave Alex some time to prepare. But it meant that, for the moment at least, she was still at a dead end.

She turned her attention to Jason Hawthorn.

For all of Anthony Hawthorn's precautions and preparations, his son showed no real signs of inheriting the same level of paranoia. Jason led the lifestyle of a rich playboy—parties and events, fast cars, faster women, lots of gambling. Most of it illegal.

And drugs. Lots and lots of drugs.

Jason may have been cleared of intent to distribute, but it was obvious he was still tapped into a very heavy vein of drugs flowing in and out of Chicago. It was also obvious that despite soaking up a considerable portion of his father's wealth, Jason had sources of money all his own. Clear signs he was still in business.

Though, to his credit, gone were the traces of weapons dealing that had gained the interest of the FBI. Jason may not have been the brightest bulb, but he'd seen the light, in that respect. He was steering clear of things that would put him back on the FBI's radar. For now.

After the digital gymnastics Alex had to go through to track and monitor Anthony Hawthorn, following Jason Hawthorn seemed almost like a joke. The guy was such an open book that it almost felt like he *wanted* to be tracked.

She followed him via his own car, mostly.

The Porsche had a GPS tracker that still used the default pass code. It took all of three seconds for QuIEK to hack into it and give Alex a precise location of Jason's whereabouts. She cross-checked that with local cellphone towers and was immediately able to pick out his phone among a sea of Chicago digital traffic. QuIEK unlocked the phone, turned on the camera and microphone, and *bam*—instant surveillance.

Too easy.

She took note of where he was headed and watched as he pulled into the parking lot of a bar called "The Hawk & Dove." It was a seedy place off of East 53rd, serving a clientele that spent its nights doing things that had to be sipped away with a stiff drink during the day.

Alex ran a background check on the place and found that local police had flagged it for illegal sports gambling and a handful of other violations on several occasions. From what she could find, the bar did exceedingly well, financially, though she couldn't quite match the level of income with the amount Hawk & Dove spent with liquor distributors.

Their patrons must be really big tippers.

Or the place was still fronting a large gambling operation, which seemed likely.

Gambling was currently illegal in the city, and thus subject to local and state taxes—unless you happened to be on a riverboat. Hawk & Dove was pretty solidly land-locked, however.

Alex rolled back through the record of locations stored in Jason's Hawthorn's GPS and found that Hawk & Dove was a frequently visited location. It seemed that Jason stopped by every couple of days. Which meant he was using the place as a front for his own business—maybe even helped the proprietor to keep the police and the DA at bay, in exchange for letting Jason run his drug operation on the premises.

This was all conjecture on Alex's part, but the facts seemed to fit. Jason clearly kept office hours here. And as far as Alex had been able to determine, the guy's only source of income, outside of daddy's pockets, was his illicit trade.

Knowing this could come in handy, and Alex filed it away for later. But right now, her goal was to use Jason, the little fish, to help her reel in Anthony, the bigger fish.

"Ok, Jason," Alex said. "Let's see if you can help me get into daddy's office."

. . .

ALEX ARRIVED BY UBER, dropped off two blocks from the bar. She was dressed down a bit, sporting a more androgynous, plain look than she'd had the last time she'd interacted with Jason Hawthorn. She didn't want him to recognize her, or to even notice her, if it could be helped.

She was wearing loose-fitting jeans and a slightly oversized sweatshirt, and had a ball cap pulled down over her brow, with a pair of cheap sunglasses to hide her eyes. Her hair was short enough that she figured it could be taken as "long for a guy," if anyone even cared to give it a thought.

She moved toward Hawk & Dove at a brisk pace, but slowed to a more casual walk when she saw the sign. She had her hands in the pockets of her jeans, and her head tilted down a bit.

Jason's Porsche was parked out front, in what seemed to be as close to a VIP spot as was possible here. She noted that a large, tough-looking man was standing nearby, his eye on the car.

Security, Alex decided. *In street clothes.*

There would be more.

She paused for a moment, leaning against a column near the door of a dry cleaner, taking out her phone. She used QuIEK to check security cameras in the area and found that surveillance was a bit light inside Hawk & Dove itself. Considering the place was a front for an illegal gambling operation and, apparently, an even more illegal drug running operation, severe discretion was to be expected.

There was a camera aimed at the front door of the place, at least, capturing the features of anyone coming in or going out. Not much to go on, in terms of casing the place. She couldn't see the lay of the land, couldn't tell how many patrons were inside. Nothing useful.

Alex shook her head.

Too many variables. Too many unknowns.

She had hoped that when she got here, she could find a way to infiltrate Hawk & Dove and go in unnoticed. But her gut was telling her this wasn't the kind of place that strangers just casually entered. Going in there would break a number of her personal rules of survival—chief of which was "always know your way out."

More than one, preferably.

She had arranged for a couple of escape paths out of the area, but she couldn't prepare for what she'd find *inside* Hawk & Dove, without being able to see the lay of the place. And given that there was security outside, it was a sure bet there was security *inside*.

For all intents and purposes, Jason was currently out of reach.

Time for Plan B.

According to Google Maps, there was an athletics store about two blocks down from Hawk & Dove. Alex made her way there now. When she was far enough away to be out of sight, she took off the cap and sunglasses and pulled the sweatshirt over her head, revealing a casual buttoned blouse beneath. She glanced around, and when she was certain no one was watching, she shimmied out of the loose-fitting jeans. She was now wearing a pair of flattering slacks. The sneakers she'd been wearing could double as business casual.

Now that she'd shed the androgynous look, she was just a local business woman, out for a walk. Good cover, but for her next move, not quite right.

She ditched the cloths in a trash can on the sidewalk, and when she came to the athletic shop she entered.

It was a small place, with a selection of mostly workout clothes, a wall of running shoes dominating one side of the store, and a set of changing rooms in the back.

Perfect.

She smiled at the clerk, who made no move to come her way, but instead tilted her head once again toward whatever smartphone app was occupying her attention.

Alex browsed a bit, but quickly selected a few items, including a small runner's backpack, and ducked into the changing rooms. She shed her casual business attire, replacing it with running clothes.

There was nothing she could do about the length of her hair, but she decided to tuck it under a new cap—one that matched her outfit. She then folded her business attire and placed it in the pack.

She was officially "a woman out for a run" now. A handy and versatile disguise that had the advantage of letting her actually run unencumbered, if the need arose.

She used QuIEK to make a couple of quick arrangements, and to check in on Jason's Porsche. According to the GPS, it was still in the same spot. She looked in on his phone, and though it was apparently in his pocket, she was able to hear some muffled conversation.

Good, she thought. *Still there.*

She left the dressing room, and when she approached the front counter, she spread a small pile of tags and barcodes out for the girl to scan.

The girl blinked and made a quizzical expression—apparently not used to people wearing the merchandise out. But she shrugged and scanned the tags without comment, and Alex dutifully paid in cash.

She left the store, and out on the sidewalk she stretched a bit, getting warmed up. She checked her phone. She tucked a pair of wireless earbuds into her ears and listened intently for any sign that Jason was about to leave.

There was no real way to time this, but she figured that if Jason started toward the front door, she could sprint from her current location to just about where the Porsche was parked before he could get in and drive away.

The muffled conversation continued until Alex thought she detected signs of exit.

She started her run.

Up ahead, as she'd hoped, she saw Jason exit the bar, motion to the man-mountain guarding his car. He caught the keys as they were tossed his way.

Alex picked up her pace just a bit and was able to time reaching the Porsche just as Jason was unlocking the driver-side door.

She stopped, making a point to huff and hold a hand over her brow, as if she'd been out running and exerting herself for some time.

"Jason?" she asked.

He stopped, looking up, then looking her up and down. "You're... that chick." He snapped his fingers a few times, then patted the front pocket of his jeans, reaching in and taking out the business card she'd handed him as she'd left Anthony Hawthorn's home.

"Ruh-gyna," he said, grinning and purposefully mispronouncing her name to sound like "vagina."

Subtle, Alex thought.

"Ruh-*geena*," she corrected, though she smiled as if she thought his joke was cute. "What are you doing here?" she asked.

"I could ask you the same thing," he smiled, then leered, eyeing her cleavage.

"I'm staying in the neighborhood," she said, waving back in

the direction of a hotel, several blocks away. She really had made arrangements to have a room there. She'd back-dated the reservation in the hotel's computers and had some luggage delivered to her room as part of a cover story. Just in case. If Jason checked, he'd find she'd been a guest for several days.

Though it was obvious the only thing he was interested in checking was her.

"I'm just out for a run," Alex said. "I was going to try to visit your father this afternoon, but I can't seem to get an appointment at his offices."

Jason was studying her, and there was something strange in his expression. Alex felt a tingle of something—a hint of an alert. Warning. She kept herself in check. She couldn't give him any hint that something might be wrong.

"He keeps himself pretty booked, when he's in town," Jason shrugged. "People set up appointments months in advance. Full calendar."

Alex nodded at this. "I can see that. I'd still like to try, though. I don't... I don't suppose *you* could help get me in? Even if I could just get into the building, I think I could convince him to chat with me again. I had some thoughts about his strategy for..."

"Sure, sure, I'll get you in," Jasons interrupted.

Alex blinked. "You will? Great!" she said. "I really appreciate it. I just need to change into something more appropriate."

"How about I give you a lift back to your hotel?" he asked.

Alex hesitated. The warning was back. Her Spidey-sense. It was only an instant, but her gut was telling her something.

She needed to keep things going, to keep Jason on the hook. This was progress.

She smiled. "Sure, that'd be great. You don't mind that I'm a little sweaty?" She motioned to the Porsche. "It's such a nice car."

He grinned. "If I can't have a sweaty girl in it, then what's the point of owning it?"

Alex resisted the urge to groan and roll her eyes. "I see what you mean," she said, smiling.

He hit the remote and there was a chirp from the car. He opened the driver-side door and motioned for her to do the same on her side.

She climbed in and buckled up, as he did the same.

The Porsche roared to life, and without much hesitation Jason slammed it into gear and accelerated.

Alex felt herself being pressed back against the seat.

"My hotel is up on the right," she said.

Jason, smiling, downshifted and took the next left.

"Where..."

"Don't worry about it," Jason said. "Just enjoy the ride."

"Jason..."

He shifted again, accelerating.

Alex felt her heart thumping. Adrenaline filled her veins. Memories of two Russians—both dead now, blood on her hands —flashed through her mind.

She felt sick.

"Pull over," she said, her tone hard, demanding. She wasn't in character now. She was just reacting.

"Almost there," Jason grinned, gunning the engine again.

They zipped through the city streets until they came to a row of warehouses. With some deft and frankly impressive maneuvers, Jason whipped the Porsche around a series of tight turns, until finally they were approaching the rolled steel doors of a warehouse ahead. Jason reached up and pushed a button in the overhead console, and the doors began opening.

The gap was only just tall enough for them when the Porsche rocketed inside, then screeched to a halt. They stopped only inches from a concrete barrier—a loading dock within the warehouse, with a concrete staircase and a smooth dolly ramp on either side, in proximity to the car doors.

It was the sort of loading dock a delivery truck would back into, and the Porsche parked on a sharp slope, its nose dipping downward. They were on a ramp.

Sunlight was quickly choked off from outside as the rolled doors settled back into place. The only light now came from the Porsche's headlights, bouncing from the concrete in front of them.

Jason turned, grinning at Alex, looking her up and down as he leaned toward her, his hand going straight for her left breast.

"Hey!" she slapped his hand away and shoved him back.

He laughed. "Oh, come on, you don't have to be like that. I know you came out looking for me."

"I..." Alex started, and was suddenly cut off as Jason leaned in, grabbing the back of her head and forcing her forward into a kiss.

The impact of it cut her lip against her top teeth. The pain shocked her, and she found herself frozen, not reacting for a moment as Jason lingered on the kiss, and then started groping her.

The memory of the Russians flashed through her brain again. That feeling, that she was in trouble, that she was caught and trapped, had been suffused with the memory of killing them during her escape—something that haunted her every night, for the past two years. She regretted it. She ran from it. The memory made some of her nights too horrible for sleep.

But worse, it made her hesitate instead of acting. Something she never did.

Finally, the feeling of fear passed. Now there was only anger and fury.

She reached out, as if greeting her lover willingly, putting a hand against his cheek.

She raked her nails down his face.

He shot back, yelling from pain and uttering a stream of profanities.

He then formed a fist and jabbed at her.

She leaned back, but the close quarters of the Porsche made it difficult to dodge. She took the hit, which connected to her chin and snapped her head back against the side window of the car.

It dazed her slightly, but she recovered in time to make a few hits of her own. Using the heel of her right hand, she jammed a punch straight into Jason's nose, stunning him just as he was lunging forward to make a grab.

He fell back, and while she had some advantage she took advantage of it, unbuckling her seatbelt and opening the door of the Porsche.

It slammed against the concrete of the ramp, just outside, only opening about half an inch.

She tried the window, but it was locked.

She looked back to see Jason running a hand over his nose, pulling a way blood, and grinning at her obscenely.

"Bitch," he said. "I'm done with foreplay."

He reached down into the space between the driver-side door and his seat, and when his hand emerged he was holding a long, black tactical knife.

Alex felt her heart pounding. She felt panic rising. And then...

For two years now, she had trained and prepared for every conceivable threat. This had caught her off guard, anyway. Something that shocked her and made her second guess herself.

Still—all that training wasn't for nothing.

The adrenaline fueled her, and she quickly snagged Jason's seatbelt.

As he lunged, feigning a swipe, toying with her, she twisted the seatbelt and wrapped it around his wrist.

"Hey!" he shouted, pulling back. There was a click as the seatbelt locked.

Alex again punched him in the nose, which made him cry out in pain and swipe at her with the knife.

She had control of that arm, however, and now she grabbed his wrist and slammed it against the steering wheel.

He cried out again, and as his grip on the knife loosened Alex grabbed it, flipped it in one quick motion, and then plunged it into Jason's throat.

His eyes widened in shock and pain, and his free hand clutched at the knife, finally, and weakly pulling it from his throat, which was gushing blood.

He made a hideous, gurgling noise that Alex knew would be folded into the recurring nightmare of dying Russians that haunted her nights. She'd have to deal with this for years to come.

After a moment, however, the noise stopped, with a sickening wet sigh, and Jason Hawthorn slumped forward, held in place by his seatbelt, which had locked in the struggle.

Alex made a noise herself—something from deep inside that she hardly recognized as coming from her own throat.

A cry. A moan. The sound of horror.

She was covered in Jason's blood.

Instinctually she tried once again to get out of the Porsche, but was still jammed in place. She felt her panic rising, and she slammed the door again and again against the immovable barrier.

Her heart pounded. Her guts twisted. She threw up, covering the dashboard with bile and breakfast.

She was losing it.

She stopped, took a breath, smelled the foul stench of vomit and blood, but kept her breathing even, measured, controlled. Slower and slower.

Until, finally, she felt calm return. She felt the cold, calculating part of her return. The part that thought through things from multiple angles and in multiple dimensions. The part that solved problems that seemed unsolvable.

She reached over, gripping the steering wheel in one hand as she put the Porsche in reverse with the other. She then clenched the leg of Jason's jeans and jammed his foot down on the accelerator.

The Porsche rocketed backwards until it slammed into the metal doors of the warehouse, coming to a jarring stop. Alex took the Porsche out of gear and reached to turn off the engine.

For a long moment she sat, stunned. The sudden silence as the Porsche's engine died was like a wave, a pressure that came over her. She sat there, stunned, for a few minutes.

Then she got to work.

She climbed out of the car, now freed from the concrete barrier, and started looking around. A large bay of switches and breakers was just inside the warehouse door, barely visible in the ambient glow of the Porsche's headlights. She flipped on the biggest of these. The warehouse was bathed in artificial light then. She could see more of the place.

She needed resources. She needed to clean up this mess. She needed to get the hell out of here.

You have everything you need, right in front of you.

Her PaPa's voice—so reasonable and practical and calm—felt entirely out of place here, and in this moment. She didn't want to hear it. He didn't belong in this place, with all of this blood and vomit and death. She didn't want him here, to see what she had done.

But he was right.

He was always right.

She calmed herself and started scouring the warehouse for everything she needed.

She first removed her backpack from the car and set it aside. She'd definitely need that, later. It's contents, at any rate.

She found a janitor's closet, with a large utility sink in the floor and racks of cleaning supplies. She took everything, rolling it out on a cart from the warehouse floor. She pulled on a pair of cleaning gloves, picked up a bucket, and got to work.

It took two hours, but when she was done, she felt she had it all settled.

The interior of the Porsche had likely never been this clean. Its leather interior had made cleaning the blood easier, but that wasn't really the goal. She needed to remove any evidence of her being there. And to that end she had scrubbed and bleached and scrubbed some more. She wiped the entire vehicle down, every inch of it, inside and out.

Jason's body was laying prone on the warehouse floor. She stripped it, taking all of his clothes and shoving them into the rolling trash can where she'd disposed of everything else.

The scratches on his face were a problem. There would certainly be trace DNA. She needed a way to obfuscate that.

It was going to be ugly.

She looked around until she found a can of sulfuric acid near what appeared to be a metal working station. This would definitely do.

She tilted Jason's head away, turning the scratched side up, and then meticulously and carefully poured acid over the scratches.

The smell, the sound, the sight of bubbling and burning skin—everything about it was sickening. She kept herself in check. She didn't want to clean up any more vomit.

Soon enough Alex felt she'd masked her scratches better than she'd even intended. Jason's face was a wreck, mutilated beyond recognition. It gave her a sick feeling inside, but the job was done. She wiped down the can and left it beside Jason's body.

Now it was time to deal with the trash.

She rolled the large trash can to the bottom of the cement loading bay, where Jason had parked the Porsche upon their arrival.

It was a pit, surrounded by cement on three sides, alienating it from the rest of the warehouse. It should be perfect.

She changed her clothes, dumping the bloody athletic gear and the backpack into the garbage can and pulling on the casual business clothing she'd worn earlier. She then poured half a dozen containers of every flammable liquid she could find into the garbage can and lit it with a lighter she'd found in Jason's pocket.

The whole thing went up in a rush of heat and smoke. Alex had disabled all the smoke detectors earlier, so there'd be no alarms. But the smoke was black and heavy down here on the floor, and she quickly made her way up and out of the warehouse, slipping out through a back door. The fire would burn down, eventually, and because it was in the pit, it wouldn't spread. Everything in that warehouse would reek of toxic smoke, but that would only serve Alex's purposes. Nothing obscured timelines like soot and smoke.

She hurried away from the warehouse, moving quickly but keeping out of sight. She used QuIEK to check for any local cameras, creating loops to mask her route and sending IP addresses for each security system to her cloud storage. She could double-check these later and make sure her exit was covered.

The adrenaline was wearing off. She was starting to feel sick and exhausted. She was starting to feel afraid.

Another death. More blood on her hands. More nightmares to come.

Again, this killing had been done in self defense, just as it had with the Russians. But she'd made things so *final*, and so *quickly*.

Could she have done this differently? Could she have fought just Jason off and escaped without killing him?

She ran the whole thing back through her mind, again and again, and couldn't think of another way out.

Every path led to blood. Every road ended with Jason Hawthorn dead, and Alex Kayne with more blood on her hands. It was inevitable.

Inevitability didn't make it any easier.

She sprinted, racing along the back alleys and side streets, staying to avenues that seemed less likely to be under any sort of surveillance. She never heard any sign of sirens and figured that meant no one had noticed or reported the fire. It would have burned itself out by now, at any rate. The smoke might linger, but it, too, would settle and vanish. The carbon from it would even help skew the timeline, once a forensics team became involved. It would make for good additional cover.

Alex thought about running. Leaving Chicago. Getting out and finding some place to lay low, far away from here.

This had been too close. There had been too much fallout. The plan—all the plans—was out of the window. She should run.

But then, what about Kenneth Hebert?

She left the back alleys and made her way to a little coffee shop, several blocks from where she'd started. One of her pickup points. A remaining fragment from her previous escape plans. At least some part of those plans had been salvageable.

She went inside, ordered ice water, and sat out on the little patio with a view of the street. When she'd stopped shaking, she called for a car.

For once she had the driver come straight to her, but she did stick to her strategy of setting up multiple pickup points. Thank God she'd created a program for QuIEK to execute this sort of thing automatically. She wasn't sure she could handle doing this manually at the moment, and it was more necessary now than ever.

She couldn't afford to deviate from her survival strategies. She couldn't risk being caught.

In all the transferring and switching rides, moving block by block until she was "home," Alex managed to get a grip. The calm came back to her. And with it, logic and reason.

She couldn't leave.

Hebert was depending on her.

And that was one of her rules, as well. *Finish the job.*

Things had certainly gone pear-shaped. And there certainly would be fallout. Anthony Hawthorn would eventually learn that his son was dead, and that would result in chaos. It would derail her plans—it already had. It would make it tougher to get what she needed from Hawthorn, to be able to help Kenneth Hebert. The job just got harder.

She would have to come up with a new set of plans. Some of what she had already put into motion would have to be adjusted, some would have to be outright scrapped. She was basically starting from scratch.

She could do this. For Hebert, she *would* do this.

But for tonight, as she arrived back at the Airbnb with darkness settling like a slow, turbulent wave over Chicago, Alex's only plan was to strip off her clothes and take a long, hot shower before triple-checking the locks on her doors and settling in to binge-watch *The Office* on Netflix.

She needed something ridiculous and cringy and escapist

tonight. She needed hours of normal and mundane, a chunk of time that had nothing to do with thinking ahead or for that matter, thinking *at all*.

She needed a fiction to let her mind disappear into, tonight.

She'd deal with reality, and the fallout from today, in the morning.

CHAPTER NINE

SYMON WASN'T much for being stuck in the office if he could help it. He preferred working from the field, finding spots mostly in hotel lobbies and bars, maybe even working from a rental car. Somewhere that wasn't rank with bureaucracy—often some place that could help put him in the headspace of the fugitive he was chasing.

At the moment, however, he and Mayher had to put on a show.

The chiefs in the FBI's Chicago branch wanted a debriefing on Alex Kayne—what sort of danger she represented, what her patterns were, how she'd been tracked to the city, why she was in this area. Symon and Mayher had to pay their dues, if they wanted to use local resources. But it always slowed things down.

The thing was, debriefing these agents on Kayne's patterns was a waste of time. She was incredibly adaptive, adjusting on the fly when things went wrong or when the FBI got too close. Anything Symon shared with them could become obsolete in seconds. Kayne's "patterns" could shift in an instant, and she'd become essentially *unknowable*, by FBI standards.

That was the part that Symon had the most trouble trying to convey. Convincing a room full of career bureaucrats that everything they thought they knew about tracking a fugitive didn't apply to this one in particular was like trying to make a river flow away from the ocean. It could be done, but it was going to take some effort.

Still, this was the job. This was the process. And Symon couldn't let his personal perspective on Kayne impact the way he did this job. Not openly, anyway.

The FBI was good at understanding criminal psychology, but it relied on patterns, on profiles, on the notion that criminals essentially stuck to established ways of doing things. Symon was continually frustrated by this idea, since his track record was a direct result of embracing how a fugitive could suddenly turn from their patterns and, essentially, become someone else.

Symon knew that if they had any real chance of catching Kayne, it would come from thinking in a new way—thinking from a new angle, accepting what *is* but also keeping in mind what *could be*, and being mindful of how the environment and the current circumstances and the current available resources might come into play.

Basically, they had to think like Alex Kayne. And Kayne was a whole different type of fugitive. A type the FBI wasn't used to tracking.

He had a theory about this. One that he'd posited to his superiors before, only to see it shot down instantly, followed by scoff and ridicule, sometimes even suspicion.

Symon believed there were "super fugitives."

There was some tangential precedence for the idea. In the world of hunting serial killers, there had long been the notion of a "super predator." This was a hypothetical serial killer who didn't conform to the usual patterns. Where most serial killers were eventually found because of certain ego traits—the need to prove they were smarter than the authorities, for example, or the need to leave a legacy, or to simply be recognized for their work—there were theories that some serial killers were devoid of those needs. They remained hidden, in plain sight, their sociopathy or psychopathy wired just different enough from the norm that they maintained their anonymity and autonomy indefinitely.

Super predators were devoid of ego and killed for reasons that law enforcement couldn't fathom.

They were immune to profiling, in other words.

And, as the theory went, they stayed hidden forever, with barely a trace of their existence become public knowledge.

Symon believed the same idea might apply to other types of fugitives—and it certainly applied to those who disappeared entirely, never to be seen again.

Fugitives like Edward Montoro—a film producer who disappeared in the 80s after taking more than a million dollars from his own company. A million sounds like a lot to most people, but it can run out fast when you're on the run. And yet, there'd been no sign of Montoro for more than thirty years.

Elizabeth Duke also disappeared in the 80s—a former teacher and radical activist, she fled with little to no resources and has eluded the FBI ever since.

Or John Ruffo, a con man convicted for a scheme to bilk the US government out of more than $350 million. The biggest single con on the federal government in US history, and the guy disappeared without a trace in the late 90s.

None of these were anything like Alex Kayne. They were completely off the radar, never showing their faces in any significant way. Never doing anything that might lead to their capture.

That was where Kayne really stood out.

In essence, the way law enforcement eventually caught a criminal was by hunting their ego. The general thinking was that all criminals ultimately wanted recognition, wanted to be *known*. They might want to be feared, or respected, or admired. They might simply want their work recognized for the "genius" that it was. Ultimately, however, criminals were most often caught because their egos turned them in.

But some were never caught. Some evaded capture indefinitely. Some were "super fugitives," playing by a different rule book than law enforcement was using, and therefore managing to stay ahead of any attempt at arrest.

That was Symon's theory.

He had been laughed at for the idea, but he still believed it. He no longer tried to push it on his fellow agents, however, but he secretly used this idea to shape his philosophy in hunting fugitives. He looked past the profiles, started looking at patterns in the *lives* of the fugitives, and changed the way he thought with each pursuit.

In essence, he did his best to adapt and think like people who thought like no one else.

It worked out pretty well. Though he was constantly challenged by the bureaucrats.

Thinking like no one else was sort of frowned upon, in bureaucracy.

How would all of this change, Symon wondered, if he joined Historic Crimes?

It was a question that nagged him, bubbling up just when he'd almost forgotten Ludlum's invitation. He and Mayher hadn't discussed the offer since a few nights earlier, but it was always at the back of Symon's mind.

How would things change for him, if he took the deal?

And a more important question...

How would things change for Alex Kayne, if *she* took the deal?

Her life would be easier, Symon thought. She'd get a better shot. Whatever this was—this nearly three-year quest that she'd been on while running from the FBI—it could finally end. Or perhaps it could finally become legitimate.

Alex Kayne could finally stop running.

Symon shook his head. It was like rooting for her, which was weird. But still, he thought it would be better for everyone, if she agreed. He didn't know what kind of pull Director Ludlum could have, to get a deal like this for Kayne. But anything had to be better than a life spent running, right?

For now, though, she *was* still running. And he was still pursuing her. And he would catch her and arrest her, because that's what he did. That was the job.

Symon and Mayher had just finished up with the briefing, and had retreated to a small conference room where they'd set up office. Mayher was already hunched over her laptop, and Symon huffed and left the room again, in search of more coffee.

When he returned, Mayher was just standing.

"I was coming to find you," she said. She had a strange expression on her face—concern, Symon thought.

"What is it?" he asked.

She turned the laptop, and Symon saw a grainy still from a security camera.

Alex Kayne, dressed in what looked like business casual clothing. She looked different from the last time he'd seen her, but that was part of her MO. Kayne changed looks constantly, making it difficult to release a description of her on an APB.

"I got this from local PD. They sent it to us when Kayne's

name came up. Someone in the department recognized her from the APB we sent."

Symon blinked and shook his head. "You're kidding? I mean... we sent that as a courtesy. This is the first time we've ever had a local actually recognize her."

"They had reason to look closely," Mayher said. She seemed hesitant, unsure of how to proceed.

Symon peered at her. "What haven't you told me?" he asked.

Mayher sighed. "There was a murder. Police identified the body as Jason Hawthorn, son of Congressman Hawthorn. He was found by a cleaning crew, in a warehouse in Southwest Chicago. He was laying close to his car, which had some superficial damage. The body was naked. Cause of death was a stab wound to the throat. But..."

Symon waited. Mayher seemed reluctant to go on. "What is it?" he asked.

She shook her head. "She *mutilated* him," Mayher said.

"What?"

"Used acid to burn his face," Mayher replied. "They identified him by his driver's license, but his face was unrecognizable. They found some remnants of clothing and a backpack in a trash can, burned pretty good. Not much usable there."

"Forensics has already been on the scene?"

Mayher nodded. "Place is clean, though, Eric. Like, seriously clean. *Spotless.* Kayne bleached and scrubbed everything inside the car. Everything else was covered in soot from the fire, but it's pretty clear she cleaned it all beforehand."

Mayher was shaking her head, and Symon thought he knew why. Murder wasn't really Kayne's thing. This wasn't like her at all.

Mayher continued. "They haven't found so much as an eyelash on the scene, but someone started pulling footage from security cameras in the area, and this still came up, emailed directly to a Detective on the scene. He recognized her. He'd just seen the photos we sent of her that morning, in his inbox. Said he'd just happened to open them and see the APB, right before he'd left for this call. It's... it *is* her, isn't it?"

Symon nodded. "It's her."

"This isn't really how she does things," Mayher said, shaking her head. "Usually she... I don't know. Does a hacking thing, gets evidence, sets someone up. This is... it's *murder*. It just doesn't fit her MO."

Symon agreed. This didn't feel like Kayne at all. She didn't murder people. That wasn't how she sought out justice.

Or was it?

Hadn't he just been thinking about this—about the possibility that Kayne and fugitives like her might be able to switch personalities and traits on and off as needed? He'd just been considering that Kayne might be a super fugitive, that the profiles and patterns and workups might not apply to her. She might be able to become someone entirely new in an instant.

So what if *this* was *that*?

What did Symon *really* know about Kayne and her motives? He had theories, and he was pretty good at profiling. One of the best in the Bureau, even if he was being modest. He had always been able to rely on his instincts, when it came to figuring out how a fugitive thinks.

But just like Alex Kayne, he was human. He could make mistakes.

Had he made one with her?

"They're asking if we can assist in the case," Mayher said.

Symon nodded. "Yes," he replied. "Tell them we're here to help."

"Do you... think she really did this?"

"I'm not sure," he replied.

Mayher considered this and turned back to her work. She called the Detective in charge and made arrangements. They would drop by within the hour, meet him at the scene, go over the details with him.

Symon sipped his coffee and thought about what this meant.

He fought the instinct to send Kayne a text. He couldn't risk tipping her off, letting her know that they were this close to her. And besides, if she really had killed Jason Hawthorn, things had just taken a turn. The game had changed.

There might be no turning back.

"Regina Royal," Anthony Hawthorn said, his voice quiet but hard-edged. His expression was angry but cold. Symon wasn't able to read any emotion from the man.

Hawthorn sipped from a glass of Scotch. "I'm absolutely sure of it."

The Congressman was slumped in a large, leather chair in his Chicago office, the glass of Scotch in his left hand, held loosely, almost dangling over the edge of the chair arm. Hawthorn's demeanor had at first seemed distant, even a little distracted. But when Symon and Mayher had shown him the photo of Alex Kayne, he'd been completely focused. The distance became something more like somber resolution. Contemplation with an edge.

The false name hadn't surprised Symon. Kayne had a litany of false identities, and thanks to QuIEK she was able to quickly set them up with backgrounds and histories that would pass even the most rigorous security checks. Kayne had managed to forge official government records and documents on multiple occasions. It would be simple for her to establish herself in an identity that would get past Hawthorn's security.

"When she was here, did she make any sort of threats?" Mayher asked. "Did she seem hostile?"

Hawthorn shook his head. "No. She seemed... efficient. She was pitching a strategy for... well, let's just say for my political career. She brought me dirt on Senator Solaira. I would never use it, of course," Hawthorn added hastily, waving the glass enough that the Scotch threatened to breach the rim. "I intended to have my people look into Ms. Royal and tell me what her story really was."

Symon had no doubt that if Hawthorn ran any sort of background check on Regina Royal, he'd get a story. He'd also get a rabbit trail that would lead him to anywhere but Alex Kayne.

Symon was standing near the Congressman's window, looking over the bustling Chicago streets below. He turned to Hawthorn. "Did Ms. Royal say anything about your son? Anything that might indicate a grudge?"

Hawthorn shook his head. "No, nothing. Jason never came up. My people tell me they met as Ms. Royal was leaving my home. As far as I know, that was the first time."

Symon had no doubt about that. It seemed unlikely that Kayne would have had any sort of personal grudge against Jason Hawthorn, or any relationship with him at all, for that matter. It seemed even more unlikely that Kayne had come to Chicago just to kill Jason Hawthorn. Her "cases" were usually more about bringing legal justice to someone who had been wronged—a powerless victim who couldn't fight back against an overpowered bully.

Occasionally, Kayne resorted to violence. But it was always more about incapacitating an enemy. There were bruises, and the occasional broken bone. And a lot of bruised pride. But rarely any blood, and never a death. Never a body.

Not since the Russians, at least. And Symon had looked at those two deaths from every possible angle. He'd seen security-cam footage of one of the Russians driving a truck into Kayne's car. Footage of her being dragged out and shoved into a second car. Footage of that car veering into traffic and coming to a stop as Kayne staggered out and ran away.

The two bodies were identified as Russian operatives, in the US illegally, both with records longer than the road Kayne had driven between Colorado Springs and Chicago.

Kayne had killed those two men in self defense, and it was obvious.

There was something else happening here, with the death of Jason Hawthorn. Something Symon wasn't yet seeing.

Not all the pieces were evident.

"In your meeting with Ms. Royal," Symon asked, "was the conversation centered entirely around your political campaign?"

Hawthorn looked up at him, sipped from his Scotch, and then placed the glass on the table beside him. He then stood, smoothed his suit, and walked over to the same window to join Symon where he stood. Hawthorn looked out onto the streets below, and Symon turned to join him in surveying the city.

After a moment Hawthorn shook his head and said, "Unfortunately, yes, Agent Symon. Our conversation was all business, and all ambition. I can provide you with recordings, if you like."

Symon's eyes widened. "You have video?"

Hawthorn nodded.

"Why didn't you mention this earlier?"

"The meeting took place within my own home. I'm a public figure, Agent Symon. I keep my private life private, as much as possible. If it helps you find the woman who murdered my son, however, I will turn that footage over to you."

Symon studied him, then nodded. "That would be helpful. Plus anything else you may have. Emails, phone records, anything. The police have already taken statements from your staff."

Hawthorn nodded. "I'll have everything sent to you." He stood observing the streets a moment longer. "Now... who is this woman?"

Symon shook his head. "That's what we're trying to determine, Congressman."

Hawthorn scoffed. "Agent Symon, it is obvious to me that you and Agent Mayher know exactly who this is. Which means this is not her first offense. She's done something to get the attention of the FBI before. So who is she?"

Symon glanced at Mayher, then shook his head and looked back to Hawthorn. "There are details we can't yet divulge, Congressman. She's a wanted fugitive, that's all I can say for the moment."

Hawthorn turned on Symon, his expression hardening, his whole demeanor changing.

"Agent, I am not some distraught victim, sinking in on myself in grief and feeling powerless. You'll find I am *very* powerful. Enough so that I won't tolerate games. I want to know who this woman is, and why she killed my son. And by God, you *will* tell me."

Symon studied him, then shook his head. As much as he wanted to keep Kayne's name out of it, he didn't want Hawthorn going off half-cocked, making things harder.

"Her name is Alex Kayne," Symon said. "She's a fugitive, and has managed to evade capture for nearly three years now. That is as much as I am authorized to tell you, Congressman, I'm sorry. If you need more, you'll have to use your own resources. As to why she killed your son, though... that's what I'm here to determine. We will investigate and we will find the answers you're wanting. Unless you decide to interfere and set things back to square one."

This last was said with equal edge and warning, matching Hawthorn's tone.

He studied the Congressman's features. Symon knew that his own position here was precarious—he really had very little clout or leverage in this situation. His authority extended only to what it would take to find and arrest Alex Kayne.

If the Congressman chose, he could make Symon's life unquestionably miserable.

So, this was a bluff.

But it seemed to work.

Hawthorn eyed him, hard, for a long moment, then nodded and turned back to the window. "Find her, Agent," the Congressman said. "Bring justice for my son."

Symon gave a quick nod and turned to walk away.

Mayher stepped in beside him, and the two of them made their way to the elevator. They rode to the ground floor in silence, and it wasn't until they were on the street, waiting for their rental car to be brought around, that Symon finally spoke.

"I'm having trouble with motive," he said.

"You mean, why would Alex Kayne want to kill Jason Hawthorn?" Mayher asked.

"Exactly. We know from her past that she tends to go after people who have wronged someone and are getting away with it. Her methods are usually on the illegal side, but she's never resorted to murder. It's just not her style. She usually focuses on bringing them down using their own rope." He thought for a moment. "I want a deep background on Jason Hawthorn. I want to know everything he's been involved in, going back as far as we can dig. And I want to know who has been victimized because of it. If there's *anything* that connects him with Kayne —anything that could lead to a personal vendetta—I want to know about it. Doesn't matter how small."

"I'll get on it," Mayher said. "But Eric, I have to tell you…

this sounds a little like victim blaming."

"Motive mining," Symon corrected. "I don't care what Jason may have done, beyond knowing what it was that brought Alex Kayne to him. When we figure out why she's here, we'll have a start on figuring out why she killed him."

"*If* she killed him," Mayher said.

"You think it's just a coincidence that she was caught leaving the same warehouse where Jason's body was found?"

Mayher shook her head. "No. It's just... Look, I'm fully onboard with bringing Kayne in. But this isn't like her. She just doesn't do this."

"She did kill two Russians," Symon reminded her. "Self defense, maybe. But she's shown she's capable of this."

"Self defense," Mayher nodded. "Which makes me wonder."

Symon peered at her.

The car was brought around, and the two of them climbed inside. Mayher took the driver's seat. Symon pulled his seatbelt on. "You're thinking that Kayne may have acted in self defense here, too," he said.

"It would fit," Mayher replied.

Symon had to agree. The only signs of violence in Kayne's history were the deaths of two Russian operatives, in the US illegally, who had abducted Kayne after ramming her car with a truck. Symon was positive that it was self defense.

And Jason Hawthorn's death could be as well.

But unless they could find evidence of that, Alex Kayne was still considered a murderer. And Symon would still do his job and bring her in.

Jason Hawthorn was their best bet for finding Kayne, at this point.

It was time to find out who Jason Hawthorn was, and who he had wronged.

CHAPTER TEN

ALEX WAS MOSTLY BURNED for getting into Hawthorn's offices using Plan A.

She felt pretty confident that she could still pull off a disguise, change her appearance enough that she could slip in and get back out unnoticed, if the circumstances were right. But the level of threat had gone up. As had the consequences. Hawthorn's people would be on the alert.

Worse, the FBI was involved now.

She had scanned the reports from Chicago PD, as well as the exchange of texts and emails between the lead Detective and Agent Mayher. She had also verified that Eric Symon was now involved. Things would get tricky now.

Trickier, really. Because all of this had gone a bit pear-shaped when Jason Hawthorn had tried to rape her.

She kicked herself for not seeing it coming.

She should have dug in more on his personal history, not just his criminal history. If she had, she would have noticed a pattern—women that Jason dated tended to end up in the hospital. They tended to end up disappearing shortly after, as well, reappearing in sunny places with fatter bank accounts and iron-clad non-disclosure agreements.

Bribes. Hush money.

Patterns of behavior, on the part of both Hawthorns, indicated something dark in play.

Alex knew that she was doing classic self-blame. She was blaming *herself* for something that was legitimately not her fault, in any way. She had not *invited* Jason to try to rape her. She hadn't made any mistakes. Hadn't done anything wrong. That was ridiculous. *She was not to blame.*

But she blamed herself anyway. And from the experience, like all experiences, she took a lesson away from it: *Do your homework, and do it right.*

She would make sure that her background checks included personality reviews from now on. Full psychological profiles. Complete histories. She would *know* her targets, to the highest degree possible, before engaging with them.

Above all, she would *never* allow herself to be put in a scenario like this again.

It was too late to do anything about it now. She had plans in motion to deal with Jason's death, and with her implication in his murder. She'd spent most of the previous morning setting things up, transferring files here, making connections there. She'd gotten the right people involved, in the right way. It had taken some juggling, some creative thinking, but now her only choice was to trust the plan.

To trust Eric Symon.

For now, she had to turn her attention back to getting into Hawthorn's offices, with even more security and scrutiny in play. She needed a new plan.

She thought she had it.

Hawthorn had changed his schedule, as a result of Jason's death. He was staying in Chicago for one more week and had postponed all of his meetings. Including his meeting with Salvatore Russo.

Hawthorn had sent an email to his secretary, asking her to reschedule everything for the next week. Alex intercepted that email and used QuIEK to make a few adjustments to Hawthorn's calendar.

His secretary dutifully contacted each appointment, but had, of course, overlooked Russo.

Alex then made sure that any emails that might be sent from Hawthorn's offices to Russo or any of his people were mysteriously bounced, without notice.

That meeting was going to happen. At least, Salvatore Russo was going to show up for it.

Alex spent the day preparing, visiting shops all over the city, getting the gear she'd need. It was more of a way to keep her brain occupied than a real, pressing need. Between keeping a low profile, dodging the FBI and the police, and shopping, the day wicked away. That night she turned in early, to get plenty of sleep. She would need the extra time—sleep wasn't coming easily.

The next morning, dressed in bulky coveralls and using a manual seed spreader, Alex waited outside of Hawthorn's offices. She was pretending to be part of the landscaping staff and was actually doing a fair job of replanting and fertilizing grass in a neglected corner of the property.

They would thank her later, she was sure, when the lush green returned.

She'd been hanging back, waiting, getting the lay of the place. And when Russo's appointment neared, she ducked into the little plastic tool shed in the back lot behind the offices. From there she pulled off the overalls and changed into a very all-business look.

Her hair had gone from auburn to blond, thanks to a wig

made from real human hair, and it was six inches longer than it had been when she'd last been seen in public.

Using some makeup tricks she'd learned from YouTube, Alex had completely changed her facial features. Her eyes appeared larger, as did her lips, and her cheekbones were more prominent. If anyone were to compare her to *Alex Kayne* or *Regina Royal*, they would be hard pressed to say she looked anything like either woman.

She was wearing a pair of high heels that gave her an extra three inches in height, and of course she had the silicone foot pads on, in case she needed to run. The skirt she was wearing was a tear-away as well—yanking it free would reveal form-fitting running shorts.

Essentially, if she needed to make an emergency escape, Alex could be wearing an entirely new look and have a completely different hairstyle in under thirty seconds. The makeup would be tougher to take off, but a pair of sunglasses would change her facial features instantly. And she had several escape routes mapped out, with resources in place.

She was as safe as she could make herself.

Newly attired, she made her way to the front of the building, and hovered near the entrance for a few minutes until Russo's car arrived.

The driver sprinted around to open the door for Russo, who stepped out, straightening his tie and tugging at his suit. He looked up at the building, as if verifying that he'd arrived at the right place.

Two men, each dressed in dark suits and wearing dark sunglasses, stepped in beside him. They made very little effort to hide the bulges of either their holstered weapons or their biceps. Alex had to admit, they were an intimidating pair. She definitely wanted to avoid having any tangle with them.

The three men moved toward the entrance, and Alex intercepted them.

"Mr. Russo," Alex said, stepping in front of the three men and smiling. "My name is Carol Grey. I am Congressman Hawthorn's liaison. I've been sent to greet you and escort you to his offices."

Russo peered at her, his expression hard and suspicious. "*Liaison,*" he said. "Never seen you before."

Alex glanced around, as if making sure no one was within earshot. Which was only partially a ruse.

"You haven't yet heard, I'm assuming..." she said. "Mr. Hawthorn's son, Jason, was murdered, two days ago. The FBI have become involved. Mr. Hawthorn felt it would be prudent to have someone act as a buffer between the two of you. For your protection, and his."

Russo's expression changed slightly, still suspicious but now amused. He glanced at his two guards. "Protection," he said, laughing lightly.

The two mooks on either side of him laughed as well.

He turned back to Alex. "Ok, *protection.* So, what's the run here? If the Feds are around, maybe I shouldn't be."

"The Congressman felt that even during this difficult time, it was best to keep his appointments with certain prominent people," Alex said. "He's taken great pains to ensure that your meeting remains private. The usual arrangements, of course. No recordings, all the cameras will be shut off. But in addition, he wants to provide you with this."

She glanced around, conspiratorially, then opened her purse and removed a device that resembled a wristwatch. She held it up for Russo to inspect. "This is counter surveillance technology. It's the same tech being used by government officials, such as the Congressman. US officials wear these when meeting with foreign heads of state. It blocks audio recordings and can disrupt video feeds, even from a distance."

She again looked around, then lowered her voice and said, "In truth, the Congressman could be arrested just for giving this to you. It's technically a violation of national security."

Russo eyed her, gave an impressed smirk then reached out and took the device. He turned it over, held it at arm's length, inspecting it. He nodded. "I like it," he said, holding it against his wrist and showing his guards. "Goes with my ensemble, yeah boys?"

The boys nodded, grinning with him.

Russo chuckled and strapped the device to his wrist, holding it out admiringly before once again smoothing the lines of his suit. "Alright, Ms. Grey. Let's do this. I like to keep my appointments, too."

Alex smiled and nodded. "This way, sir."

She led the three of them into the building, and when security recognized Russo they did what they always did—they let him and his entourage pass without pause or question. A standing order from the Congressman, no doubt. One that was very convenient.

No metal detectors, no identification. In fact, Alex noted that one of the security guards reached under his desk and clicked a button.

That would be the signal to turn off cameras in the building, for the duration of Salvatore Russo's visit.

Alex was holding her phone in her left hand, and tapped the screen. QuIEK engaged several pre-arranged protocols.

She led them to the elevator and then stopped as the doors opened and the three men stepped inside. "Enjoy your meeting with the Congressman, Mr. Russo. I know that even in his grief, he's looking forward to it."

There was a brief swipe of some expression on Russo's face.

Something Alex couldn't quite read. He recovered quickly, his expression going neutral.

"I'll offer him his condolences for his loss," Russo said, nodding solemnly.

The doors closed then, and Alex turned and walked down the corridor, glancing toward the front of the building before she opened the door to the stairwell and rushed inside. With no cameras in operation, she only had to worry about human eyes watching. Most were focused on the entrance to the building. No one was looking her way.

Security was on the second floor, and this was where things would get a little risky.

She checked her phone. The watch she'd given Russo would do a couple of things—none of them actually blocking anything he said or did, though it did temporarily mask him from local security measures.

In actuality, as long as Russo was wearing the device, anything with a microphone or camera within 20 feet of him not only became fully active, it would use any available internet connection to send information to half a dozen Smokescreen modules all over the country, storing the footage in the cloud until it could be compiled and sent to the FBI.

Alex was pretty sure that Russo would decide to keep the little trinket that supposedly protected him from surveillance. She was also pretty sure that it would capture *something* that the FBI could use to put him away. A bonus, she figured.

The second thing the watch was doing was bridging any local devices to the Smokescreen network—essentially using QuIEK to install software on any computer, smartphone, or smart tablet the watch passed by, with a command to join any open WiFi within range. This new virtual network would give Alex all the access she needed once she made her exit from Hawthorn's offices. She'd have a back door into all of his digital records. Which, until now, had been air-gapped from the local network, making them impossible for her to reach, even with QuIEK.

Salvatore Russo was the Trojan horse—or maybe a better description was "Patient Zero." Every time he came near an electronic device, he essentially infected it with QuIEK.

To that end, Alex's primary mission here was accomplished. Now she just needed to take care of one more detail.

Within the building's security offices there were physical documents. Alex needed access to those.

Paper was more or less Alex's kryptonite, since QuIEK had no power over the physical world. No *direct* power, at any rate.

Alex suspected there might be something in the physical files that she could use, though, and that meant she'd have to put physical *eyes* on it. Or digital eyes, since her plan was to record 8K video as she opened and scanned through every file she could find. That would allow her to grab everything in a quick seep and make a fast exit. She could examine everything later, at her leisure and from a safe distance.

She glanced at her smartwatch. She was still on track with her timeline. Russo was currently seated in a waiting room outside of Hawthorn's office, likely annoyed at having to wait while a panicked and confused receptionist scrambled to get Hawthorn on the phone.

Chaos would break out soon. Alex needed to get the lead out.

She pulled the wallet and badge from her bag. It was a pretty impressive forgery of FBI credentials, especially considering the timeline in which she'd had it made. It would certainly do for getting Hawthorn's security team to cooperate, though. They'd already been primed by the visit from Agents Symon and Mayher. Her plan was to pretend to be on follow-up duty.

She had ID ready when she knocked on the door.

When the door opened, however, she froze, her jaw dropping.

"Hello Ms. Kayne," Anthony Hawthorn said.

Two armed security agents trained weapons on her as they rapidly moved out in the corridor, flanking her from either side, keeping enough distance that she had no way to take one on without being shot by the other.

Hawthorn was also keeping his distance, though he stepped forward as Alex was ordered to step back and turn to face the wall.

Alex did nothing to resist as the two guards brought her hands around behind her back, cuffing her. They turned her, roughly, to face Hawthorn.

"We were hoping you'd drop by," the Congressman smiled.

CHAPTER ELEVEN

Mayher whistled. "Our boy Jason has a guardian angel." She paused for a moment, then made a face. "*Had*, I guess."

She was scanning through the stack of files they'd procured from Chicago PD, as well as information pulled from the FBI database.

"He certainly seemed to have someone making sure he didn't spend much time in prison," Symon replied. He was sitting at the desk in the little office they'd been given at Chicago's FBI headquarters. Before him was his laptop, more stacks of police files, and an empty coffee cup that had seen at least a dozen refills over the past few hours.

"My money's on the father," Mayher said, glancing back at the file she had in hand.

"And I'm betting *his* money is in the pockets of a few dozen officials," Symon added. "From what I'm seeing, Jason Hawthorn spent the better part of his life getting the wrong kind of attention. The Bureau was just about to put the hammer down on him, use him as an asset, when he got busted for intent to distribute."

"I was just looking at something about that," Mayher said, looking up, pausing, tossing her current file aside and digging through the stack. She pulled up another file, folded it open, and read for a moment. "Here," she said, handing it to Symon.

He took it and read.

It was essentially the same story, same details he'd just picked through. But this was a report from the arresting officer —Detective Kenneth Hebert. Symon nodded. "This was quite a collar," he said. "Enough drugs to make this a pretty tight case. Should have been a slam dunk."

"Except Jason barely served any time for it," Mayher said, leaning back. "And Detective Hebert was busted a few months later for extortion."

Symon read through the report, then turned to his laptop. He brought up everything he could find on Detective Hebert's arrest and plea deal.

His brow furrowed as he read through the files. The "plea deal" wasn't much of a win for Hebert. It still cost him time behind bars, plus every scrap of everything good in his life, from what Symon could see. His career was over. His friends on the force abandoned him. What family he had wrote him off as well.

And it seemed Hebert had a change of heart, nearly from the beginning of his sentence. Symon scanned through letters and statements, filings from Hebert's attorneys, a digital stack of Hebert recanting his plea.

It seemed pretty obvious what had happened.

Jason Hawthorn had a guardian angel, alright. From what Symon could figure, his father was bribing people up and down the governmental food chain to keep the heat off of his son— and therefore off of his own political career.

There was every indication that Hawthorn was making a bid for the big chair, in the Oval Office. It would hurt him significantly to have a son sitting in prison, when that bid came due. If Symon had to guess, Hawthorn leveraged his pull with the state, amplified by his rising star on the national stage. He used his influence to dismantle Hebert's case and win Jason his freedom.

It hadn't taken long, or much looking on Symon's part, to discover Hawthorn's relationship with Salvatore Russo, or to get a pretty revealing overview of Russo's history. Russo Waste Management had been on the FBI's radar for decades, and there were files going back to before Symon was born. Racketeering, extortion, bribery, kidnapping, murder—all alleged, never proven. Close calls that somehow got swept away, just as Russo was facing life behind bars.

Russo seemed to have a guardian angel of his own. Or maybe a succession of them. And his current angel, by all indications, was Congressman Hawthorn.

There was no evidence to support it yet, but Symon suspected that Hawthorn had Russo take care of his Kenneth Hebert problem.

Killing a cop would have brought on too much heat and attention, and wouldn't necessarily give Hawthorn the story he needed—that his son had been tagged by a corrupt cop, and that in bringing Hebert down, true justice had been served.

Tales of police corruption were *en vogue* at the moment, and a story about a Congressman taking down a corrupt Detective would come with quite a bit of *cachet* that Hawthorn could leverage. The story would gain him even more public favor, but only if the cop lived, and only if he served time while Jason Hawthorn walked free.

For his part, Hebert had actually gotten a cushion of a deal from the DA, considering the charges and the circumstances. Though it wasn't without its share of troubles.

Hebert had served two years on a conviction of extortion—

always a very rough scenario for a former cop—and he would be on pretty strict probation for years to come.

This would limit some of his options, for sure. Finding work and making a living would be a challenge, for a start. Symon knew that as a dirty cop, Hebert would have some serious trouble just getting by, here in Chicago. His former line of work, or anything even related to it, would be completely out of reach. Background checks would preclude him from any decent job in the city. He'd be left with only the lowest of the low hanging fruit, having to eke out a living doing whatever odd jobs he could get, from the sorts of establishments that weren't particular about either their employees or their clientele. Most would pay close to nothing in salary, but would demand long, grueling hours in dangerous environments.

Symon looked up at Mayher, who was still leaning back, rubbing her eyes. She noticed him. "What is it?"

"Jason Hawthorn was arrested and convicted on a pretty open and shut case, but a few months later Detective Hebert gets arrested on charges of extortion, and Jason goes free. Anthony Hawthorn supplied some of the evidence used against Hebert in the case. Evidence that indicated that Hebert had been extorting Jason as well."

Mayher leaned forward. "You're thinking Hawthorn arranged to get Hebert busted so that Jason's conviction would be thrown out?"

"That's exactly what I'm thinking," Symon said.

Mayher considered this. "Not just Jason, though. A lot of Hebert's cases got shuffled off. Jason wasn't the only one who went free."

"Even worse, then," Symon said.

Mayher shook her head. "I agree, it seems pretty convenient for the Hawthorns."

"We need to find Hebert. Pay him a visit."

Mayher nodded and turned to her own laptop. In moments she had an address. She sent this to Symon's phone, and the two of them were on their way.

HEBERT WAS HOME, in a tiny rental that Symon thought would need a coat of paint just to get up to *dilapidated* status.

The neighborhood itself was decrepit to the level of being dangerous. It had one of the highest murder rates in the city and was a veritable Mecca for drug trafficking. This was no place to live. It would have been better for the whole place to be leveled to the ground. A fresh start, from razed earth.

Symon couldn't help feeling sympathetic toward the former Detective. In many ways, he was currently living a life worse than a prison sentence. With no chance of parole.

Hebert let them in and sat at a rickety kitchen table. There were only two chairs, and Symon and Mayher opted to stand and conduct their interview.

They started with the photo.

Hebert examined it, and Symon thought he sensed a spark of recognition there, though Hebert made no immediate indication that he recognized Kayne.

"She wanted for something?" Hebert asked.

"Murder," Mayher said, "among other things."

Hebert glanced up, a look of shock on his face. "Murder?"

"Jason Hawthorn," Symon said, watching him.

Hebert looked at him, the shock evident. He shook his head. "No," he said quietly. "That wasn't..."

He stopped himself, glancing between the both of them.

"We know you didn't hire her to kill Jason Hawthorn," Symon said, guessing at what Hebert was thinking. "She was here to... well, she approached *you*, didn't she? To help you?"

Hebert looked nervous. He hesitated, then apparently

came to some decision. To Symon it looked like resolution.

Maybe he figures it'd be better to go back to prison than to stay here, Symon thought.

Hebert nodded. "She said she was a consultant with the FBI. She never showed me any ID, though. I... didn't push it. Didn't ask for it. I thought..." he shook his head. "Stupid. I was stupid."

"No," Symon said. "You were hopeful."

Hebert looked up at him. "*Hopeful,*" he said, quietly. He nodded. "Yeah. Definitely hopeful." He looked around at the squalor of the little apartment. It was part of a duplex, barely habitable by Symon's estimate. The pantry, which had no door, looked well stocked.

"She's paying you, isn't she?" Symon asked.

Hebert tilted his chin toward his chest. "Yeah, she is. Had me quit my jobs so I could stay home. Stay... safe."

"While she took care of Jason Hawthorn?" Mayher asked.

Hebert's face shot up, his expression angry. "I didn't ask her to kill the guy. She told me she was going to find a way to get me cleared. That's it. I don't see how *this* does *that.*"

Symon didn't see it, either. Which was exactly the problem.

Kayne's usual MO was to find someone like Kenneth Hebert and then start picking apart the person who had wronged him. She did this through fairly benign means—at most committing a series of white-collar crimes that ultimately uncovered some bit of evidence that could be used against the offender. Something that could put the victim back in good graces, and resolve the problem, bringing some sort of justice.

Non-violent solutions, mostly. A few assaults, typically if Kayne was confronted by security or somehow physically threatened. These resulted in bruises, mostly. A fractured jaw or finger or elbow, at most. No blood. No severe injuries.

Never murder.

Not until now.

They spent the next hour asking Hebert for as much information as he could give them, regarding his interaction with Alex Kayne. How and when had she first made contact? How much money had she given him? How was it transferred? Did he have a way to reach her?

He did, as it turned out. An email address that used the FBI's domain. Kayne had set up a fake FBI email address.

Of course she had.

Symon was pretty sure they'd find absolutely nothing when they tried to trace that email, but he made a note of it all the same.

It was clear that Hebert was playing straight with them on this. He seemed appalled and even distraught that Kayne had murdered Jason. He was taking all the blame for it onto himself.

"I had no idea," he kept saying, shaking his head, his expression angry. "I would never have done it. I had no idea."

"I believe you," Symon said gently.

This seemed to make Hebert even more angry.

"Does me no good," he said, his voice a growl. "Killing that boy does me *no good*. Why would she do it?"

Symon glanced at Mayher, who had apparently been watching the two of them.

She shook her head, confirming what Symon was feeling.

None of this made sense.

Time for a new tack.

"What about Jason?" Symon asked. "You were the arresting officer. What put you on to him in the first place?"

Hebert slumped back a bit in the little kitchen chair, which creaked and protested from his weight. He shook his head. "It was a lot of things, but mostly it was the girls."

Symon arched his eyebrows. "The girls?"

Hebert nodded. "Every now and then, someone would file charges against that kid, and they'd just sort of go away. The charges, but the girls, too. I was looking into that, making sure there wasn't something there, ya know? I'd gotten a call from a parent, the mother of one of them. She'd been concerned that her little girl suddenly moved away, and wouldn't come home. She wasn't the only one."

Hebert leaned forward, resting his beefy elbows on the kitchen table, another creak from the chair. "I tracked a few of them. They all left Chicago, relocating to someplace far away. Usually California, or someplace like that. None of them would talk to me over the phone. They seemed scared. One of them said she couldn't talk because of some contract, but she wouldn't give me any details. But then there was Monique Simmons."

Symon jotted the name in his notebook. "What about her?"

Hebert shook his head. "She came back to Chicago, visiting her folks. I just happened to call, dropping by while she was there. She got real scared. Panicked. Kept asking me how I'd known she was there. Said she'd been so *careful*."

"I told her it was just a coincidence, and I managed to get her to sit down with me, at her parents' house. They sat with her, while she talked. It was... she was a mess. Cried through the whole thing. Told me some pretty bad stuff about Jason Hawthorn."

"What kind of bad stuff?" Mayher asked.

Hebert looked up at her. "He raped her," Hebert said, bluntly. "Got her stoned at a club and took her to some warehouse. She went to the hospital right after, got a rape kit and everything. And that went missing, right around the time she did. She told me she got a visit from a lawyer, and a couple of toughs. They made her sign something, told her that if she

talked, she'd go to jail or worse. Talked about her parents, and
what a shame it would be if something happened to them. That
kind of thing. And then they gave her a bunch of money and a
plane ticket for Santa Barbara."

"They paid her off and sent her out of town?" Mayher
asked.

Hebert nodded. "She filed charges, she said. Before the
lawyer paid a visit. But I couldn't find any record of it. Rape kit
was gone. Jason's file was clean. Of that, anyway. He was dirty
for other stuff. Nothing I could really use against him."

Symon shook his head. "Ok, so how did you get from
Monique Simmons to busting Jason for drug trafficking?"

Hebert leaned forward again. "Monique was drugged,
which gave me an idea that there might be a way to get to Jason
through that. I couldn't do much to help her with the rape. I
wanted to. I told her that if she could help me get him some
other way, it might at least put him away. Make him pay for
what he'd done. It took a little convincing, but she gave me
some leads."

"She told me that Jason spent a lot of time hanging out with
some pretty shady people, when the two of them dated. They'd
only been together for a couple of weeks, but he'd taken her to
the city's slimiest hot spots. Made himself look like a big shot
among the city's biggest low-lifes. I dug around, ran down some
of the locations she gave me. Found out some stuff. He'd set up
some kind of import business, here in Chicago, and was
running it out of a few different locations. Bars and clubs,
mostly. I started looking into things and eventually picked up
some threads. Put some heat on a few bartenders and found out
that Jason had a warehouse where he was stashing just moun-
tains of drugs. All ready to go. Packaged for individual sale. He
was supplying dealers all over the state, maybe even the country." Hebert leaned back then, holding his hands out, palms up,

fingers flexing and grasping. "I... I *had* him. Witnesses, video, DNA even. Fingerprints all over everything. I could put him in that warehouse and at those clubs, I could show him literally handing drugs over to distributors. Nailed him, dead to rights. Shouldn't have been no way for him to get out of that."

Hebert shook his head. He clenched his fists. *"I had him."* He looked up at them, his expression haunted and pleading. "I never had to *plant* anything. I would never do that! That place was in his name, and that junk was there when me and my team raided it. I tried to get all of those boys to testify to that, but I think Hawthorn got to them. Half of them moved away, the other half just shut their traps and said nothing, went out on brand new fishing boats or took early retirements. They just let me dangle in the wind."

Hebert's voice was tense, bitter. Symon could see the fury rising within him.

Symon was thinking.

"This warehouse... was it anywhere near East 53rd?"

Hebert sighed, slumping forward slightly, his hands unclenching. He shrugged. "Yeah, couple of blocks from there. I heard he got it back, after the conviction was overturned. After I went to prison."

Symon exchanged a glance with Mayher, who nodded.

There were follow-up questions. Notes were taken. Assurances were made, though Hebert seemed to consider these to be empty and hollow. Symon couldn't blame him. So far, the system hadn't done much to help him. Things had just gotten worse, not better.

They thanked Hebert, and after getting contact information for Monique Simmons, they made their way to the door.

Before leaving, Symon stopped in the doorway, facing Hebert.

"Keep doing everything you've been doing," he said.

"What do you mean?" Hebert asked.

Symon motioned toward the kitchen, its pantry bulging with food. "Keep laying low. If she reaches out, tell us. But don't change anything. Keep taking any money she offers. Keep doing whatever she tells you. We'll have someone close by, watching. But we don't want to tip her off."

Hebert huffed, shaking his head. "I swear to God, Agent Symon, I never would have let her help me if I'd known she was going to kill Jason Hawthorn. I hate the guy, I really do. But... I know it doesn't look it, but I'm still a cop, right? I don't have the badge, but I'm still a cop."

"It's ok, Mr. Hebert," Mayher said. "We're not looking at you on this. Alex Kayne has a history. We're going to find her, and we appreciate any help you can give us."

Hebert nodded at this, and Symon and Mayher left, getting back into their rental car and driving away. Symon drove as Mayher sat in the passenger seat, watching the unseemly neighborhood pass by, slowly transitioning into a more upscale landscape.

"That warehouse was his hunting ground," Mayher said. She looked at Symon. "Jason did this more than once."

"You think he tried it on Alex Kayne," Symon said.

"You don't?" Mayher asked.

Symon shook his head. "Just making sure we're on the same page."

They took a turn, moving in the general direction of the FBI offices.

"I want to talk to Monique Simmons," Symon said.

"I'll find her," Mayher replied.

"And any of these other girls," Symon said. "I want as much information as we can get. I don't think we should leave Chicago, though. Let's get some field agents on this. Do some drop-bys. And I want a full record of anything we can dig up regarding that warehouse. There was no sign of drugs when Jason's body was found, so it's clear he's not using it for that purpose anymore. Find me any other properties he owned."

"What about his father?" Mayher asked.

Symon nodded. "Him, too."

They drove on, and Symon silently contemplated what all of this could mean.

If Jason Hawthorn had tried to rape Alex Kayne, that would explain everything. It would certainly explain why she killed him.

Of all the women to mess with, Kayne definitely would not have been a good choice.

She was no murderer. Symon was convinced of that.

She was no helpless victim, either.

Alex Kayne fought back.

They turned into the parking garage for FBI headquarters. It was going to be a day of phone calls and searching databases, Symon knew. A day of being stuck in an office, with bad coffee and occasional scrutiny from the branch Director. Questions he didn't want to answer, and leads that took them nowhere.

The hunt for Alex Kayne had taken a turn. Things had gotten more complicated than they were twenty-four hours ago.

Somewhere out there, though, Kayne was still doing what she did. Symon was sure of that. Her history showed that she wouldn't leave until the job was done, and he didn't think killing Jason Hawthorn resolved anything. If he saw that, then Kayne certainly would.

Which meant she wouldn't leave town. She needed to redeem Kennth Hebert, even if it put her at risk.

To that end, Symon's job was no different than it always was: Find the motive, and they'd have a trail for finding Alex Kayne.

He just hoped she was ok.

CHAPTER TWELVE

ALEX WAS IN TROUBLE. *Big trouble.*

Hawthorn had left the room shortly after she'd been cuffed and shoved into a chair. The two guards stood at the door, facing her. There was no chance she could get free and take them out, under the current circumstances. She might be able to take down one guard, but in these tight quarters, the other guard could get off a shot with no trouble. For the moment, she was hooked.

They searched her, taking her phone and other possessions. They turned the phone off and tossed it, along with the little Swiss Army knife she carried, onto a table along one wall of the room. When they realized she was wearing a wig and tear away clothing, they removed all of these and added them to the pile as well.

She sat now, hands cuffed behind her, wearing only the tight-fitting runner's outfit. They'd even taken the silicone footwear.

Big trouble.

She wasn't sure how much time had passed, but eventually

the door opened and Congressman Hawthorn entered, along with Salvatore Russo and his two mob mooks.

It was Russo who approached her first, his expression amused but dark. "Well, hey, Ms. Grey. You looked better, down on the street. You know, I don't appreciate being... waddya call it..." he snapped his fingers a few times, then smiled. "*Misled.*"

Alex said nothing. She was busy.

Watching. Thinking. Assessing.

Things looked bad, but there was always a chance, if she kept her cool. PaPa Kayne had drilled that into her head, and she needed it now more than ever.

Hawthorn joined Russo, standing before Alex, looking down on her with his hands clasped behind his back. "This is the woman who killed my son," Hawthorn said. He turned to Russo, "My friend, I have a favor to ask."

Russo smirked and held up a hand. "Say no more," he replied. Then he chuckled, "It's always best not to ask certain favors out loud!" He glanced knowingly to his two boys, who chuckled with him.

Hawthorn nodded. "This has caused me quite a bit of personal pain, but it has also complicated things for me professionally. So I trust you can take care of things in a discreet way?"

Russo shrugged. "Of course."

Hawthorn again nodded, then turned to Alex. "Ms. Kayne. I've learned a lot about you. I suspect I know what brought you here. My son's... *dilemma* with Detective Hebert. Is that it?"

Alex peered at him. "*You* framed Hebert for extortion," she said. "Jason was never my target."

Hawthorn's expression hardened. "So you intended to murder *me*, is that it?"

"Jason attacked me. Tried to rape me, and tried to kill me," she said. "I defended myself." She paused, never breaking eye contact with the Congressman. "You know how that goes."

"I do," Hawthorn nodded. "We often do all sorts of things, to defend ourselves and what's ours. Or to avenge those we've lost. You took my son from me. He could be a lot of trouble but he *was* my son. *Mine.* Now... this tragedy can only help me in the polls. The public will have deep sympathy for me, especially when they learn that a wanted felon was behind the murder. But the pain you've caused me can't go without punishment. And I'm afraid that prison just isn't enough. My friend here," he nodded to Russo, "will make sure I see justice done."

Alex took this in. "Justice," she said, nodding. She looked from Hawthorn to Russo.

"Swordfish," she said.

Russo made a face and shook his head. "What, you want a last meal or something?"

Alex said nothing.

Russo shook his head and turned to give a few veiled instructions to his men. Hawthorn and Russo had one final conversation, with a few details about Alex's fate getting a loud enough mention that she knew she was supposed to be afraid.

She was not afraid.

Opportunities are just resources you can't hold in your hand, her PaPa's voice echoed in her mind.

The clock was ticking.

Hawthorn left the room, along with his guards. Alex knew that, officially, she was no longer in Hawthorn's custody.

Russo had her now.

He motioned toward her and toward the table where her things were piled. One of his boys grabbed her by the arm and pulled her roughly to her feet. The other grabbed everything on the table, shoving it all into a garbage bag pulled from the little waste bin under the table. Alex was then yanked along as the four of them exited the room, making their way to the stairs.

It was a rough go, as she was half dragged, half shoved, stumbling her way along down the stairs until they reached a door on the ground floor. A glowing *EXIT* sign hung above it, and another sign read *ALARM WILL SOUND.*

The mook with a grip on her arm pushed the door open.

No alarm sounded.

Alex found herself being pulled along over the asphalt behind the building until they reached a van.

Russo's boys must have called ahead and made arrangements.

Alex was pushed into the side of the van, her escort joining her. He tossed the garbage bag onto the floor of the van, in the back corner.

The other guard went around to the driver's side and found the keys in the visor.

"Do it somewhere outside the city," Russo said, leaning in to talk to the driver though the window. "She's a felon, turns out. Leave her somewhere that the Fed's can find her." He glanced at Alex, a smirk on his features. "Later," he said.

"Yeah, boss," the driver replied.

Russo turned and walked away as the van started and then pulled out into the street.

Alex said nothing during all of this. There was nothing to say. She knew what was coming next, and unless she thought of something, soon, things would not turn out well. Her initial plan was going to take some time to play out, so she couldn't rely on that to save her. What she needed was a miracle.

We make all our own miracles, PaPa Kayne's voice said in her head. *They start by thinking things through.*

Alex was thinking.

Since the plan was to take her out of town, she would

have some time—for what good it did her. But since her life seemed to have come down to minutes, she'd take all she could get.

The cuffs were a problem. Restricted hand movement was a serious hindrance. She'd done some training for this kind of thing, though. There were ways.

That left dealing with the two mooks, not getting shot, and escaping a locked, moving van.

Piece of cake, she thought.

Despite the obstacles, however, a plan started to form.

The mook was watching her, which made this even more difficult. She started to squirm.

"Settle down," the guy said.

"I... need to pee," she complained.

"Go ahead," he replied.

She shook her head. "Classy guy."

He said nothing, but he did look away, turning to peer out of the windshield.

Seconds now. That's all she'd have.

She had practiced this particular maneuver a thousand times, but never in a moving vehicle with an armed bad guy just a couple of feet away. Still, there were certain reflexes involved. Certain muscle memory.

She rocked forward, put her feet on the floor of the van, and brought her knees up. She then pushed off into a hop, her entire body leaving the floor at once as she rolled her chest forward, against her knees, and pushed her shoulders downward, stretching and moving her arms forward and under her bottom.

It was enough. She managed to get the cuffs over her butt and then had her ankles through in an instant. The end result was that her cuffed hands were now in front of her, and she was in a crouch, facing the front of the van.

The mook had noticed the sudden movement and turned to face her. He made a noise and started to spring toward her.

She didn't waste that momentum.

Her hands shot upward, wrists pulling apart so that the metal links of the cuffs were stretched between them. She had her fingers clinched, palms up, and as the guy came forward, she jammed the cuffs into his throat, adding some extra oomph by pushing upward with her feet.

The impact was sickening, and the guy made a strangled, choking sound, falling to one side as he clutched at his throat.

Alex again slammed the cuffs into his throat, for good measure, then reached into this jacket and took out the gun holstered there.

She hesitated.

She knew this was life or death. Them or her. Just like it had been with the Russians. She hadn't hesitated to shoot them, to save her own life. It might take the same with these two mafia enforcers. It should be a simple choice.

But the memory of Jason Hawthorn was too fresh. The memory of the two Russians was still in her head, in her nightmares.

The blood. The deaths.

She didn't want more on her hands.

She turned the gun toward the front of the van and fired into the dash.

The driver let out a yelp and yanked the wheel, screeching to a halt. He turned and Alex fired again, this time directly into the steering wheel.

The airbag deployed.

The mook on the van's floor was recovering and starting to rise. She slammed the butt of the gun into his right temple, then did it again for good measure.

He fell back to the floor, eyes glassy.

Alex fumbled with the handle of the van's side door, forced to drop the gun as she slid the door open. She turned quickly, grabbing the garbage bag holding her stuff, and then rolling out onto the street just as a shot was fired from the driver.

She clutched the bag, running at full tilt for any cover she could find.

The street was busy, and people screamed and ran at the sound of gunfire. Drivers who had stopped to see if there was anything they could do, at the scene of this accident, suddenly sped away. The scene was chaos.

Good.

Alex concentrated on running and ducking into the crowd, keeping low, trying to remain obscured as people ran frantically for cover. She would be easy to spot, dressed as she was and still handcuffed, but if she kept low among all the moving bodies, she could stay hidden.

Up ahead she saw scaffolding and construction. A building being remodeled.

She made for it, bursting through the door of the building and racing past startled and confused construction workers.

She eventually came to an area where stacks of building materials were being stored. She ducked behind a pile of 2x4s and tore open the trash bag.

She turned on her phone first and shoved this and the Swiss Army knife into the purse she'd been using. She unclipped one side of the strap and slung the bag crosswise over her body.

Next she pulled on the latex foot covers. She'd need all the traction and foot protection she could get, and though getting these on took some effort, they'd be worth it. She hoped.

The rest she left in a pile, hidden behind some construction debris.

Moving now, dodging past the General Contractor who

was yelling for her to stop and answer some questions, Alex sprinted into an open stairwell and made her way upward. She wasn't sure what she'd do once she got to the top. But given her options, she figured this was her best bet.

She kept her eyes open for any sign of tools, or anything she could use to cut the cuffs. She could really use her hands right now. But so far, there was nothing.

She could still hear shouts from below, and then they changed.

Alarm and panic, she thought.

The mooks had arrived.

They'd be armed. They'd shoot. No hesitation. She knew this. Knew she was in trouble.

She was nearly to the roof, but instead of continuing upward she ducked through an open door to the top floor.

Plastic sheeting dangled over unfinished walls, and again there were more piles of building materials. She could potentially hide here, but it wouldn't do her much good. They'd find her, eventually. She needed to start building some advantages, and fast.

In one end of the room there was a stack of plastic pipes and hoses, part of retrofitting the building with new plumbing. The hoses were lashed with a thin strip of metal.

Alex dropped down beside this, bending the loose end of the metal strip outward. She then held her wrists over it and aligned the tab of metal to the gap in one of the cuffs. She shoved the tab into the gap, putting pressure on the cuff, pulling.

It loosened, and in a moment she had her hand free.

She glanced at the door, across the room.

She worked on the second cuff, and it, too, came free.

She tucked the cuffs into her purse. Just in case.

Hands now free, she felt a lot more confident. Though the feeling quickly faded.

She had no weapons. Nothing but a Swiss Army knife. There were boards and plastic pipes and hoses all around her, but nothing she felt she could use to fend off two armed mafia enforcers.

She stood and raced around the room, taking everything in. She pushed through one sheet of plastic and discovered that an entire section of wall had been opened here, gaping out to open space, likely in preparation for installing a larger window.

She could see the street below. A construction dumpster was several floors down, with a temporary garbage chute leading to it. She briefly considered a leap into the dumpster, but dismissed the idea. It was full of jutting, sharp debris. She's be a pin cushion, and no better off than if she turned to fight.

She could hear sirens in the distance.

"Hey!"

She turned to see that the two guys had made it to this floor. They'd spotted her. They had their guns out.

She turned back to the opening.

No choice, then. Her options had been narrowed to zero. Or one.

Her only shot was the leap.

She took a breath... and jumped.

She heard the gunshots as she sailed outward, bullets piercing the sheet of plastic that obscured her exit. In the next instant, she was clutching the side of the garbage chute , climbing up and onto it.

Down was the most obvious direction to go.

She went up.

She ducked, laying flat on the top of the garbage chute , and peering over the edge to see the two enforcers standing at the open segment of wall, looking down to the street.

She couldn't hear them over the sounds of the city, particularly over the sirens that approached quickly from down the block. They were now so close they were echoing from the city canyon all around her.

The mooks noticed this as well. They eyed each other, then holstered their weapons and left the edge, disappearing back into the building.

Alex counted to five, then climbed the rest of the way up on the garbage chute . She had to make a bit of a leap to reach the scaffolding and then used that to go up and onto the roof.

From there she ran to the other side and leapt from this rooftop to the next. She found a doorway leading to that building's stairwell.

She took her time going down, being cautious, inspecting everything as she went. She used her phone to look in on any cameras she could find locally, especially in this building. There wasn't much, but it was enough. She could get a general idea.

She was more or less in the clear.

Down on the street she sprinted away, dodging through the growing crowd until she was in a spot where she felt she could take a break, to call for a car.

She had the driver drop her off six blocks from where she was staying, eschewing her normal circuitous route. At this point, she needed to get to someplace safe, and fast. She would have to take a risk.

This had been close. Too close.

Hawthorn had taken her by surprise.

She had underestimated him. That was a big mistake. One she didn't intend to repeat.

As she ducked into the Airbnb, she peeled the silicone footwear off, tossing it into the trash. It was shredded, from all the activity. Useless. She'd make new ones.

She dropped onto her bed, breathing heavy, shaking with adrenaline.

When she'd calmed down enough, she lifted her phone, checking the stream of data and camera feeds.

It was all there.

The data from the new bridge in Hawthorn's offices had been compiled and saved. She might not have accomplished her mission, to put eyes on the physical documents. But she had managed to sew up every available digital device between the front door of the lobby and Hawthorn's office.

She had data. She had surveillance. Video and audio footage had been captured. GPS tracking had been enabled.

Things were in motion now.

She'd go through all of it later.

She smiled at that.

This plan had gone to hell, but it was going to bring some hell back with it, for Salvatore Russo, at least.

One bad guy down wasn't a bad day's work.

But the main bad guy was still out there. And he'd won this round.

Next round, Alex thought. She got up from the bed, peeled off her clothes, and took a long, hot shower. She'd nurse her bruised body and ego over a cup of coffee and some late-night strategizing and planning.

The next round—the final round—was coming soon now, and she intended to win it.

CHAPTER THIRTEEN

SWORDFISH.

Agents Symon and Mayher were interviewing Monique Simmons when the text came through. The preview on his smartphone showed the password, and a URL.

It had to be Alex Kayne. She must want to talk to him again.

He slid the phone back into his pocket. He'd get back to her later. He knew from experience that she was patient. She had to be, considering her life.

Plus, Symon had a job to do, and it didn't include jumping at every text sent from a known fugitive. He indulged Kayne quite a bit, but he wouldn't let her dictate his schedule. There had to be boundaries.

For now, he needed to focus on Ms. Simmons.

He had let Mayher take the lead on questioning. Considering the sensitive nature of Monique's case, Symon didn't think it would be productive for him to be the front person.

The front *man*, to put a fine point on it.

Despite his hesitation, however, Monique seemed more than willing to talk to both of them.

"I couldn't believe it, when Detective Hebert got arrested," she said.

She was seated on a rattan loveseat, her knees pulled up near her chin and her feet on the blue Hawaiian print cushions. She was smoking a cigarette, but was careful to turn her head and blow the smoke away from where Symon and Mayher were seated.

She was dressed in yoga pants and a hoodie. Her feet were bare. She looked normal, in every respect, but the way she held herself told Symon a lot. She was scared. Protecting herself.

She was brave, he decided.

Symon hadn't said much during their conversation, but now he spoke up. "Ms. Simmons, you told us that you were threatened by Jason Hawthorn's attorney. What made you come back here?"

She looked at him, then took another drag from the cigarette.

A nervous habit, Symon decided. *Doing it to calm her nerves.*

"My parents, mostly," she said. "My dad..." she hesitated, and Symon caught a note of something in her voice. Grief. Worry. "He's sick," she said, a tiny catch her in voice. "Cancer." She glanced at the cigarette and shook her head, leaning toward the little side table to grind it out in an ash tray. "I'm not supposed to be smoking around him."

"That's a good enough reason to take a risk," Symon said, sympathetic. "Coming back to take care of him."

Monique nodded, and her bottom lip curled. Tears rimmed her eyes, and she wiped them away with the cuff of her sleeve. She nodded. "Yeah, I don't care what happens to me. I want to see my dad. But... I also came back because..." she shook her head, as if unsure what to say. She took a rattling breath. "I heard about Detective Hebert, and I thought, maybe I can help somehow? I don't know. I was just sad, when I heard. He was... he was the first person to believe me. Besides my parents. And he tried to help, and they set him up."

"What makes you believe they set him up?" Mayher asked.

Monique looked at her, and then glanced at the ash tray, her expression regretful. She shook her head. "Had to be. I only talked to him a few times, but he was good, you know? Kind." Her eyes softened, and she stared down at the outdoor rug of the patio.

"Monique," Mayher said, "when Detective Hebert talked to you, he says you told him you were raped. But when he investigated, the rape kit and the police report were missing. Can you confirm that you filed charges on Jason Hawthorn?"

Monique was still staring at the rug, but nodded vigorously, closing her eyes tight and again wiping at the tears with the sleeve of her hoodie. "I did. I totally did. And they..."

She didn't finish.

Symon leaned forward, his elbows on his knees. "They shut it down," he said. "Hawthorn's people came and made it all go away. Including you."

She looked at him, her face setting in an expression that was angry and determined. She nodded.

Symon made a note in the little notepad. Some things to follow up on. "Did you get the name of the attorney?" he asked.

"She didn't tell me her name," Monique said. "God, I'm so stupid. I should have made her tell me."

Mayher reached out and gently put a hand on Monique's knee. "She wouldn't have told you. She was here doing something illegal. She may not have even been an attorney. You didn't do anything wrong, and you didn't do anything stupid."

Monique nodded, not meeting Mayher's eyes. "They didn't

even say they were from Mr. Hawthorn," she said, shaking her head. "I just... *knew.*"

"Their job was to intimidate you," Symon said. "To get you to leave and be too afraid to say anything, or to even come back. But you came back anyway. Twice. That says a lot about you."

"That I'm an idiot," she said.

"That you're brave," Mayher replied.

Monique laughed and shook her head, then reached into the pocket of her hoodie and pulled out a pack of cigarettes and a lighter. She shook a cigarette loose and put it to her lips, lighting it and then setting both pack and lighter on the side table—a sign that she was far from done with smoking.

A sign that she was starting to feel stressed.

"Ms. Simmons," Symon said, his voice gentle. "You gave Detective Hebert some leads about Jason's drug dealing. It was what ultimately led to Jason's arrest. Can you give me any names or leads that you shared with the Detective?"

She nodded and began reciting a list. Symon took it all down, clarifying where needed, making note of all of it. They'd follow up on these later, though he was pretty sure it would lead nowhere. That trail was long cold.

"The warehouse where Jason took you," Symon asked. "Was it near 53rd street?"

She nodded. "Yes. One of them was."

"One of them?" Mayher asked.

"There were two. I never really knew where the second one was. I... Jason... he drugged me."

"It's ok," Mayher said. "But any details you can give us may help."

Monique wiped her eyes and took a long drag from the newly lit cigarette. Symon watched the line of ash grow until she turned and tamped it into the ash tray. "I don't think he owned that one," she said. "I think it was owned by whoever runs the Hawk & Dove."

"The bar?" Mayher asked.

Monique nodded. "I remember seeing their logo on a bunch of stuff. And... there were..." she waved vaguely, trying to call up a memory obscured by her having been drugged. "There were bottles. Crates of bottles. Booze."

"So this could have been a supply warehouse?" Symon asked.

Monique shrugged. "I don't know. I'm sorry."

"Did you share this with Detective Hebert?" Mayher asked.

Monique considered this. "No. I think I didn't really remember until later. I... I feel so stupid, you know? I don't know why I started seeing Jason. He was... kind of slimy, you know? Said some really gross stuff. It was just... he was rich and hot and..." She shook her head. "Stupid. I'm so stupid."

"You remembered the second warehouse after you talked to Hebert?" Symon asked.

She nodded.

"But you didn't say anything?"

She shook her head. "By then, Jason had been arrested. I thought it was over. So, no point."

Symon noted this as well.

They continued chatting with Monique for another half hour, but it became clear that they'd gotten all they could. Symon worried that they might be pushing her too hard, and he didn't want that. She'd been through enough—was still going through it. He rounded things up.

They stood, the three of them, and Monique walked them to the gate. Symon stopped, turning to face her. "You did everything right," he said to her. "You aren't stupid. You didn't do anything wrong. Jason Hawthorn may have been able to get out of his sentence, but he isn't going to be a threat anymore."

She looked at him for a long moment, then nodded.

Symon and Mayher left, Mayher driving as they made their way back toward Chicago. Out here in the suburbs, things seemed so clean and peaceful. Everything seemed in order. It was troublesome that just a few miles away, so much could be so wrong.

He and Mayher were chatting, going over leads they would follow up on. The Hawk & Dove was definitely on that list. They'd check for any properties under the same ownership.

Symon picked his phone out of his pocket, intending to do a quick lookup, when he once again spotted the text.

He opened it and clicked on the URL that Alex had sent.

It prompted him for a password.

He smiled and typed in *Swordfish*.

The screen refreshed.

His eyes widened.

"My God," he said.

"What is it?" Mayher asked.

"Pull over!"

She immediately put on a blinker, turning into the parking lot of a gas station. She put the car in park, and the two of them watched Symon's phone.

He had selected just one of hundreds of links arrayed on the site, and this one had opened a video.

It was a multi-angle compilation of footage featuring a man in a tailored suit, accompanied by two bulky bodyguards. As they watched, the man moved through what appeared to be Congressman Hawthorn's offices. Symon turned up the volume, and they were able to listen in on all of his conversations.

Hawthorn's personal assistant referred to the man as "Mr. Russo."

Salvatore Russo.

Russo's name had come up more than once as Symon and Mayher pored over case files. He was a local mob boss, fronting his operation with a waste management service. He was Teflon —in and out of penitentiaries over the past few decades, with stays that would be considered short even by Airbnb standards. Nothing stuck to the guy. Just like Jason Hawthorn, Salvatore Russo seemed to have a guardian angel.

Seeing Russo in Hawthorn's offices told Symon this was no coincidence.

The footage appeared to be grabs and screen captures from multiple security cameras, mobile phones, laptops and more. It was all spliced together in an unbroken timeline, tracking and following Russo and his men as they moved through the building. Symon started skipping ahead as the men sat in a waiting area, and soon he stopped the footage and let it play at normal speed.

Russo was suddenly greeted by Congressman Hawthorn, who led the three men to an elevator and, eventually to a room on the second floor.

There was no footage from within the room, but there was audio.

Hawthorn. Russo. And, Symon was shocked to discover, the voice of Alex Kayne.

He and Mayher were intent on the audio, listening closely, playing back clips to make sure they'd heard correctly. They made notes.

Kayne said the word "Swordfish."

A code word, Symon realized. The signal for QuIEK to send a link to him, to give him the page where all of this footage was being recorded and stored.

Suddenly the video reappeared, and this time Russo and his two men were accompanying Alex Kayne—handcuffed, being dragged by one arm. She'd been stripped to a set of form-fitting workout clothes, her feet bare.

This did not look good.

"Get on the horn to the home office," he said to Mayher. "We need people on the scene."

Mayher immediately started making calls as Symon continued to watch.

The footage followed Russo as he moved back into the building, where he ultimately had a conversation with Hawthorn, in Hawthorn's office. Symon noted details from this conversation as well. And then Russo left, meeting up with two more flunkies in the back alley behind the office building, where the conversation got heated.

Russo became irate, tearing into the two enforcers.

Kayne had escaped.

Symon felt a wave of relief. He knew Kayne was capable, and could certainly take care of herself. But things hadn't looked so good for her, for a minute there.

He began skipping ahead in the video and realized suddenly that he'd caught up to the current moment. Live footage of Russo was still being captured, from what was apparently his home. A mobile phone was recording him, though the angle wasn't very good. The audio, however, was coming through loud and clear. And as Russo moved around in his home, the footage would disappear and periodically return, apparently switching to a camera from a laptop or some other device.

Somehow, Alex Kayne had set things up so that every camera or microphone Russo passed instantly captured and transmitted whatever he said or did. The footage was being updated in a continuous livestream on the site Kayne had sent to Symon, along with the code word *Swordfish*.

Alex Kayne liked her tropes.

Symon quickly scanned through other files, and found that though most were not video or audio, there were plenty of digital documents from Hawthorn's offices. Personal files. Business files. Government files.

This was dangerous territory, Symon knew. This information was definitely being obtained illegally. But Symon was merely the receiver. Alex Kayne was the whistleblower—a fugitive and potentially a confidential informant, if Symon played things right.

Without looking through every file on the site, Symon wasn't sure if there was anything they could use against Hawthorn directly. It was a data dump. Too much information to scan through while sitting in the passenger seat of a rental car parked at a Chicago gas station. It was going to take time and a tech team to parse all of this.

The footage of Russo, however, was damning all on its own. For Russo, for certain, and possibly for the Congressman.

They would have to play this carefully.

"I have people on their way to Hawthorn's offices," Mayher said. "ETA is about twenty minutes."

"Tell them to hang back," Symon said. "Watch. Follow Hawthorn if he leaves."

"What about Kayne?"

"She's safe," Symon replied. "She got away from Russo's men."

"You know where she is?"

He shook his head. "Just that she got away. But I think she was worried for a minute there. Taken by surprise." He motioned to his phone. "This isn't her usual style. This is a complete data dump. Just everything she had on both Russo and Hawthorn. She usually compiles everything. Builds a case. This feels more like a contingency plan. Like pulling an emergency chute."

"So Kayne got into trouble and had everything dumped to you?" Mayher considered this. "She must have been pretty scared."

"Tell our people I want someone on Hawthorn 24/7. Same with Russo. No direct interaction. Gather intelligence, look for anything that might give us an excuse to get warrants for either or both of them."

"Don't we have a mother lode of evidence from Kayne's data dump?" Mayher asked.

Symon shook his head. "Too slippery. Nothing admissible. Hawthorn's lawyers could slide him right out of this. And Hawthorn might do the same for Russo. Our best play is to use this to help us build a case Hawthorn can't wriggle out of."

Mayher was already dialing, nodding her head. She held the phone to her ear and looked at him. "What about us? What are we doing with this?"

"Sitting on it for the moment," Symon said. "There's nothing we can do until we start finding some direct evidence on our own. That's what the surveillance is for. For now, first thing's first. I want to follow the leads we got from Monique Simmons."

He locked his phone and shoved it into his pocket.

"I want to check out Hawk & Dove."

CHAPTER FOURTEEN

The Hawk & Dove was pretty much what Symon would have expected from a Chicago dive bar. Though security was a little tighter than he would have thought. As he and Mayher entered, they were scrutinized by two very large men seated near the door.

"No guns," one of the men growled, eyeing the bulge in Symon's sports coat. The man's voice was deep and resonant even over the music and chatter.

Symon and Mayher both showed their badges and FBI credentials, and the guy gave a brief nod. Though the glare continued. Possibly even intensified.

They moved to the bar, and asked for the manager, again showing their IDs. The bartender was an amicable-seeming guy and nodded to a door in the back with the words "PRIVATE" and "KEEP OUT" stencil-painted on it.

Symon and Mayher exchanged glances and moved to the door. They knocked, and moments later the door opened, revealing a woman in her forties. She was wearing jeans and a button-up, sleeve's rolled to the elbows, and a tie hanging loosely around her neck. She had a cigarette in her mouth and puffed it just before reaching up to take it between the forefinger and thumb of her left hand.

"Need something?" she asked, her voice husky and gravelly from years of smoking and talking over bar noise.

The badges came out for the third time. "We'd like to ask you some questions about Jason Hawthorn," Symon said.

The manager looked from their IDs to their faces. She nodded and stepped aside, motioning for them to enter.

The office was a small, dingy closet of a space, with walls lined by filing cabinets and shelves stacked with boxes and crates of booze. The manager's desk was a small, wooden table scarred from decades of cigarette burns and coffee spills and any number of other dings and marks. It was stacked with invoices and accounting books. No computer.

Symon was willing to bet that Kayne had been a little frustrated with this place. So far, he hadn't seen a single security camera inside. No computers. No sign of WiFi or any other internet connection. Even the registers at the bar were old school, a bell chiming with each open of the till.

"What can I do for ya?" the manager asked, dropping into a tattered office chair that creaked as she leaned back, facing them.

There was nowhere else to sit in the space.

"We're investigating the death of Jason Hawthorn, Ms...."

"Name's Ronnie," she said. "*Just* Ronnie."

"Ronnie," Symon nodded, making a note. "I assume you knew Mr. Hawthorn?"

"Didn't know he was dead," Ronnie said, picking up the cigarette and taking a long drag. She shook her head as smoke poured from her nostrils. "Figures, though."

"Why's that?" Mayher asked.

She looked at Mayher, her eyes making a quick run up and

down. "Guy was always in trouble. Figured eventually it would catch up to him."

"He was a frequent visitor here, wasn't he?" Symon asked.

Ronnie looked at him and shrugged. "Well, yeah. I mean, he owned the place."

Symon and Mayher again exchanged glances, and Symon made another note. "We haven't found any record of Hawthorn as the owner," he said.

Ronnie smirked. "No, I'll bet. Things here tend to be... off the record. But we got a deal. *Had* a deal. I guess it's up now."

"What kind of deal?" Mayher asked.

"This place was mine until about six years ago. Jason started coming here, doing... *business.* I didn't like it. Told him he'd have to leave. Didn't want that kind of trouble in my place. So he made me a deal. He had his lawyer draw up a contract."

She paused, thinking, then stood and pushed past them to a beat-up filing cabinet just inside the door. She opened the top drawer and rummaged through it until she pulled out a manilla envelope.

"Gave me six-hundred grand," Ronnie said, turning and handing the envelope to Mayher. "Papers say he's the owner. If anything ever came down, it was on him."

"You're saying that he was running some kind of illegal operation here, and you were letting him?" Symon asked.

Ronnie chuckled and dropped into her chair, once again picked up her cigarette from an ash tray, and took another drag. "Only thing I do is run this place. Don't know nothing about what he does here. Don't care. He owns the place. Or did. Papers say I'm his beneficiary, so I guess that means it reverts back to me, now that he's dead."

Symon watched her. It was clear she knew a lot more about Jason's business dealings here than she was saying. Maybe they could drag it out of her eventually, but it wouldn't be worth it.

This place was just an office for Jason Hawthorn. With him dead, whatever he did here would dry up.

"What about other assets?" Symon asked.

"What assets?" Ronnie asked.

"Does the Hawk & Dove have a warehouse offsite? Somewhere nearby?"

Ronnie took a longer drag, finishing off the cigarette before stubbing it out in the ash tray. Smoke once again poured from her nostrils. She nodded. "Yeah, there's a place. Got set up after he took over. We don't got much need for large inventory, as you can see. Barely three people in this place at any given time."

"Must make it hard to earn a living," Mayher said.

Ronnie shrugged. "I got other investments."

"Six-hundred grand worth, right?" Mayher asked.

Ronnie smirked at her, a lustful expression on her face. "I get by."

"Do you have the address for the warehouse?" Symon asked.

Ronnie nodded and turned back to her desk, sorting through the stacks of invoices and papers there. She picked one up, held it at arm's length under the ailing desk lamp, then turned and handed it to them.

It was an invoice for delivery—more than sixty crates of whiskey—with the address for a warehouse only a few blocks away.

It was close to the same warehouse where Jason Hawthorn's body had been found.

Symon noted the address and handed the invoice back to Ronnie.

They followed up with a few more questions, but it was clear they'd gotten everything they could. When they'd finished, they walked out of the little office, and Ronnie closed and locked the door behind them. They passed the two guards on their way out.

"An off the books business with an off the books warehouse," Mayher said.

"Which means Kayne likely knows nothing about it," Symon said. "For once we're ahead of her on intel."

"What do you think we'll find there?" Mayher asked.

Symon wasn't sure. He shook his head as he climbed into the driver's seat and started the car.

"We'll just have to see," he said as they pulled away.

CHAPTER FIFTEEN

ALEX NEEDED to check in on Hebert.

She'd learned about the visit from Agents Symon and Mayher, more or less by accident. She'd been scanning through any digitized notes they had on Jason Hawthorn and found something on Mayher's phone.

The missing details—the fact that it was such a scant reference, and that nothing appeared in any of the official records—told Alex a lot.

Symon had told Hebert to keep playing along.

In a way, this was good news. It was still best to keep Hebert out of this, and out of sight. And he was much safer—and much better off—if he wasn't reporting to a handful of crappy jobs each day. The money she was diverting his way made it possible for him to just stay home, out of the line of fire.

Alex wondered, briefly, if Symon had thought the same.

It wasn't entirely clear how little or how much Symon trusted Alex's "mission." In the brief conversations they'd had, over the phone or via text messages, he certainly seemed to get that she was trying to help people. She knew that would make zero difference to him, if he could find a way to arrest her. Agent Symon would do his job, without hesitation. It was one of the things Alex respected most about him.

But if he got that she was trying to help and protect innocent people, he might at least try to safeguard her clients.

That could be what he'd done here, with Hebert. She found herself hoping that was the case, for Hebert's sake as much as her own. More than her own.

Alex was standing between two duplexes across the street from Hebert's home. It was night, and there were very few streetlights here. There were porch lights on some of the homes, and those that weren't broken were filthy, casting a sickly yellow glow onto the gravel drives and weed-choked little lawns.

Alex was dressed like a ninja.

Not precisely, but it was pretty close. Form-fitting black Gore-tex leggings, black all-terrain running shoes, a Gore-tex top covered by a black hoodie, and a pair of black gloves. She even had a black gaiter mask around her neck, which could be pulled up to cover half her face in an instant.

It was helping her stay out of sight in the shadows, but shouldn't draw too much attention if she needed to blend in on a busy street. Most important, though, she could *move* in it. The material didn't hamper any of her parkour or fighting moves.

Lately it felt like this was a bit more necessary than usual.

Clinging to the shadows, Alex peered out toward Hebert's home. She'd been here for hours now, and she'd picked up on a few things.

There were two cars parked at either end of the street, both oriented toward Hebert's home, and both occupied by FBI agents.

That part was an assumption, but given what she knew about how Agent Symon did things, it seemed like a safe bet. Either way, it was clear they were law enforcement, which meant she would need to stay alert and cautious.

Each car had two agents, and as Alex had observed from her hiding spot, there had been a shift change. Another vehicle pulled up, there was a brief exchange as the new team was brought up to speed, and then the first shift drove away as the second settled in.

This might be good news.

With four FBI agents watching, Hebert should be safe. With Symon telling him to keep taking the money, all of Hebert's needs should be taken care of.

This all worked out for Hebert, and for Alex's plans.

She could relax.

She was preparing to leave when two more sedans pulled up to Hebert's place.

One had government plates.

Alex felt a sick twist in her stomach as she hunkered down, watching. It was too soon for another shift change, and the FBI had been using completely unmarked cars.

This was something else. Someone didn't mind being spotted. Which meant something was about to go down.

The sedans parked, and from the first a pair of suits climbed out and moved in opposite directions along the street, walking toward each of the two FBI vehicles. As Alex watched, each man held up identification and then leaned in to chat with the agents. Moments later the two FBI vehicles left, and the men in suites walked back to the sedans.

They stood to one side as the back door of the government car was opened.

Congressman Hawthorn stepped out, along with more dark-suited men flanking him.

Alex cursed and stepped back into the filthy alley, taking out her phone and using QuIEK to see if she could figure out just what the hell had happened here.

How had Hawthorn gotten on to Hebert? There was nothing in the official reports from Symon and Mayher. Had they mentioned something during their meeting in Hawthorn's offices?

Alex doubted that Symon would share specific details about the case, but Hawthorn was a US Congressman, and well connected in Chicago. He had ways of learning what he needed to know.

As she scanned through everything she could find, she came across an official request from Hawthorn's office to the USCP—the United States Capitol Police—a division of law enforcement charged with protecting members of Congress.

The request detailed an imminent threat to the Congressman's safety—Alex Kayne herself. There were details of Jason Hawthorn's murder, Alex's fugitive status, photos and surveillance video showing her intrusions into Hawthorn's home and his offices. Plenty of rope to hang her. But the implications of it all were worse than the threat itself.

Hawthorn knew who she was. And he'd used his pull and resources to figure out her game.

Hawthorn was no idiot. He'd put two and two together once he knew it was Alex on his tail. Her MO was part of her record with the FBI. He must have read through it and realized she was here to help Hebert—a publicly disgraced former cop that Hawthorn had framed to get Jason out of prison. It wouldn't be hard to make the leap.

Alex wasn't concerned with all of that, though. Her worry was what Hawthorn would do to Hebert.

She watched intently, trying to figure out what her options were. At the moment, they were extremely limited.

She could rush the place, try to fend off the USCP officers —five of them, by her estimate—as well as Hawthorn himself. That seemed like a fruitless and pointless plan, though. What would she do then, even if she somehow overtook them? Hebert would be in the soup, anyway.

She could hack her way into the USCP's systems and revoke the order for their presence, but that would likely raise suspicions from the officers on site, and the order would be verbal from that point. It was a useless plan.

Other ideas rose and fell, but nothing seemed promising. Hawthorn had her, for the moment.

After nearly a quarter of an hour the Congressman finally emerged with one of his guards at his side. The guard opened the rear door of the government Sedan, and Hawthorn climbed in.

Next, the four USCP officers emerged, with Hebert between the front two. He was cuffed, hands out front, and was being escorted to the other sedan. They placed him inside, closing the door behind him.

Everyone loaded up then, and the two sedans started and pulled away.

Alex stood in the darkness, cursing and watching. Shaking.

Rage. Fear. A heaping portion of both.

Hebert was now suffering even more injustice. And it was thanks to her. She had managed to make his life even worse, while trying to bring him justice.

Unacceptable.

She slipped back into the darkness, moving along the alley until she came to the next street over. She pulled the hood down to cover her face and started running. Her pickup point would be six blocks from here, according to her original plan. She'd already mapped out the circuitous route to get home. She could meet up with the Uber and be back at her place in about an hour.

From there, she'd spend the rest of the night going through options.

The plan had just changed. Again.

Now it was time to improvise.

CHAPTER SIXTEEN

SYMON AND MAYHER ARRIVED AT the warehouse by mid-morning, nearly 10 AM. It had taken that long to get the warrant.

The trouble and challenge had come down to a lack of just cause.

Jason Hawthorn had been cleared of all charges regarding drug trafficking. The Hawk & Dove was clearly the center of something suspicious, but Symon and Mayher currently had no evidence to support any specific charge. Getting into this warehouse was going to take something more than vague suspicions and hunches.

In the end, getting the warrant came down to Alex Kayne

He hadn't liked it, but Symon used Kayne's implication in Jason's murder to convince a judge that there was a reason to look into this place—a warehouse tied to Jason Hawthorn, so close to the scene where Jason's body was found.

Symon built a case around the idea of this potentially being Kayne's hunting ground. He shared some of Kayne's file and history with the judge, to show that Kayne often infiltrated the places of business of the people she targeted, even co-opting their resources to use against them.

Essentially, Symon implied that Kayne might just be holed up at the Hawk & Dove warehouse, and at the very least it should be eliminated as a potential site. In the end, that did the trick. It was enough to convince the judge to issue a warrant.

There was absolutely no chance of finding Kayne in this warehouse, Symon knew. But it was a convenient enough button to push just to get them in the door. Whatever he and Mayher discovered about the victim while investigating his murder was admissible and relevant even in tangential cases, as long as it was obtained legally.

The warehouse in question was less than a block from the scene of Jason Hawthorn's murder. Symon suspected that the only reason Jason kept the other warehouse was as a sort of camouflage—since the authorities knew about it, and it had been the scene of his supposed framing by Detective Hebert, keeping it on the books made sense. It was just a place of business, nothing more sinister than that.

It also was *his* hunting ground, Symon knew, where Jason took girls he picked up in clubs and bars. Serial criminals tended to favor patterns, and this warehouse was part of Jason Hawthorn's pattern. It explained why he'd brought Kayne there.

After the close call of being arrested and sent to prison, Jason had wised up and started separating business from pleasure. The warehouse where he had died had been his place of pleasure. The Hawk & Dove warehouse would be where he conducted his business.

At least, that was the theory Symon was gambling on. They'd know if that gamble paid off once they were inside.

They weren't breaching this place alone. As part of the warrant, Symon had requisitioned a team to help with the infiltration. Officers and agents surrounded the warehouse and meticulously marked and guarded exits. The place was monitored from every angle.

Alex Kayne was a dangerous and elusive fugitive, after all.

Symon and Mayher were the last to enter, as the team swept inward to check and clear the entire space. They found no one, which was not a surprise. From every angle, this was just a warehouse with industrial shelves reaching floor to ceiling in multiple rows, from wall to wall. The shelves were filled with crates, each marked under various brands of alcohol or other bar-related inventory.

A *lot* of inventory.

Taken at face value, there would be enough booze here to restock every bar in Chicago for a week. Far more than a dive like the Hawk & Dove would ever need.

"Start opening those crates," Symon ordered.

The team got to work, taking down crates row by row, prying them open and revealing the cache inside.

There was barely a drop of booze in the warehouse, that Symon could determine.

But there were lots of drugs.

And more chilling, lots and lots of weapons.

Mayher whistled. "Our boy Jason was into the heavier side of the night life."

Symon knelt to inspect the contents of one crate, picking through it with one gloved hand. This one contained neatly spaced rows of magazines, each loaded with .223 rounds. "AR-15 ammo," Symon said.

"Enough to go to war," Mayher replied.

Symon stood. "The FBI's file on Jason said they were closing in on him about weapons dealing. Looking for his supplier. They were going to turn him."

"But Hebert busted him for drugs instead," Mayher nodded.

"Why did the FBI let the case drop?" Symon replied, shaking his head. "They had him in a cell. They could have leaned on him. Gotten his source, even if he was burned as an asset."

"Maybe they didn't quite have the evidence they needed," Mayher shrugged. "This place was off the books. We only knew about Jason's ties to it because Ronnie told us."

Symon considered this. It didn't quite gel. The FBI would have kept digging, would have questioned Ronnie, would have eventually found this place.

Unless someone interfered.

Someone on the rise in the halls of Federal government.

Symon sighed. "Ok, so this tells a story about Jason. Let's see what else we can get out of it."

"Agent Symon?"

Symon looked up to see one of the field agents approaching. "We've found a server and security system." He pointed up to the rafters. "There are cameras all through this place. We think there's footage we can backtrack."

"Good," Symon nodded.

"We also found something else. Kind of weird."

He handed Symon a leather-bound ledger.

Symon took it, shaking his head. "Old school," he said. He flipped it open and started studying the handwritten entries. "Seems to be written in code."

Mayher stood beside him, peering over his shoulder. "What would be so sensitive that Jason Hawthorn would keep it off of digital records but still stash it in his super secret warehouse full of drugs and guns?"

Symon shook his head. "Something bigger than drugs and guns?"

"Like what? Nuclear weapons?"

Symon was studying a page of entries, trying to puzzle out what he was seeing. There were dates and numbers that might correlate with some sort of manifest. The rest of the information was just gibberish.

"Let's get our hands on any local shipping manifests and cargo logs," he said, flipping through the pages. "Airlines, ports, all of it. See if we can get any of these dates and numbers to line up."

He handed the ledger to Mayher, who nodded. "I'll start making calls." She took out her phone and left Symon standing among the open crates of contraband, and the FBI agents cataloging it all to create an inventory.

Symon was considering the scene, and everything they'd found here. This would be a big green check mark for Symon and Mayher, but it didn't quite answer any of the questions they'd come here for. It just created more.

"What were you into, Jason?" Symon asked as he looked around at the warehouse.

And then a more chilling question occurred to him. One he didn't yet dare ask aloud.

How much of it does your father know about?

CHAPTER SEVENTEEN

ALEX HAD SPENT much of the previous night backtracking camera footage, scouring every feed she could find, trying to track Kenneth Hebert.

Getting footage from near Hebert's house had been a challenge—what few cameras she could find online were usually vandalized or had terrible coverage at best. It was a pretty rough area of Chicago.

She had noted the license plates from Hawthorn's visit to Hebert's home, and with that information she eventually managed to catch the cars on surveillance, via a combination of ATM and traffic cams and QuIEK running character recognition on the fly.

Even with QuIEK handling the heavy lifting, it was still grueling, piecemeal work that had taken hours. It was a big city, and even narrowing things down to a finite number of paths, there were still thousands of cameras to access and sift through. It was the wee hours of the morning before she had any solid hits.

But those hits had paid off. And now that she had it sorted she was able to track the cars and their passengers from A to Z.

The Congressman's sedan had split off and taken Hawthorn to his home. The sedan carrying Kenneth Hebert had taken its time and a number of convoluted turns until reaching a secure holding facility in downtown Chicago.

She couldn't be certain, but it seemed like they were trying to shake her from tracking them.

Despite all measures taken to hide their route, however, Alex had been able to follow them virtually, with QuIEK tracking their plates from camera to camera throughout the city. After a bit, Alex was able to "fast forward," jumping ahead from footage to footage without having to track them in real time. Eventually, QuIEK showed her footage taken from their final destination.

From there, she essentially had an open access pass to every digital system in the facility where Hebert was being held.

So much for trying to throw her off their trail.

Alex pored through video feeds, using QuIEK to gain access to every corner of the place, and was able to watch as Hebert was booked, searched, and escorted to a room where he would sit and wait. For what, and for how long, was anyone's guess. But Alex suspected the USCP had orders to hold and observe him for a few days. The specifics of all of this were a mystery, but the purpose of it was obvious.

Kenneth Hebert had just become Alex Kayne bait.

Congressman Hawthorn was setting a trap, using Alex's client to lure her into the open so he could sic the USCP on her and have her tossed into a deep, dark hole somewhere in the world, held indefinitely, far removed from being any hindrance to his plans—and punished, of course, for taking his son from him. Though, Alex suspected that was probably a secondary offense in Hawthorn's eyes.

This was obviously meant to trip her up, to get her out in the open, where she would presumably make a mistake and the USCP would put her in a cell for the rest of her life.

It was *obvious*.

The trouble was, it was *working*.

Kenneth Hebert was an innocent man, and now—thanks to Alex—he was facing even greater punishment for something he didn't do. His life had already been ruined by the Hawthorns, and now Alex had gone and made it much worse.

There was no telling what would happen to him, when this was over, especially if she were caught. Alex suspected that his misery would be amplified a hundred fold, thanks to being on the bad side of a crooked Congressman, slighted and injured in the name of "justice" as a result of Hebert seeking *actual* justice.

It was too cruel. Too ugly. She couldn't let this stand.

She had to *do something*.

That was the impulse screaming into her brain—the voice demanding that she take action and *fix this*. Alex wanted to obey that impulse, wanted to make a run on the USCP facility, to free Hebert and then, maybe, do something in retaliation.

All stupid ideas.

When your plans go sideways, Papa Kayne's voice whispered in her head, *stop and look at things from that new angle.*

New perspective. That's what this was. New questions to ask. A new set of circumstances and resources to consider.

She knew this was a trap, which gave her some advantages. She also considered that this could be the best path for her client, for the time being.

For the moment, Hebert was cooling his heels in a government cell. Maybe not ideal for him, personally, but at the very least, he was safe, even from Hawthorn. The USCP would feed him and protect him, making sure his physical needs were met.

So there was that. And since he couldn't go anywhere, and no one else could get to him, it would take a bit of worry off of Alex's shoulders.

Hebert was safe. And so was Alex, as long as she didn't try to bust in there and rescue him. Calm and reason took over from impulse, and Alex felt the adrenaline and anxiety subside, replaced by that cool, calculating part of her mind that tended to ask the right kind of questions, and give her a better plan to follow.

So what now?

Hawthorn.

Unlike Hebert, Alex knew exactly where Hawthorn's sedan would have gone. No need to track him across the city. But that wasn't what she needed, anyway. What she needed was dirt.

She shifted her attention, dipping back into the bridge she'd installed at Hawthorn's home and his offices. QuIEK was running a series of AI-guided searches, looking for any information with a high relevancy score. She was getting back a lot of interesting hits, but nothing she saw as a smoking gun.

Out of frustration, she turned on the live video feed from Hawthorn's home.

This feed was built from a roving combination of cameras from mobile devices and laptops, overlaid with the security cameras from around the property. Alex had everything playing in small windows on her desktop, aligned with a blueprint of the house. This gave her a way to orient herself, to see where a scene was taking place.

In a slightly larger window she had a tracking pattern running—the AI was following Hawthorn as he moved about in his home, switching automatically to whichever camera could keep up with him from room to room. There was the occasional blank spot, filled in somewhat by audio from Hawthorn's smartphone. For the most part, it was fairly continuous coverage.

Alex sat back in the little kitchen chair she was using at the small desk. She had a cup of coffee and a bowl of roasted almonds, and she munched at these absently as she thought about her next move. She was watching the footage, but things were barely registering. Nothing notable seemed to be happening on-screen.

Until...

She paused in mid-nibble, then leaned forward to examine the screen of her laptop.

"Where the hell?"

She placed the coffee cup and the bowl of almonds off to the side and started navigating on the laptop. She pulled up the blueprint of the house, with its little windows of video associated with each room. She scanned back and forth from the live view to the blueprint.

Hawthorn had just entered a room that had a camera covering the space from one corner. The footage was crisp and clear—at least 4K. The data streaming from the feed was incredibly high. A real bandwidth choker.

Whatever happened in this room, someone wanted to be able to see every single detail.

This room was not on the blueprint of the Hawthorn home.

The layout Alex was using to generate her virtual landscape came from the official plans for Hawthorn's estate. She'd found both the original set for when the home was built, and the revised set for when Hawthorn had purchased and remodeled the place. Alex had reconciled the two when she'd set up her overlays of video.

Neither set featured this room.

Alex moved the main live view aside and opened the recorded feed, backtracking and tracing until she could spot where Hawthorn had transitioned from the house's layout and into this secret, unmarked space.

It had happened during one of the blank spots.

Alex cursed, and started sorting through the feed again, stopping when she got the next camera angle, from just before the blank in the footage. Hawthorn had a number of fancy camouflaged doors in his home—just like the one in his study, when Alex had met him. He'd gone through one of these from the corridor leading off of his master bedroom and had entered a zone that had no camera coverage.

Alex made a note of the entrance and its general location on the blueprint.

She turned back to the live feed.

"What are you up to?" she asked quietly.

On-screen the lights slowly rose, illuminating the space as the Congressman moved deeper into the room. Hawthorn stopped and stood in the center.

The space was interesting. It was set up almost like an apartment, with a sofa and table, and a couple of chairs. And, at the far end, a bed.

Someone was in the bed, covered to the neck by blankets. Their face wasn't visible from this angle.

Alex leaned in, her heart racing. She wasn't sure who this was, or why the scene was triggering something within her. But she felt a sick twist in her gut.

Something was definitely wrong.

"I'm afraid Jason won't be coming to visit you anymore," Hawthorn said to the lump in the bed. "I'm sure that's actually something of a relief to you. But it presents me with a problem. One that I'll have to solve soon."

The lump didn't move. There was no sound. Hawthorn stood for a moment, watching. Then he shook his head and turned, pausing at the door for a few seconds before it opened, allowing him to retreat back to the main house.

The camera showing the room went dark as the lights faded back to black.

Alex felt the sickening twist intensify.

Who was in that room? Were they a prisoner? And how was Hawthorn going to "solve" this problem?

It was too soon to tell. As sinister as this looked, there could be any number of explanations. But given what she knew of Jason Hawthorn's history, Alex couldn't shake the dark instinct that had come over her.

She sat back, shaking her head.

What were you into, Jason?

Regardless of the answer, there was nothing about this scene that could be good. Jason Hawthorn was into something nasty here.

And Congressman Hawthorn knew all about it.

Alex shook her head again. She glanced at the live footage of Kenneth Hebert, then at the footage of Hawthorn moving through his house.

Her eyes fell once again on the black video feed from the room that didn't exist.

There was someone in there. There were *answers* in there.

She had to get into that room.

CHAPTER EIGHTEEN

This was dangerous. More dangerous than usual.

Alex had been sneaking around in the dark for years, breaking and entering into the homes and businesses of her targets so often it had become routine. There was always some element of danger—getting caught, getting arrested, getting shot. She took her chances because it was what the work required. It was how she helped people who had no one else to turn to. Dangerous situations were a small price to pay for bringing justice to the powerless.

But this was pushing the line.

Congressman Anthony Hawthorn's estate held secrets that Alex couldn't dredge up using QuIEK. There were blind spots in this place that Alex couldn't prepare for. And the Congressman had already shown a proclivity for trying to get her killed. All of those things combined to make this one of the most dangerous places she could be. She should be *anywhere else*—her survival instincts screamed it with every step.

But she had to get into that room.

Getting past Hawthorn's home security wouldn't be as

challenging as just getting to his house in the first place. The long, winding drive she'd taken in the rental car, just a few days earlier, was completely out of the question as a means of approach this time. There were dozens of cameras along that path, each equipped with night vision, and each pinging each other in succession to ensure they were getting live, uninterrupted coverage.

While Alex figured she could use QuIEK to fool even that elaborate setup, she believed there was a better way.

The property leading up to Hawthorn's home was filled with forest growth—some of it cultivated and placed intentionally, and some left to run wild, mostly uncultivated land that had been standing nearly untouched since before the estate was built. In her research of the property, Alex had found that the original owners of Hawthorn's estate had been budding naturalists and preservationists. Hawthorn, on the other hand, appeared to have "self" preservation as his motive for keeping the forest growth intact.

Aside from its natural beauty, all the wild underbrush and thick tree cover provided a great deal of privacy for Hawthorn's estate, as well as a fierce barrier to entry for anyone casually trying to navigate the property. Using satellite imagery, however, Alex had found that there were trails carved throughout the woods—a network of manmade gravel paths that she suspected were meant for property maintenance.

Some of the estate's infrastructure was sheltered in these woods—water treatment, sewer management, and similar systems were all kept discretely out of view. Grounds staff would need access to these from time to time, and so the paths provided it.

Of course, paths went two ways—in *and* out.

Scanning the local security grid with QuIEK, Alex had

determined that though the facilities in the woods were covered by video surveillance, none of the trails had cameras.

If she could push her way through the thick brush from the road to the water treatment building, staying to its West side, she could stay hidden from the cameras by skirting the edge of the clearing. Then she could join the gravel trail that led back out to the main property.

Easy. Except for the part where she had to push through half a mile of unkempt, wild forest and undergrowth in the middle of the night.

It had taken almost two hours to get to the gravel path she'd targeted. That was an hour over her estimate, which meant she was woefully behind schedule. She was also covered in scratches and bug bite, sweating from head to toe, and generally miserable.

None of that mattered, however. She'd made it. And the trail gave her a quick and easy jog to one of the outbuildings on the property, where she could pause and assess the situation. It had been a slog, but she'd made it. She was within a sprint of Hawthorn's house, and no signs of a security team ready to pounce on her.

She had a different plan in mind for getting away from the estate, when her work was done. One that would be a lot faster, but also a lot more noticeable.

She made the quick sprint to the main house, then used QuIEK to digitally unlock a door before entering through the kitchen.

The house was dark, but there was enough light from various innocuous sources that Alex could navigate without a flashlight with no trouble. She'd also memorized the layout of the place and knew every door and every hiding spot—and every camera angle. QuIEK had taken over that network and was using real-time selective masking and looping to hide Alex as she moved.

Basically, QuIEK was isolating Alex on the footage, frame-by-frame, and replacing her with a frame of video from seconds before she stepped into view. It caused a minor lag in the signal sent to the monitoring equipment—not enough that anyone should notice. If anyone was watching too closely, they might spot a blip as the image was manipulated, but otherwise it would be fairly seamless.

Roving digital camouflage that worked like a cloak of invisibility for security cameras.

She hoped. It was kind of a new trick, and she hadn't had much time to shake out the bugs.

No help for it now, though.

Alex moved through the same set of corridors Hawthorn had taken to get to the hidden room, using the route she had memorized.

The house was quiet, and to Alex it seemed like every step she took echoed loudly throughout the entire home. She knew she was just hyper alert to noise, but she found herself moving at a slower pace, taking more cautious steps, making sure to place her feet on carpets and rugs rather than uncovered wooden floors.

This all slowed her down even further, but it was hard not to lapse into caution.

She checked the time on her smartwatch, touching the screen to activate it.

She was still good. Her window was narrowing, but she had time, if she hurried.

She took a few quick, calming breaths, and then picked up her pace, moving quickly to the hidden door.

This was where things went off book.

She had no idea where the trigger would be to open the

door. In fact, thanks to a blank in camera footage for this corridor, she wasn't even sure what the door would look like. Now, as she faced what appeared to be an ordinary wall in a darkened corridor, she wasn't sure what to do next.

She frowned and started running her fingers along the wall's surface.

There were definitely seams here. Several, in fact. Any of them could be a contender for a secret opening. But no entrance presented itself.

She stepped back, thinking.

From the footage Alex had intercepted, Hawthorn had paused for a few seconds before exiting the room on the other side of this wall. He hadn't used any sort of keypad or device, that Alex had seen. He'd simply moved to the door, waited, and then exited when the door opened.

No keypads. No keys. No fingerprint or retina scanners. But there was definitely something gatekeeping that door. Something that could tell the difference between Congressman Hawthorn and his "guest."

Alex's money was on proximity sensors.

The specific flavor of the system could be anything, but there had to be something scanning whoever was near the door, determining their permissions, and then unlocking and opening. Since there were no cameras aimed at or away from the door on either side, that meant it wasn't facial recognition. There was some other type of scanner.

Alex took out her phone and used QuIEK to start poking around for any signs of a system embedded in the wall, anything transmitting. It took a few seconds, but eventually the AI connected to something—an RFID reader.

Similar to the systems that scan car tags on a tollway, the RFID reader embedded in the wall here would look for a specific transponder signal.

Hawthorn must have had something on him that the system could read, as he entered and exited. It could be anything, right down to a microchip on a credit card. Small, innocuous, and easy to hide. Someone from the outside could look right at it and never know it was a key to a secret room.

Alex could replicate it easily, using QuIEK, and in just a few seconds she heard a satisfying click from the hidden door, then saw a crack open along one of the seams.

She was in.

She entered the darkened room on the other side of the wall, and found that she was standing in a short corridor, about six feet long. Another door, more obvious than the first, was set into the far wall here. Again, Alex used the RFID she'd cloned to open the door with no trouble, and exited the corridor—an airlock of sorts—into a larger space.

At first it was pitch black, but she had already programmed QuIEK to find and raise the lights. As she stood in the doorway, the room illuminated like the dawn, a slow rise in the lights that brought with it the details of the space.

This was the room she'd seen on the video.

As she had entered, QuIEK had gone through the process of finding the room's 4K camera and looping the video feed. If anyone happened to be watching, they'd see the same pitch black as before she'd walked in. Though Alex noted that the camera did have an infrared mode as well.

Hopefully no one would try to activate that—it'd be a dead giveaway that something was wrong, if no video showed up. The live-looping she was doing with the cameras outside this room wouldn't work because there'd be a moment, as the camera modes switched, where QuIEK wouldn't have an empty frame of video to use as camouflage. For a flash, Alex would be visible, plain as day.

She was counting on Congressman Hawthorn keeping this

room out of the loop for security monitoring. It was obvious that this was a secret only he and Jason had known about until Alex stumbled onto it. So unless the Congressman himself was monitoring the room at this late hour, and decided to turn on the infrared, she *should* be safe, just looping dark-room footage.

It was a gamble. But so was this whole enterprise.

Next, Alex turned her attention to visually scanning the room, looking for signs of life. She hadn't seen anyone on the footage she'd sorted through earlier, just signs of movement from the bed across the room. At the moment, however, the bed appeared empty. The covers were tossed aside, lying in a heap at the foot of the bed. Whoever had been there had moved.

There was a noise from beside her, a groan that sounded almost feral, and before she knew it she was thrown to the ground, a figure landing on top of her, striking her with something heavy and hard.

Alex raised her arms in defense, protecting her head, and saw that the person on top of her was a young woman, maybe in her twenties, holding what appeared to be the leg of a chair.

The girl raised the chair leg above her head, making a guttural cry, and Alex quickly snaked her hands up to take hold of her wrists. She held them there, without much effort. The girl seemed weak and frail—likely as a result of prolonged captivity. She cried out, frustrated and afraid, and it was a wail that broke Alex's heart.

"I'm a friend!" Alex shouted. "I'm here to help! I'm here to rescue you!"

The girl was beyond listening. She screamed and thrashed, pulling her hands free from Alex's grip and springing to her feet. She ran for the back corner of the room, wedging herself between the bed and the wall, the chair leg held up like a sword before her, an attempt to ward Alex off.

She slid down along the wall until all Alex could see were

her eyes, wide and fearful, and the wavering stump of the chair leg.

Alex moved carefully, cautiously. She edged closer, her hands held out and visible. "It's ok," she said calmly. "It's ok, I'm here to help you."

The girl pushed even further back into her hiding space, and Alex heard another wailing cry, low and inhuman.

My God, Alex thought. *What did they do to her?*

She moved closer, but stopped at the foot of the bed, making sure to keep it between her and the girl.

"My name is Alex," she said, putting the palm of her hand against her own chest. She had to be careful here. She had to appear completely unthreatening. The girl's fragile state was going to make this difficult, and Alex was afraid they were already running out of time. "I'm here to take you home."

The girl made a choked noise, then swallowed and said something Alex didn't recognize. Another language, perhaps?

Alex shook her head. "I don't know what they've done to you here, but I know it's horrible. We have to get you out of here."

The girl watched her, and Alex could see the tears streaming down her face.

It took several minutes to coax her out of the spot, and several more before she would sit on the bed and let Alex come anywhere near her.

This was bad.

When Alex had seen the footage, with Congressman Hawthorn standing and talking to someone in here, she knew that the reasons for it would be something horrible. But she hadn't quite anticipated how bad this would be.

She had to get this girl out of here. *Now.*

"What is your name?" Alex asked, slowly and deliberately.

She again patted her chest and said, "Alex. My name is Alex." She motioned encouragingly to the girl. "What is your name?"

The girl still looked terrified, maybe even in shock. But she seemed to understand the gesture. "Natalia," she replied, her hands staying at her side. She sat, rigid, only making quick glances toward Alex. She seemed ready to bolt at any second.

Alex noted an accent. Russian, maybe? The name was typically Russian. Alex wasn't sure. Definitely not American.

"Natalia," Alex said gently, smiling. She thought for a moment, then carefully reached into her pocket and removed the little pod that contained her wireless earbuds. She made sure that Natalia was paying attention, and showed her the buds as she placed one in her own ear. She offered the other to Natalia.

The girl hesitated, but as Alex smiled and continued to offer, she took the earbud and placed it in her own ear.

Alex took out her phone and brought up QuIEK, doing a few quick passes with her fingers over the screen, making connections to various databases and subroutines. QuIEK's AI was smart enough to figure out what she was trying to do and assisted with the heavy lifting.

"There," Alex said after a moment. "You should hear me in Russian now. I'm assuming you speak Russian?"

The girl's eyes widened as QuIEK interpreted and translated. She nodded. "Yes," Alex heard from the earbud as Natalia spoke. "I am from Russia. St. Petersburg."

Alex nodded, smiling. "I visited there once, years ago."

The girl looked at Alex and suddenly burst into tears.

It was a risk, but Alex moved closer to her and tentatively reached out a hand, touching Natalia's own. It was a simple gesture, but it seemed to be enough.

"Natalia," Alex said gently, "I know you've been through a lot. I don't know what they've done to you but I... I can guess.

I'm here to get you out of here, though. And I'll need your help to do it. Can you come with me?"

Natalia was crying and sniffling, but nodded. "Yes," she said. "I want to go home."

This last was so sad and pathetic sounding that it broke Alex's heart all over.

"Yes," Alex replied. "Home. Let's get you home."

They stood, and Alex led her to the door where QuIEK activated the RFID scanner. The door opened, and Alex moved through, cautiously, into the short corridor. She motioned for Natalia to follow, and the girl padded into the hall, a bewildered look on her face. Alex's guess was that the girl had never actually seen this corridor, or the house itself.

Alex clicked the hidden door closed behind them and took Natalia's hand as she led the two of them back through the darkened house. They stepped carefully, just as Alex had on the way in. Natalia was clinging close now, and Alex could feel her shaking as she walked.

In time they approached the kitchen.

A light snapped on just as they were entering.

There was a moment of blindness as Alex's eyes adjusted, but as she blinked her vision cleared. Standing before them was Hawthorn's butler or valet or whoever he was—the man who had introduced Hawthorn during Alex's first meeting with the Congressman, several days earlier.

There was a pause as the three of them stood, staring at each other, recognition and comprehension dawning on them all. Then...

"Intruders!" the man shouted, as he leaped for a panel beside the kitchen door.

Before Alex could reach him, the man had already hit the panic button, and an ear-piercing alarm cut through the entire house.

"This way!" Alex said, gripping Natalia's hand and yanking her past the butler, through the kitchen door and out into the darkened grounds of the estate.

They didn't remain darkened for long, however.

Lights snapped on all around Alex and Natalia, sweeping spotlights mounted on the roof came to life, emitting powerful white beams that Alex could feel as much as see.

Headlights also lit the grounds as security raced toward them in vehicles. There were electronically amplified commands shouting for them to halt, to drop to the ground, to stay where they were.

Alex had no intention of staying where she was.

She yanked Natalia along, practically dragging the younger girl as they raced in the direction of Alex's escape plan.

She had memorized the layout of the property, both from Google Earth shots and from her own 3D map, built using the various security cameras and sensors that monitored everything on the estate grounds. She'd plotted this escape route down to the slightest detail—though she had hoped she wouldn't be running from security on her way out.

Natalia, for her part, was doing an admirable job of keeping up. She trusted Alex now—they were bonded by a common threat, and Alex was her only hope of getting out of this place.

Trust was good, because Alex needed her hands free for a moment.

She released Natalia's hand and took out her phone, tapping an icon on the home screen. This started a process she had pre-programmed for QuIEK, and things got going quickly.

Lights started flickering on and off all around the estate, accompanied by the sounds of sirens and even music blaring on and off, switching frequently. The cacophony was meant to be a distraction, and it helped.

Doors also opened and then re-locked themselves, creating

a clear path as Alex and Natalia stepped through, helping to facilitate their run while slowing down their pursuers.

Hawthorn's over-dependence on digital security was playing right into Alex's plans. The estate was over-reliant on digital locks, which worked in Alex's favor, and each door opened as if by magic. Each also stubbornly locked behind them once they passed through, its digital codes scrambled, as security tried futiley to follow.

It wasn't impossible for security to break through, but it slowed them enough to give the girls a lead.

Eventually Alex and Natalia burst through a door leading into a large garage—a space lined with expensive automobiles.

Jason Hawthorn's Porsche had been wrecked during Alex's final encounter with him, but she'd learned he had a collection of other vehicles. It was another passion of his—something else he possessed to give himself the illusion of being more than just a scumbag.

The vehicle Alex wanted was on the far end of the garage, and QuIEK got it started and waiting for them as they sprinted toward it.

It was a bit much, Alex would admit, but she had selected it for its speed and maneuverability.

Also, she would confess, because it was *bad ass.*

She and Natalia skidded to a halt and stood before a Dodge Tomahawk V10 Superbike—a half-million-dollar motorcycle that looked like something Batman would have drooled over. Its engine purred insistently as they approached.

"We're leaving on that?" Natalia asked, the Russian translating in Alex's ear.

"*Da,*" Alex nodded, grinning.

Natalia blew out a breath and made no objection as Alex hopped onto the bike and pulled her onto the seat behind.

Alex took a deep breath, then waited.

The garage door opened, rolling upward with a whir.

Before it had even reached the top of the ceiling, Alex gunned the Tomahawk, and they were out.

The thing moved like a diving falcon—speed and grace, a terrifying screech of power, leaving no question that you were witnessing a predator in motion.

Alex had ridden motorcycles before, and had practically grown up on one. Papa Kayne had restored old bikes as a hobby. But nothing Alex had ever ridden had been half as powerful as the Tomahawk. It had so much power it scared her.

She *really* liked it.

She gunned the engine, accelerating at a ridiculous speed, and turned to race up the drive leading away from the garage.

Security vehicles had the drive itself blocked, and guards were out, aiming weapons at them as Alex and Natalia raced forward.

"Hold on!" Alex shouted.

She felt Natalia squeeze her waist tighter.

The Tomahawk, somehow, managed to go even faster.

Moving like something out of a comic book movie, Alex zig-zagged through the barricade of guards and cars, blowing past them so fast and loud she was sure she'd just introduced some of the guards to religion.

She raced along the drive now, the Tomahawk's headlights barely keeping pace with the speed of the bike. As they approached the front gate Alex was relieved to see that it was already standing open. QuIEK had done its job, clearing the path that would continue on out of the estate and through the neighborhoods, towns, and cities beyond.

In an instant they were out, leaving Hawthorn's property and racing along the back roads. QuIEK was working ahead of them the whole way, tuning traffic lights, diverting traffic, making an open road for them. In a very short time they passed the Chicago city limits, moving into the city like a pulse of light.

It was only minutes later that Alex pulled into the emergency lane of a local hospital. QuIEK had done its work here, too, because as they approached a team of nurses and orderlies and doctors raced out of the ER with a gurney.

Alex held the Tomahawk up at a slight angle, though it was a remarkable feat of leg strength to do so. She turned, twisting and leaning back so she could see Natalia, who was still clinging to her.

"Go with them," she said. "They can help you. Tell them everything that Jason Hawthorn and Congressman Hawthorn did to you. That's who had you—*Jason and Anthony Hawthorn*. Can you remember their names?"

Natalia nodded. "Yes," she said.

"You can trust these people," Alex said, nodding to the ER personnel. "And soon you'll be visited by two FBI agents— Agent Eric Symon and Agent Julia Mayher. When they come to you, use the word *Swordfish*. Got it?"

Natalia made a strange expression. "*Swordfish?*"

"Exactly," Alex smiled. "They'll understand." She hesitated for a moment, took a deep breath, glanced at the orderlies and nurses and then back again." Natalia... I'm so very sorry that this happened to you. But if you can be brave, and tell Agent Symon everything you know, I promise you, the people who did this will pay." She hesitated for a second, then said, "I trust him."

Natalia was helped off of the motorcycle and up onto the gurney.

A nurse tried to get information from Alex, and even tried to keep her there, but with a loud gunning of the Tomahawk's engine, startling everyone into hopping back a step, Alex was out onto the street in seconds, on her way deeper into the city.

She would ditch the bike.

Which was heartbreaking. But her life didn't allow her to keep toys, these days. And this one was way too conspicuous, anyway. Though, for a moment she considered it—the thing was so fast it might make for some handy exits.

She sighed. It just couldn't be. She gunned the motor again, felt the press of acceleration, and lamented the necessity of having to give it up.

QuIEK had already sent word to Symon and Mayher, so Alex knew she could count on them to show. She'd arranged that ahead of time. The code word would be verification that this had been her work.

And her work here was done. This part of it, anyway.

She parked the bike and then sprinted away—now feeling like she was moving at a slug's pace. She wound through a pre-arranged route to the first of several pickup spots. She would network her way through the city, from pickup to pickup, and be home in just over two hours. Then she'd start monitoring for the fallout from this evening.

There were still things to deal with—problems to solve, inevitable hiccups in her plan that she would have to compensate for. But this was a big blow against Hawthorn. A big win for justice.

She hoped. She prayed.

The only thing that mattered, though—for now—was that Natalia was safe. That part of the plan, at least, had come up as a win.

But there was still work to do.

CHAPTER NINETEEN

SYMON HAD a translator sit in as he interviewed Natalia. Even with the delay between answer and translation, the story that unfolded had him riveted.

And turned his stomach.

This *had* to be enough to bring the Congressman down. Didn't it?

Maybe, maybe not.

The fact that it was Alex Kayne who had liberated Natalia from whatever sick scenario was unfolding at the Congressman's estate—that made things complicated. Especially considering that the Congressman had recently engaged the services of the USCP.

Symon was getting some details from Mayher on all of that now, and it wasn't looking good.

"Basically, the Congressman is spinning this as Kayne setting him up," Mayher said. "He's denied any knowledge of Natalia being in his home, and because he had already engaged the USCP to protect him from Kayne, his attorney is making a case that she arranged this as part of targeting him. It's making it tough to get a warrant to search the premises."

"Come on," Symon replied, incredulous.

Mayher shrugged. "He's got pull. No judge in this town is willing to sign that order. Not yet."

"So what's it going to take?" Symon replied, bitterly. "We have someone who says she was there, held captive, assaulted. Worse."

"She can't identify the Congressman," Mayher replied, shaking her head. "We showed her a deck of photos, and she couldn't pick him out. Same with Jason. No positive ID. She was kept in the dark most of the time, and apparently Jason liked to keep his conquests drugged to the eyeballs. Toxicology shows pretty heavy traces of sedatives and psychotropics. She's been on a trip for a very long time. What details she remembers are all scattered and hazy. There's nothing we can use to definitively put her in Hawthorn's home."

Symon blew out a breath. He shook his head, turning to stare toward Natalia's hospital room. "I knew the Congressman was dirty, but I wasn't expecting this."

"My money is on this being all Jason's thing, and the Congressman just enabled it," Mayher replied. "There's some history of him covering for his son."

Symon nodded. "Right. Makes sense." He stared at the door for a moment, blew out another breath, squared himself and turned to Mayher. "Ok, so this isn't going well. We need to find a way to put Natalia in that house, prior to Kayne's arrival, with strong enough evidence to support a warrant."

"Maybe we can get someone on his staff to crack?" Mayher asked.

"If they haven't so far, I don't see them doing it anytime soon," Symon replied. "The Congressman has hired some very loyal people. And they all lawyered up the second this went down. Even the butler who spotted Kayne and Natalia in the kitchen will only speak with an attorney present. We're getting nothing useful out of any of them."

They continued to chat for a few minutes, and then Mayher went in to ask some follow-up questions of Natalia. The hope was to get something—*anything*—that could be used as enough evidence to justify a warrant.

Symon knew it was futile.

From Natalia's story, she'd been abducted in St. Petersburg, drugged and shoved into a cargo container. She had vague, hazy memories of the trip—lots of wailing, crying, gagging. The smell had been sickening. She recalled vomiting, feeling weak, going in and out of consciousness. And then, one day, she woke up in a dark room, where she was visited regularly by someone Symon assumed was Jason Hawthorn.

At first she hadn't even realized she was no longer in Russia, and that revelation had brought shock and tears.

Every memory she had was skewed by a continual drug haze, which only ended after Jason's death. She'd had an IV in her arm, when she awoke, and whatever cocktail Jason Hawthorn used must have finally run out in the days after his death.

Natalia had come out of the stupor just hours before Kayne had arrived to rescue her and had fashioned a weapon by breaking a chair. It was the first real moment of lucidity she'd had since her abduction.

She couldn't provide much for them to use to counter the Congressman's claims, that Kayne had brought Natalia to his home herself, as a way to frame him. Given that he'd already filed complaints and engaged law enforcement, following Kayne visiting his home and his offices, and the murder of his son, it was easy for him to make his case. Kayne was obviously a threat, obviously out to get him. She was capable, dangerous, and deadly.

His attorneys had all of this stitched up.

If only we could use the video evidence Kayne gave us, Symon thought.

Evidence that, he knew, was completely damning to the Congressman, but was also completely inadmissible for how it was obtained.

It was frustrating. They knew Hawthorn was dirty. They knew he was into some pretty evil stuff. But nothing they had could be used against him. Not yet.

Symon left the hospital, driving the twenty minutes back to the hotel where he decided to spend some off-duty time in the bar.

He needed sleep.

No, what he really needed was a *distraction.*

He needed to do something that would take his mind off of all of this, long enough that the blocks could come down and some new idea could rise up. He needed something that could shift his thinking, let his mind unclench.

The hotel bar was the best he could come up with, and since he was off duty, he ordered a whiskey sour to help move things along.

"Mind if I sit?" a woman asked.

Symon gave a quick glance at the blond. She was wearing a red evening gown, low-cut and revealing. Certainly a distraction, but not quite what he was looking for.

Hooker, his mind supplied.

"I'm a Fed," he said, his eyes locked on the drink on the bar before him, set to ignore her and send her on her way.

"Yeah, so I'm told," the woman replied.

Symon looked up at her then, his face quizzical. His eyes widened when he recognized her.

Alex Kayne.

He started to move, to reach for his gun or his badge—he wasn't entirely sure which.

Before he could do whatever his FBI training was telling him to do, however, Kayne plopped down on the barstool next to him, pressing against him so close that her body hampered his movements.

It was uncomfortably intimate. He could feel the heat of her on his arm. He could smell her—not perfume, she would avoid that. Nothing that could easily identify her. Just the scent of her, like evening air.

He had mixed feelings about all of this.

"Eric," she said, leaning in close, whispering. "I have at least ten different ways out of here. And I could have you either on the floor or flung over the bar before you could get your hand out of your coat. You may catch me some day... this isn't your day."

He looked at her, then sighed, nodded, and relaxed. She was right. The last time he'd had her this close, she showed him exactly how well she could handle herself. This time, with no backup, no plan, not even the advantage of surprise, he had no real shot at capturing her.

She sat back, keeping herself oriented toward him.

"Been awhile," she said, a smile touching her lips.

"We talked just a couple of days ago," Symon replied.

"But we haven't seen each other in the flesh since Orlando. This is a nice change of pace."

"If you turned yourself in," Symon said with a casual smile, "we could chat face-to-face more often."

"Just isn't the same with a half-inch sheet of plexiglass between us," she replied.

He laughed lightly. Then, after a pause, he glanced around,

looking to the eaves of the bar. "If there's any video of this, my career is over," he said.

She made a derisive sound. "Please," she said. "Did you just meet me? Footage doesn't just *get out* when I'm involved." She smiled sweetly. "It becomes part of a strategy."

"This does seem to be the case," Symon nodded, raising his drink for a sip. He smacked his lips slightly as he placed the glass back on the bar. "Alex... what are you doing here? This seems like a pretty big risk. What's your angle?"

"My angle is that I want to bring down Congressman Hawthorn and get Kenneth Hebert's life back on track."

Symon was watching her face, considering. He nodded again. "Yeah, I think we're almost in full alignment, for once."

"More often than you think," Kayne smiled. "But yeah, this time I think your job and my job are overlapping pretty close. Heck, maybe we'll both have the *same* job soon, if this whole Historic Crimes thing happens."

Symon had nearly forgotten about Historic Crimes, and Dr. Ludlum's offer to both him and Kayne. "Have you made a decision on that? Is this you coming in from the cold?"

Kayne shook her head. "Not yet. I don't know what will happen if I decide to take Ludlum up on that offer. But I can't risk being locked down when Hebert still needs me. And when scum like Hawthorn is doing this kind of thing to innocent girls."

"You think it was the Congressman who put Natalia in there?"

Kayne shook her head. "No. That was Jason. But the Congressman enabled him to do it and is still enabling it now."

Symon nodded, then shrugged and took another sip of his drink. "Hawthorn has us roadblocked at the moment. Because of you."

"Me?" Kayne asked.

"He's claiming this is all a setup, and that you brought Natalia to his home to make it look like he was involved. Since he had already gone to the USCP about you, all the judges in Chicago think this is plausible."

Kayne sighed. "I figured that might be it," she said. "Damn, this guy is slippery."

"It seems like he's had a lot of practice," Symon said. "One thing though... we did manage to nail Salvator."

Alex's eyes widened, and she smiled. "Really? That's great!"

"It was a lot easier to get warrants on him, based on the evidence you slipped us. The stuff we could link to a warrant came in handy. Thanks for that. Also, I am officially telling you to keep out of FBI business."

"Noted. I'll remember this fondly the next time I'm handing some bad guy to you, all tied up in a bow."

"As expected," Symon said, nodding, tipping the whiskey sour toward her in a mock toast. He looked at her for a moment, shook his head, and said, "Alex... what kind of life is this? You have to be exhausted. Don't you want all of this to stop? Why are you doing this?"

Kayne seemed as if she were about to answer, then stopped, closed her mouth, shook her head. After a brief moment she said, "I wish I could say I had this all figured out, but the truth is I've been making things up as I go for more than two years now. I think... I do this because no one would do it for *me*. I think that's it."

"You didn't give anyone a chance to do it for you," Symon said. "You ran, right out of the gate."

"Can you honestly say I'd have gotten a fair shot, if I'd let them take me into custody? I was framed for *treason*, and the only thing anyone seems to care about is getting their hands on QuIEK."

Symon nodded at this. "True," he said. "I can't say what would have happened, really. Maybe you're right. Maybe you'd be buried in a hole somewhere. I'm just saying you never gave it a shot."

"Fair enough," Kayne said. "But it doesn't change much. I do what I do because these people fell through the cracks. Justice isn't being done, because... well, because the law isn't set up for *justice* these days. It's set up for ass-covering, mostly."

Symon laughed. "I think everyone else in my life would disagree. But I can see your point."

"You should," Kayne said, her expression serious but soft. "It happened to you, too."

Symon wasn't looking at her. He kept his attention focused on the drink, on the bar, on his hands.

"I've seen all the files," Kayne said. "The whole thing that went down with Director Crispen. How it blew back on you."

"It was a long time ago," Symon said.

"Not that long," Kayne replied. "You're just starting to get your career back on track."

"And doing a smash-up job of it," Symon smiled, looking at her. "My top fugitive is sitting three inches from me, and I still can't nab her."

"*Nab* me? What are you, the Hamburglar?"

"Cheeseburgers don't flip the Hamburglar over bridge rails and make an escape that Tarzan would envy," Symon replied.

Kayne nodded. "Fair enough. Look, Eric... I'm sorry for things like that. I'm sorry for all of it."

"Sorry enough to turn yourself in?" Symon asked.

She smiled, shook her head. "Never that sorry."

He shrugged. "Worth a shot."

He thought for a moment, staring over the rim of his glass as he swished the whiskey in a circle. "I have all the footage and evidence you've gathered against Hawthorn, and I can't use any of it," he said. "It was all obtained illegally. It's poison to this case."

"I know," Kayne said. "That isn't how I normally do things. It became kind of a necessity, after Hawthorn had Salvator's goons grab me."

"It's getting tougher to get justice for Hebert," Symon added.

"I know," Kayne repeated.

Symon hesitated before making his next statement. "Alex, if you turned yourself in, I could use that evidence to nail Hawthorn. I could say we obtained it during your arrest."

Kayne studied him for a moment.

"Ok. I'll keep that in my back pocket," Kayne said, finally. "Plan B."

Symon sighed, nodding. "Fair enough. So what's your Plan A?" He looked up at her, stared at her. "You always have one. You think twenty steps ahead, have all your exits and strategies and options worked out." He motioned vaguely to the surrounding bar, as if in example. "So what is it this time? What's the trick you have up your sleeve, to bring down Congressman Hawthorn?"

She looked at him, then leaned forward, her eyes locked on his.

Symon felt his heart thump, and though he knew perfectly well why, he still couldn't just *accept* it.

Kayne was a fugitive. She was a criminal, or accused as such. She was on the run, and he was the one chasing her. That made her unattainable, in more ways than one. It made her dangerous. Here she was, inches from him, and she might as well be miles away. She was untouchable. She was radioactive. She was...

Reaching for his drink.

She leaned back, tossed the remaining whiskey sour down

her throat, and stood, placing the glass on the table. "No tricks," she said. "I'm not that kind of girl. But I do have a plan. And I need you to help me with it."

Symon was staring at her, then he shrugged. "Ok, I'll play along for now, if it can bring Hawthorn down. What can I do?"

"You and Mayher have been requesting shipping and air freight manifests."

"How did you..." he stopped himself. Of *course* she knew.

"I think they're keeping what I need on paper somewhere."

"Paper," Symon smirked. "Your kryptonite."

"Exactly," she smiled. "So I need you to digitize everything you find."

"And send it where?" Symon asked.

She laughed. "Eric... come on."

He shook his head. "Right. What was I thinking? Ok, I'll call Mayher and have her get that going, starting tonight."

Kayne nodded. She looked past Symon, motioning for the bartender who approached to ask what they needed. She looked down to Symon. "I'm sorry, I don't know what you ordered," she said, motioning to his empty glass.

Symon nodded and turned to the bartender, telling him what he wanted.

When he turned back, Kayne was gone.

"When did I become Commissioner Gordon?" Symon said, scanning the room to see if he could spot Kayne's red dress and blonde hair. Knowing Kayne, she'd probably torn away the outfit and pulled the wig off, transforming completely just seconds after Symon turned his head.

She's good at this part, Symon thought. *Escaping. Running. Hiding.*

Was she capable of leaving that behind? Coming in from the cold? Could she walk away from this life, now that she'd been a part of it for so long?

Joining Historic Crimes would mean shifting the way she did things. She'd have to trade some autonomy for a more legitimized freedom. She'd trade some liberty to stop the ongoing hunt.

Could Alex Kayne, super fugitive, really become Alex Kayne, agent on a leash?

The bartender placed a freshly poured whiskey sour on the bar, and Symon thanked him, paid and tipped him, and then left the drink sitting there as he rose and left.

He had work to do.

He was officially back on the clock.

CHAPTER TWENTY

Alex ran optical character recognition over all of Mayher's scans of paper shipping manifests and transport logs. A great deal of this was handwritten information, from people who were less than proficient with the English language. This made digital translation dicey. It took a boost from QuIEK to get the accuracy up to 100 percent, but even with that it still took some time to get the whole thing translated.

Now Alex pored over the logs, running relevancy searches, scanning and reading, looking for something—*anything*—that she could use against Hawthorn.

These manifests represented the best chance they had at nailing the Congressman.

For a start, the FBI had initiated this search, without her direct involvement. She might be giving it an assist, but that information need never be revealed. If she delivered a digitized version of these paper manifests to Symon and Mayher, along with notes on any anomalies she found, it would be easy enough for any judge to assume the FBI had used its own resources to gather this data.

They had, after all. Mayher had scanned these paper manifests and, well, Alex was kind of an FBI resource, wasn't she?

It did help a lot, however, that Mayher had done all the legwork in getting this stuff pulled together.

Alex had to admire Mayher for her work—she really was a good agent. She paid attention to the details, and she was thorough. But more than that, Mayher really seemed to *care*. The people she was helping remained *people* to her, judging by the notes Mayher kept and the reports she filed. Alex could see it in every syllable. Mayher had a passion for ensuring that people were never objectified.

She always used their names, for one. It was rarely "the victim" or some other euphemism or overly clinical term. Mayher seemed to go out of her way to make sure she kept the name with the individual, from start to end. Alex liked that.

Mayher's detailed notes also gave Alex some shortcuts in scouring the manifest for useful data. For a start, she could eliminate a large chunk of irrelevant data thanks to Mayher tracking down date ranges and correlating the shipping manifests and the inventory logs at Jason's secret warehouse. This gave Alex a complete list of dates already cross-referenced to existing data. Half the work done, right there.

But there were gaps, mostly due to inconsistencies in how various workers tracked incoming and outgoing shipments. QuIEK was helping to fill in some of those gaps, applying AI-determined relevancy scores to the information as it was translated from handwriting to digital characters. Anything that didn't fit the criteria Alex had specified got sifted. But as the matrix of data grew, and the relevancy web expanded, connections would sometimes be made that brought what might otherwise be "irrelevant" data back into the mix, while eliminating rabbit trails that led nowhere.

It was complex, and took time, even for QuIEK. But it cut hours or even days off of the search.

To narrow things down even further, Alex started focusing only on shipments that had arrived from Russia and surrounding regions. This seemed like a good way to get the number of entries down. At first.

It turned out there were too many to get her head around.

She'd had no idea how prolific import and export had been between the US and Russia. Gauging by these shipping records alone, there were hundreds of incoming flights per day containing cargo from Russia, and a nearly equal amount of cargo by boat. There was a constant flow of materials, going in and out of the port, by the hour.

Too much info, with too much overlap. It was no wonder an operation like this could exist, unnoticed, for so long.

She was going to have to narrow this down further.

QuIEK could help with this as well, to a degree. Alex set it to the task of cross-referencing all the logs with the Hawk & Dove inventory, and in just a moment she had things down to a more comfortable and manageable level. Still, there were thousands of data points to consider.

Hawk & Dove got shipments from all over the globe, and considering that the warehouse was a front for running drugs and weapons, this made sense. Inventory like that wouldn't have a single point of origin. It was kind of the point of smuggling. This stuff would be routed to come in from all over the world. There were shipments representing just about every country on the planet.

But the shipments from Russia were what interested Alex the most, for the moment. She eliminated everything else, narrowing the results down to a few hundred.

Better.

Looking into these, it was clear there was something else

going on, even beyond the other illegal activities that Jason had been into. At a level of meta so deep it would give Christopher Nolan an *Inception* headache, something was happening off of the *off-the-books* books. It went deep, and it was a crazy amount of detail to sort through.

The manifests for each shipment were all over the place, with booze being a part of it. None of that booze was going to Hawk & Dove, however. Not booze from Russia, at any rate.

She dug in and discovered that there were cargo containers coming into the Port of Chicago that were strictly "contents unknown." This wasn't unusual—a lot of cargo came through the port that was either unidentified or only vaguely described. It was kind of alarming to think about.

There could have been *anything* in those containers.

According to the manifests, each container was about 40 foot long, and eight foot wide by ten foot tall. That was a lot of space, when you really thought about it. Anything could be in there.

Or any*one*.

Alex had been mentally dancing around this ever since she'd liberated Natalia from Hawthorn's estate, but it was time to admit what she was really looking for—she was pretty sure Jason Hawthorn was importing more than drugs and guns.

He was running a human trafficking operation.

It made sense, with Jason's appetites and proclivity for incapacitated women, he was bound to have connected with other perverted monsters in the world. A community of monsters—and a market for what Jason could deliver.

He certainly had the means. With his father's money and connections, not to mention links to the mafia, Jason had a direct tap into a world of power, money, and influence. He also had some business savvy, and an eye for the sorts of businesses that were high personal risk, but even higher financial gain.

Drugs were an evergreen business. Weapons could make big cash, fast. But *people*... selling people was where the real money was at.

Alex wanted to vomit.

The deeper she dug into this, the more Jason Hawthorn looked like human waste. And the less she regretted having to kill him.

She wished she really believed that, though.

Every death was a stain on her, even Jason's. Even the two Russians who were clearly intending to kill *her*. Killing people was not a casual thing, not something she wanted to get used to, even if it was necessary. Even if it was *deserved*.

But if it *was* necessary, maybe it was better that someone who was reluctant to do it was the one pulling the trigger?

A flimsy justification. And no salve whatsoever to the wounds in her soul. But it was enough of a useful fiction to let her shift away from dwelling on the deaths she'd caused. Enough to let her sleep at night. Most nights.

Alex checked Mayher's and Symon's notes from their interview with Natalia. The poor girl had a vague recollection of the date she was abducted, and Alex used this to narrow down the records even further. It took a minute, but she was able to track a shipment from Russia to the Port of Chicago, and from there to the Hawk & Dove warehouse, all under a single manifest number.

A mistake, she was sure. It was too much of a direct line, from A to B, and Alex was certain that someone had screwed up. In her favor, at least.

She was absolutely certain that Natalia had been in that shipment.

But she wouldn't have been alone. It was too big, too much wasted space for just one girl.

More girls would have been in that container, Alex was

certain. More human lives would have been snatched and traded for money.

And if there was one container, there would be others.

Alex sat away from her laptop, thinking, running through the math in her head.

Jason Hawthorn had been dead for nearly a week now.

A sudden thought occurred to her, followed by a twisted dread.

She started sifting through the records again, looking for specific details, making intuitive leaps.

She found it.

A container, arriving from Russia, to be picked up by the transport service used by Hawk & Dove.

She looked into that service now, using QuIEK to speed things along.

It was a subsidiary—a second-tier business, owned and operated by Russo Waste Management. The service made deliveries from the port to various businesses all over the greater Chicago area.

But that transport would be moved only when the service was told to pick it up—no order, no pickup. And with Jason dead and Salvatore Russo in prison...

Alex bolted from her chair, grabbing her things. She started making plans as she moved, scanning the port using QuIEK from her phone. She brought up any cameras she could find and started mapping a route even as she called a car to pick her up a few blocks away from the AirBnB. She'd run to it, skipping the usual caution.

There was no time left to waste.

After a flat-out sprint in the street she arrived, huffing and panting, at the pickup spot just as the Uber was pulling in. As she climbed inside, she sent a text to Symon, along with all the information she'd just gathered. She needed him to see it, and *now*, so she had QuIEK force his and Mayher's phones to ring and buzz continuously until one of them finally opened the message app.

Get to the port NOW! I think there may be a container filled with girls there! Bring EMS!

She included addresses, shipping info, and anything else she could find.

And there were prayers. Lots of prayers.

She hoped to God that whoever was in there was still alive.

CHAPTER TWENTY-ONE

THE PORT WAS DARK, and might have been pitch black if not for the irregularly staggered pools of halogen lamps, and what little ambient light could be seen from the city itself. Alex clung close to the corrugated walls of the warehouses and shipping containers, staying to the shadows as she moved closer to the slip that was her target. She watched for signs of anyone else— dock workers or the FBI. Or maybe someone worse.

This was dangerous. Maybe stupid. She was completely exposed here and had no proper plan of escape. Not her usual MO. She had rushed this, once she realized the danger, and that meant being in danger herself.

But if her hunch was right, there wasn't a second to waste. It might already be too late.

She found the slip after a moment, and lingered back, watching, wasting precious moments out of a sense of caution, berating herself for it the whole time.

She had a decision to make—play cautious or be willing to sacrifice herself, in the hopes of saving lives.

She had alerted Agent Symon before coming here. It

occurred to her that if he really was set on catching her, this would be the perfect time. He could swoop in and have her in cuffs and still be able to save whoever might be in that cargo container.

Maybe that was for the best.

He was right, after all. If Alex were in custody, the FBI could use all the evidence she'd given them to take Hawthorn down. It would be easy enough to claim that it had all come as part of the arrest. She could save the day and stop the bad guy by sacrificing herself. This could be her chance to do that.

She shook her head.

If it came to that, she would. She'd rather be free, rather keep going, to help more people. Maybe she was being selfish— it *felt* selfish. But it was her sense of mission and purpose that kept her from just giving it up, when the odds were against her, and that didn't change just because turning herself in was the easy button for justice.

Putting herself here, knowing the FBI were on their way, it was a big risk.

Doesn't matter, she thought.

It just didn't matter.

If Symon took advantage of this scenario to bring her down, anyone in that container would still be saved. Investigating how they got there would produce the same trail Alex had followed. It should... *should*... move the FBI closer to bringing down Hawthorn, at least for this. It was worth the risk. And she had taken the gamble because she couldn't be sure there was any time to waste.

It was worth it, she kept reminding herself. If this was the end, it was worth it.

She moved.

It meant stepping into the light, being visible, but there was no turning back now. She rushed over the wooden planks of the docks, her feet rapping loudly, echoing from the water below, from the canyon of cargo containers and metal buildings around her. When she reached the container she was after, she stopped, looking it up and down.

It was one of hundreds, but she had the numbers for this one memorized. She went straight to it.

There was a padlock on the handle, and she looked around for something she could use to get past it. She found a piece of rebar, and wedged this into the lock, leaning all of her weight into it. She bounced a few times, and the lock gave way suddenly, sending her sprawling to the ground.

She got to her feet, dusting herself off, and then gripped the rebar like a weapon as she unlatched the door of the container and swung it open with a loud creak.

Light poured in from the street lamp, and Alex stared inside the darkened container. She heard a cough, and the sound of crying. A smell wafted out of the container, making her cringe and gag.

She recognized that smell. An awful, ugly smell.

The smell of death and decay.

"Hello?" she asked. Then shook her head. *What's the word?*

She struggled to remember what rudimentary Russian she could, then said, *"Privet?"*

There was no response but the continued soft crying. "I'm... I'm here to help," she said.

But she had no idea how to do that. She wasn't sure what to do at all. She'd spent the past two years doing everything she could to help people who were helpless, and now she stood looking into the darkened maw of the cargo container, wondering what she could possibly do.

"Kayne," a voice said from behind her.

She turned to see agents Symon and Mayher, weapons drawn.

Drawn on *her.*

Guess he decided to kill two birds after all.

It didn't matter. The realization of that came on her like warm bath water. *It doesn't matter,* she thought.

All that mattered was that the people in this container were safe. She might be buried for life, in some government-guarded hole in the middle of God-knew-where, but at least she'd know that she did this. She saved Natalia, and she saved whoever was in this container. If that was the end result of her life's work, it was more than enough. She could live with that. Even if living with it meant she was a prisoner for the rest of her life.

Kenneth Hebert might still be screwed, though.

That thought ate at her. Failing Hebert—it was her only real regret. Between that and the lives she'd taken, she was in for some long, sleepless nights, wherever she ended up.

Maybe Symon and Mayher could find a way to exonerate him, through all of this. A faint hope, but if she were going to prison, she'd take any hope she could get.

Mayher clicked on a flashlight, illuminating the interior of the container. It was all Alex could do to keep from screaming.

There were dozens of girls inside, pressed against the far end of the container, soiled and hugging each other. They looked dazed, exhausted. Alex figured most of them might still be drugged, or at least feeling the lingering effects of the drugs, depending on what was used in their abduction.

Some girls were completely immobile, and Alex knew why, even as her brain tried to go back to being naively confused by it. It was too late. She'd already eaten that particular fruit of knowledge. The evil was evident.

The smell, the stillness, the pallor of skin...

Symon picked his phone out of his pocket and spoke to someone on the other end. He hung up and looked at Mayher. "Ten minutes."

Mayher nodded.

Symon turned to Alex. "You'd better leave."

Alex heard him, but stared, blinking. She glanced at Mayher, who was avoiding eye contact.

"This..." Alex started. "Look, Eric, I'm ok. It's ok. I'm busted. I get it."

"Kayne..." Symon started, then shook his head. "Alex... there's a lot more happening here than I can deal with at one time. We all know you have some super organized escape route. A zip line to a speed boat or a catapult or something. You'll wiggle out at the last second. I'd rather you just left now, instead of making me look like an idiot when my team gets here."

Alex blinked again, shaking her head. She opened her mouth to say something, but Mayher interrupted. "Kayne, go."

Alex looked at her, then back to Symon, and then sprinted away without another word.

She took to a dead run until she was deep enough in the shadows that she thought she could safely turn around. She inspected the spot where she was hiding, and saw a ladder mounted to the wall of one of the warehouses nearby. She scaled this, climbing quickly until she reached the top. From her new perch she could see Agents Symon and Mayher helping the young girls out and onto the pier. In a few minutes a parade of police and FBI vehicles arrived, red and blue lights flashing, reflecting from the water and illuminating the buildings in a nightmarish disco pulse. Emergency personnel flooded the scene, raced to the girls, guided them to seated positions.

Some entered the container, their movements slow, cautious. Their faces covered, to guard against the smell.

Alex watched, taking in every detail, wishing she could be down there, helping. She felt powerless. Here, on the roof of a warehouse, staring out over the pulsing light show of emergency vehicles, the dance of rescue workers and police and FBI agents, she felt like a coward.

She would run, because Eric had told her to run. Because Agent Mayher had told her to.

But it felt like cowardice.

When she felt things were handled, she raced away from the scene, hopping the gap to the next rooftop and taking a ladder on the opposite side to get to the ground.

She found a safe spot to spend time arranging her usual array of rides to get home. She engaged Smokescreen to take over every local network she could find and let QuIEK erase her from all the local security footage.

As she made her circuitous route home, switching cars often, she thought about what had happened tonight.

What did it mean that Symon and Mayher had let her go?

It was out of character for both of them.

But it was a second chance, and Alex was going to take it. She took out her phone, making arrangements for the data to go to the right places. A lot of this had already been delivered to Agent Symon—the data pulled from the shipping manifests would be enough for him to justify the last-minute rush to the shipping container. And it would be easy enough to link that to the Hawk & Dove warehouse.

Jason Hawthorn's guilt would be established. Dead or not, there was that, at least. And once that story went public, it might be a black eye to Congressman Hawthorn, causing some headaches as he was forced to talk to reporters and face the public. A ding in his reputation.

But it wasn't enough.

Hawthorn and his attorneys would spin it, twist things, make it look like a frame-up, or even throw Jason under the bus while the senior Hawthorn disavowed any knowledge of his son's illicit business. With the right spin, Hawthorn could come out of this smelling like a rose.

No, none of this would be enough to set things right for Kenneth Hebert. None of it would do a thing to bring justice down on Anthony Hawthorn.

It was time to take drastic measures.

"You're sure that was a good idea?" Mayher asked.

"You're not?" Symon replied, watching her.

Mayher shook her head, shrugged, then said, "It was. I think Kayne may be the key to bringing Hawthorn down for this." She motioned toward the cargo container, where dozens of girls had been liberated from their hellish prison. Paramedics were treating them, giving them water and medication. They were being carted away to the hospital a few at a time.

The dead were being brought out as well.

Seeing this, knowing that the Congressman was at least partially responsible for it, made the decision to let Kayne run an easy one.

"I think you're right," Symon said quietly.

"And what about us?" Mayher asked. "What do we do now?"

Symon opened his mouth to speak, then closed it again. He shook his head. "For now, we follow this case. Go where it leads us. We have enough threads to link all of this back to the Hawk & Dove, and to Jason Hawthorn. It might not be enough to implicate his old man, but with Natalia's testimony..." He shrugged, shaking his head. "Maybe."

Mayher nodded. "Maybe."

Symon watched her face for a moment, as she stared after the girls being treated and cared for by paramedics. So far, there were four dead—dehydration seemed the most likely culprit. It was hard to say until the autopsy reports came back.

Symon shook his head and turned away, feeling sick. Feeling angry.

No... feeling *enraged*.

Anthony Hawthorn was a US Congressman. His son was clearly a monster, but Hawthorn was covering for him, and apparently had been for years.

For what? Political ambition? Preserving his reputation? Keeping himself in office?

Didn't that make Hawthorn the bigger monster?

Symon and Mayher communicated with the team on site, gave instructions, and made their way back to the rental car. There was more work to be done.

If they couldn't get a warrant to search Hawthorn's house over Natalia's abduction and imprisonment, maybe they could get one by linking Jason Hawthorn to this atrocity. It was the best shot they had.

Symon got on the phone to the District Attorney, followed by a judge. Getting the "yes" took a lot of convincing—more than it should have, in Symon's opinion. And in the end, it all hinged on evidence that had been handed to Symon and Mayher by Alex Kayne.

Shaky ground. Thin ice. Very thin.

It was all they had, and it could fall apart any second. But until then, they had their warrant.

Lucky for them Jason Hawthorn—drug dealer, gun smuggler, human trafficker—still lived at home with Daddy.

CHAPTER TWENTY-TWO

"MY CLIENT WILL COOPERATE FULLY with the letter of the warrant."

Hawthorn stood well behind a wall of attorneys, as well as a couple of USCP officers, remaining silent. Which, Symon mused, was his right. Hopefully he'd have the chance to read that right to the Congressman soon.

"Good," Symon replied.

"And according to the warrant," the attorney continued, "you are to be given full access to Jason Hawthorn's legal residence."

Symon didn't like the sound of this.

"If you will follow us," the attorney continued, leaving through the front door of Hawthorn's home, with an entire team of lawyers in tow.

Symon exchanged a glance with Congressman Hawthorn, who gave only the slightest smirk before turning to retreat deeper into his home. The USCP officers took up position outside of the door the Congressman passed through, making it clear that the FBI agents would not be gaining access.

Dammit, Symon thought.

They'd been had.

It was clear that Symon and Mayher and their agents would only be given access to the specific residence that Jason Hawthorn had occupied—which turned out to be a guest house elsewhere on the property. Symon was whispering with Mayher, who was on the phone with the DA.

She shook her head. "The place has its own address," Mayher said. "He was essentially a tenant. We can search his home and the immediate property surrounding it, but none of the outbuildings, and definitely not Hawthorn's main estate."

Symon cursed under his breath and tried not to notice the lead attorney's obvious smirk.

They were led to Jason Hawthorns house, which occupied a corner of the Hawthorn estate. It was completely separate from any other part of the property, with its own low brick fence surrounding an Olympic-sized swimming pool. The house was small in comparison to Hawthorn's main home, but would still be considered palatial by most standards, sprawling over most of an acre. It was a two-story, modern-style building that had to contain at least a dozen rooms and living spaces.

Meaning that though this was not the house they needed to search, it was still going to take the better part of the day to search it. And it was going to be a fruitless search, Symon was sure. Everything they were after was in Hawthorn's main house, which was off limits. The Congressman and his attorneys had pulled a fast one.

Despite that, and despite knowing that real, hard evidence was still in the Congressman's home, this was the hand Symon and his people had been dealt. There was nothing to do for it but to get started.

When eating a toad, it was best to start head first.

Symon directed agents to scour the place from top to

bottom. "I want DNA samples, fingerprints, anything you can find. Bring me every scrap of paper and ever stray hair in this place. Find any video feeds, laptops, mobile phones, anything and everything."

"Problem," Mayher said, approaching with one of the tech guys. "There were obviously cameras and a monitoring system here, but they're gone."

"Cables were ripped right out of the walls," the tech said. "We found a server rack in one of the closets, and it's been stripped clean. Sheetrock has been ripped down and there's no trace of cables left in the wall."

Symon looked angrily at the lead attorney. "Your client is interfering with a federal investigation."

"My client had the home stripped and cleaned days ago, well before your warrant was issued," the attorney sniffed derisively. "Before this attempt to railroad him and defame his son was even started. There's no law against cleaning out a property my client owns, especially since there was no open investigation at that time."

Symon opened his mouth to reply, but gave it up. This was useless. They would be right, at least according to the letter of the law. They had this all taken care of, scrubbed squeaky clean. Every button buttoned, every thread tied.

His team wouldn't find a single thing here that could be tied back to the Congressman.

Hawthorn had won again.

"Agent Symon?"

Symon looked up to see one of the field agents leaning over the stair railing. "We've found something."

Symon shot a quick glance at the attorney, who had a confused expression that he quickly hid.

That fleeting expression was all the hope Symon needed.

They moved upstairs, with Symon in the lead and a passel of attorneys following closely behind.

"We almost overlooked it," the agent said. "But there's a fake wall here. Floor plan shows a closet off of this hallway, so we cut into the wall. This is what we found."

Symon stepped through the neatly cut gap in the drywall, and stood before a glittering array of blinking LEDs, like stepping through a portal into a high-tech Christmas village.

A server rack—jammed top to bottom with hard drives and control boards. Behind it, a line of cables running into a conduit in the wall. Perhaps a line to a video feed?

The real question, and the one that gave Symon a thrill of hope, was *where does that cable lead?*

He turned again, glancing at the lead attorney, who had gone somewhat pale.

His smile widening, Symon turned back to the field agent. "I want everything in here moved to FBI headquarters and cracked open." He took a small flashlight out of his pocket and used it to peer behind the server rack. He traced it along the wall, highlighting the neat bundle of cables that disappeared into the conduit.

"I want that line followed to its source," Symon said. He straightened, and while looking at the lead attorney he spoke to his agent. "I suspect we'll be very interested in where the other end of it turns out to be."

ALEX SCRUBBED hard to get the paint off of her skin. No matter how careful she was, how many painter's suits and tarps she used, she always, somehow, managed to get paint on herself. Always had.

But especially when she was in a hurry.

It had been hours since she'd left the Hawthorn estate, and

several more hours still since she'd managed to painstakingly sneak drywall, tarps, and paint into Jason's little house, along with setting up the server rack crammed full of recordings and data she'd mined from Hawthorn's security feeds. Especially the feed in Jason Hawthorn's little thrill room.

It hadn't been easy, and she'd been working against the clock. She'd had to piggy back on the team Hawthorn had hired to strip the place.

She had realized immediately that it would only be a matter of time before Hawthorn had the place stripped and scrubbed clean. While Symon and Mayher were going through official channels to get their warrant, Alex could see that the Congressman was playing by a less official rule book. The Smokescreen network she'd set in place in his home was still active, and she'd used QuIEK to generate a quick summary of the Congressman's activities. The order to bring in a crew and clean Jason's home was one of the first things she'd found.

The Congressman had someone on the inside, giving him a heads up about the warrant. She'd look into who that was in a bit, but the immediate need was to make sure that the Congressman's ruse failed. She couldn't keep him from diverting Symon's team to Jason's house, and she wouldn't be able to stop the cleaning crew from removing evidence. But she could make sure there was more evidence to find.

The fun part was using QuIEK to alter the cleanup plans a bit. Now, as part of their work, the crew-for-hire was instructed to deliver a crate of materials to the small storage shed behind Jason's home. Stashing it there had helped to conceal it from the hasty inspection by Hawthorn's attorney, when he'd done his pass through to make sure the place was clean.

Alex had used some of her old tricks to gain access to the house, disguising herself as one of the crew and doing some cleaning work herself. It had been easy to blend in—everyone was required to wear a disposable clean suit and mask. No one had bothered to count the number of workers entering or leaving.

Once the crew was done, Alex had ducked into the storage shed, and waited.

The instant the attorney did his walk-thru and left, she started hauling materials into the house.

Getting the cables from Jason's spare closet to the security panel of Hawthorn's estate had been the hardest part, with the most risk. She'd done the bulk of the work beforehand, sneaking a line to the security panel inside Hawthorn's home, piggybacking on the existing lines. It took some work to bridge the gap between Jason's place and the main building, but once it was done, the trail was in place. She ran the remainder of the cable into Jason's house after the cleanup crew left, routing it through an attic access and dropping the line to the closet from above.

From there, it was mostly hoisting, carrying, dry-walling and painting. Then, escaping and spending the better part of a morning scrubbing paint off of her arms and face, waiting for the FBI to show up on Hawthorn's doorstep, to be smugly directed to Jason's place by Hawthorn's team of attorneys.

Alex used QuIEK to tune in on the scene, tapping into various body cams and mobile phones of the agents and lawyers present, stitching together a picture of what was happening. She was able to watch as the FBI cut into the closet, and then again as Agent Symon inspected it. He'd done exactly as she hoped he would and found exactly what she'd intended him to find.

The conduit of cables leaving that closet included a line that led directly to the camera in Natalia's cell. Tracing that would give Symon and the others all they needed to legally enter Hawthorn's residence. And Alex could see that the 4K video feed was still active, the cell was still there. Hawthorn had been rushed and hadn't had time to dismantle and clean his son's perverted little project.

Between that live feed, matching Natalia's description of the room, and the reams of data Alex had crammed on the server hard drives, Hawthorn's attorney's would be powerless to block the FBI from searching the main house.

They had him now. They could link him to all of it now. They'd won.

Except...

It was an instinct, but Alex had the feeling something wasn't right. She trusted that instinct, always. And so, she checked.

The Smokescreen network she'd installed in the Congress-man's home was still feeding video and audio from dozens of sources. She still had the virtual map of the Congressman's home. She ran through it, searching, using QuIEK to run facial and biometric recognition to help her home in on where Hawthorn was, waiting—whether he knew it or not—for the FBI to take him in.

The trouble was, Hawthorn was nowhere to be seen.

She cursed and widened the parameters of her search. QuIEK started looping through the recorded footage now, looking for the last instance of Hawthorn moving around in his home. It took a few seconds, but Alex finally got to the footage of Hawthorn walking away from Symon and his team in the foyer of the home. From there, she was able to trace his path, through the home, through one of his little secret doors, and out to a car waiting for him behind the house.

She cursed again.

Hawthorn climbed into the car and it rolled away, at which point Alex lost track of it. There were no cameras on this side of the house, aside from the one aimed at the drive. Hawthorn's car disappeared into the woods, riding along a winding road that led away from the estate. A back exit, basically.

This footage was nearly half an hour old. Wherever the Congressman was headed, he'd likely gotten there by now. And to find him, Alex had to waste *more* time.

She got things moving. QuIEK was sifting through video feeds along possible routes, looking for the license plate of the car Hawthorn had gotten into.

Too long. It was taking too long. All the confidence Alex had over finally nailing Hawthorn was being spent on anxiety as she wondered what he was up to. What trick had he managed to pull now? He was too smart to think that by just evading the FBI he'd manage to stay out of prison. So what was his plan?

QuIEK found his trail a few miles from the estate, via an ATM camera. From there, Alex watched as the car made its way into Chicago, and then to the facility where Kenneth Hebert was being held.

She felt a cold dread come over her.

She began rapid switching between views, checking in on Hebert first, then back to the Congressman as he emerged from the car. He didn't immediately enter the facility, but instead waited as another car approached.

A black sedan arrived, and two suited men stepped out. Alex recognized one of them—one of Salvatore Russo's men.

The Congressman, now escorted by two mob enforcers, entered the USCP facility.

From within, she saw the Congressman speak with someone on duty, presenting papers. The two enforcers took out what looked to Alex like government IDs—she captured a frame of the video and used QuIEK to zoom in and up the resolution.

The image was grainy but readable.

Forged badges, identifying the two men as official USCP agents.

She sped through the rest of the footage, watching as the Congressman and his two "agents" were shown to Hebert's cell. They retrieved him, putting him in handcuffs and escorting him. out of the facility and into the town car. Both cars pulled away.

Alex raced through footage now, making QuIEk jump ahead using logic routines meant to "guess" the most logical route. Before the AI could suggest a final destination, however, Alex already had it figured out.

They were heading to the Port of Chicago.

The Congressman was planning an escape? Or was he shipping Hebert somewhere? Either way, things were going off the rails, and fast.

There was no time to waste.

Alex huffed a few times, then grabbed her backpack—her bug-out bag. This had everything she'd need for a quick escape. It also had a few other things that might come in handy. Some things she hoped she wouldn't have to use.

One thing in particular that she'd hoped, beyond hope, that she'd never have to use. A thing of nightmares. A thing that was the last of last resorts.

They were in the endgame now.

Whatever came next, she'd need to be ready. She no longer had the luxury of keeping her hands clean.

Hebert's life would depend on what she did next, whether Alex could live with it or not.

CHAPTER TWENTY-THREE

It was a different part of the port, far from where the girls were recovered, which was to be expected. The Congressman would stay away from the spot where the FBI had uncovered evidence that could link him to human trafficking. Especially as the heat was on.

But his resources at the port would be pretty extensive. His reach, his contacts, especially those from the seedier underbelly of Chicago, gave him plenty of options. Even as his kingdom crumbled around him, Congressman Hawthorn still had plenty of power.

Alex had done something she wasn't proud of to get here as quickly as she could. Something that also burned any chance of returning to the AirBnB.

Her neighbor's Suzuki GSX250R had been liberated, in the call of duty.

She'd make up for it with a sizable deposit into his personal bank account, first chance she got.

She really hoped she'd get the chance.

There just hadn't been any time to waste. QuIEK had

managed to isolate Hawthorn's vehicle, and track them to this spot, but there was enough lag that Alex figured she was arriving about 15 minutes after they had. It had been a harrowing ride across the city, cutting through alleys and one-way streets, gunning the motorcycle at top speed to get here as quickly as she had. And it still felt like it might be too late.

She cut the motor as she zipped through the barricade, dodging the swing arm through a narrow gap. No one appeared to be manning the security booth here, which was a blessing.

Her momentum carried her along for a good stretch, straight toward the pier where QuIEK had the car pinged. Before she got too close she braked, kicked the stand down, and left the motorcycle with the keys in the ignition. If it was still here when she came back this way, it might make a nice escape vehicle. She wouldn't count on it, but it was good to keep options in mind.

Padding her way as silently as possible across the pier, ducking behind cargo containers and around the corners of warehouses, she finally spotted the car, and its former occupants.

Kenneth Hebert was cuffed and standing barefoot at the opening of a cargo container. The two mob enforcers Alex recognized from the surveillance footage were on either side of him, each holding an arm. Hawthorn was standing at the edge of the pier, looking out over the water as he talked on a mobile phone.

Alex couldn't hear the conversation from her position, but that didn't keep her from listening in. She popped her wireless earbuds in and used QuIEK to intercept the call.

"...to look like he was killed in a deal gone bad," a male voice on the other side of the phone was saying, as Alex tuned in.

"That's precisely what I'm saying. But it has to go a great

deal deeper. I need paperwork, records. I need something the FBI can discover that not only implicates him in this, but shows that he tried to frame me for it."

"Shouldn't be too tough," the voice said. "We got him on framing your kid once. We can make this look like a revenge thing. What about the girl? Kayne?"

"She's been trouble, but I believe we can use her to our advantage," the Congressman said. "Hebert hired her, but I don't have anything that proves that."

"I can make that happen."

"Good," Hawthorn said. "And I can make sure your re-election happens."

"I appreciate your support, Mr. Congressman."

"It's no trouble, Mr. District Attorney." There was the definite sound of a smile in Hawthorn's voice. It made Alex want to rush him and send him into the lake.

"How does this impact the business?" the DA asked.

"Slows things down considerably. My son complicated this. I should never have let him keep his playthings in the house. But I believe we can recover. What about Russo?"

"He's going to prison. Nothing I can do about that. Not yet. I'm working on it. There's some questionable activity going on with the FBI's evidence, and I think I can tie that to the girl. I can leak some things to your attorneys..."

"*Russo's* attorneys," Hawthorn corrected.

The DA chuckled. "Right. Sorry. I can leak some things that will definitely create reasonable doubt. Stuff I could definitely counter, in any other case, but Russo's team will get... lucky."

"That's what I wanted to hear," Hawthorn replied. "I'm going to be leaving for DC in a couple of hours. The FBI is searching Jason's bungalow, and one of my staff has informed me that they've found something to get them into my home. I had the place scraped clean, but apparently my team missed something. I intend to be difficult to reach until the evidence implicating Detective Hebert goes public."

"Good plan," the DA said. "I should have everything you need before you even board your flight. Where will Hebert's body turn up?"

"I'm going to have him floating near one of the cargo containers. The FBI are already here, nearby. With the paperwork and records you're generating, and the bodies on the scene here, I think it will make all of this quite convincing."

"How many did we lose?"

Alex felt a sick twist in her guts at the question.

How many did we lose?

She was putting it together, and it was horrifying to realize what—no... *who*—the DA was talking about.

She prayed she was wrong, but she dreaded what would be found in that open cargo container.

"Ten total," Hawthorn said, glancing back at the container. "Easily replaced. Plus the four Russians we had Russo's men dump here. Weapons, spent shells, even some papers on one of them. You did an excellent job."

"Practice makes perfect," the DA said.

"Now, let's get the rest done," Hawthorn replied, turning back to the water. "We'll put a few bullets in Hebert, drop him in the lake and be on our way. Get the evidence to the FBI as soon as possible. And make arrangements for an anonymous tip about this site. Shots fired, that sort of thing."

"I'll even have someone give sworn testimony that they saw Hebert get into a tussle with the Russians," the DA replied.

"Good man," Hawthorn said.

They hung up, and Alex felt the sick twist in her guts turn to rage.

He's going to get away with it, she thought. *Again. All of it.*

And Kenneth Hebert will pay the price.

It was too much. Too unfair. Too unjust.

Hawthorn, Jason, Russo, and now the DA—the corruption, the pure evil of all of it was too much to stomach. The thought of ten dead girls in that cargo container...

And Hebert would be next.

In seconds, Alex realized, Hebert would be next.

She sprinted back to the motorcycle, shucking her bug-out pack as she ran. She reached inside, grabbed what she needed, checked it, and then hopped on to the motorcycle.

The time for stealth was over.

The time for hesitation was gone.

She knew, once she used this thing, there was no going back. Not for her.

This was a choice she'd hoped she'd never have to make.

She held her phone near her mouth and said "Swordfish" before shoving the phone back into her pocket. Then she started the motorcycle's engine, gunning it loudly and repeatedly before kicking the stand up and jetting in the direction of the cargo container.

She had not gone unnoticed.

The two mafia enforcers had stepped away from Hebert, their weapons out and ready, each drawing a bead on her as she approached. Hawthorn, she noticed, hurriedly sprinted for the car, which sped away from the scene even before he'd managed to close the door.

There was the sound of gunfire, and Alex ducked low on the motorcycle. The engine drowned out every sound after that, and she had no idea if they were still firing at her or not.

But she was definitely firing at them.

The Glock 18 in her hand had been a special order. They were tough to get—primarily because they were a full-automatic pistol. The Glock could fire 1,200 rounds per minute, which meant that even with the extended 100-round drum she'd procured for this one, she could easily be out of bullets in a blink. Accuracy was less important when you could sweep 100 rounds across a small space, though, so that was an advantage.

The trouble was Hebert.

She could see that he'd turned and ducked behind the outside edge of the cargo container, which meant he would be out of the line of fire. The 9mm rounds in the Glock wouldn't be able to penetrate the quarter-inch steel of the container, so he should be safe.

She couldn't say the same for the two mafia guys.

As bullets pinged the tank and frame of the motorbike, one grazing Alex's leg in a searing stripe, she raised the Glock and its drum, took general aim, and let loose a stream hell on the men before her.

She braked, skidding the bike sideways while keeping her aim fairly level as she merely swept her arm across her field of view.

The 100 rounds evacuated the Glock in half a second.

When they were gone, all Alex could see was smoke wafting from the barrel. All she could hear was the now idling motorcycle.

The smoke shifted and moved in a breeze from the lake, and after a moment the air cleared enough for her to see the carnage she'd brought.

The two enforcers had gone down like grain sacks, their own weapons falling beside them.

Both were still.

The only movement came from the water, the light swaying pulse of light reflected from the port.

Lucky shots. There weren't really any other kind, in a scenario such as this. But luck or not, these men were dead.

The motorcycle died as well, the result of its motor taking hits that damaged the inner workings. Alex rose to her feet, and winced, putting a palm on her injured leg. She drew away blood, and the stinging told her this was a scarring wound.

As she looked at the bodies on the ground before her, she knew the scar would run deep.

She limped away from the bike, the Glock leveled at the two enforcers even though it was dramatically empty. She was hoping she could bluff them, if it turned out they were still alive after all.

But there was no need. Both were dead. Multiple wounds. Blood in pools that spread like a blight over the ground.

She kicked at the bodies to be sure, then stooped to pick up one of their weapons. She rifled through each of their pockets as well, until she found a set of handcuff keys.

"Kenneth," she said. "It's ok. It's me. Alex Kayne."

There was no sound, and Alex worried for a moment. "Kenneth, we have to get you out of here. They're trying to frame you for... for this. For all of this."

"I heard," Hebert's voice said from behind cover. He stepped from around the side of the cargo container, looking down at the two enforcers, then back to her. His expression was unreadable. "The FBI said you were a fugitive."

Alex studied him, then nodded. "That's true."

There was a pause. Silence. "Did you do it? Whatever it is they accused you of?"

She shook her head. "No. I was framed. Just like you."

Another pause. Then, Hebert nodded. He stepped forward, holding out his hands so Alex could uncuff him. He then stooped and pulled a shoe from one of the bodies at his feet. He held it against his bare foot. "Close enough," he said, pulling on the shoe and then grabbing the other one. He also picked up the other enforcer's weapon, checked it, and chambered a round.

Alex turned away from him, stepping to the edge of the cargo container. Its doors were wide open. She took out her phone and used the flashlight to scan the inside.

She regretted it immediately.

There was nothing to see her but death. Horrid, wretched death—an unspeakable offense rounding off a series of unspeakable offenses.

Ten girls. Ten lives. Ten nightmares to cling to Alex for the rest of her days.

"They shot them when we got here," Hebert said from behind her, his tone somber but resolute.

"I couldn't save them," Alex whispered. "I didn't even know they were here."

"You couldn't save them," Hebert repeated. "But that isn't your fault. This is Anthony Hawthorn. And he's going to get away with it."

Alex turned on him. "No," she said, her voice a razors edge of steel. "He's not."

Hebert shrugged. "He's got the money, the power, the connections. I figure he'll pin all this on me. Only reason I can think of for bringing me here. So how do you think you'll stop him?"

"He's going back to DC tonight," Alex said. "Or so he thinks. I can make sure his plane never leaves the ground."

"Neat trick," Hebert said. "Doesn't change much."

"Depends," Alex said.

"On what?"

"You like swordfish?"

CHAPTER TWENTY-FOUR

THE PLANE WAS JUST STARTING its taxi down the runway when a swarm of government vehicles surrounded it. Pulsing blue, red, and white lights reflected from every surface. Loudspeakers demanded that the plane shut down its engines and open its doors.

A similar order was being given over the radio.

Symon's favorite part was how he'd ordered everyone to use the Congressman's name repeatedly in the orders.

As their car pulled up to the organized chaos, Symon stepped out from and walked toward the plane, followed closely by Mayher. He already had his badge and his weapon out and ready. Strictly speaking, they weren't necessary. But he was enjoying this, and wanted to play things to the hilt.

As the door of the private jet opened, tilting toward the ground to form a set of steps, one of Hawthorn's aides emerged, hands visible. He was ordered to step down, and once he reached the ground, he was roughly patted down by armed agents wearing gear emblazoned with the bright yellow FBI logo.

"Congressman Hawthorn d-demands to speak to the USCP," the aide said, his voice a bit shaky.

Symon made a scoffing noise, and then mounted the steps, taking them two at a time before barging into the interior of the jet. His badge and gun were raised. He expected no trouble and encountered none. The Congressman, along with two more aides, sat in the plush leather seats of the aircraft. Hawthorn looked casual, while his aides seemed terrified.

"Congressman Anthony Hawthorn," Symon said. "You are under arrest, and will be charged with human trafficking and multiple counts of murder, not to mention a half dozen other crimes we're still cataloging."

"Preposterous," the Congressman said, not bothering to even rise from his seat.

Symon smiled as two of his agents pushed past to lift the Congressman by his arms and cuff him.

"You've run out of roadblocks," Symon said. "And allies. The DA just confessed and turned over recordings of your phone call this evening. We have you on audio outlining your plan to frame Kenneth Hebert for your crimes, not to mention your plans to murder him. And we have you confessing to the murder of ten girls and four Russian citizens. Your words, Congressman. Looks like you get to hang by them."

The Congressman's face went white, and his mouth opened slightly, as if he were about to speak. Then, apparently thinking better of it, he simply said, "I would like to speak to my attorney."

"Happy to arrange it," Symon smiled. "Though you may want to hire a new one. Yours has been implicated in all of this as well, thanks to the DA. We have people picking up half your legal team as we speak."

Hawthorn said nothing, but was escorted from the plane just as Mayher came to stand beside Symon.

He couldn't help himself. He was grinning by the time the plane was cleared.

"What do we figure made the DA flip?" Mayher asked.

Symon shook his head. "No idea."

Which was not, strictly speaking, a true statement.

Symon did have a pretty good idea.

When he'd gotten the automated message from Kayne, along with recordings and details showing what had happened at the docks, and what Hawthorn's plans were, he'd figured it would be another round of "can't use that." But when he'd gotten the call from the DA, everything changed.

The man had been contacted anonymously and given explicit instructions.

"I'm supposed to say the word 'swordfish,'" he'd said miserably. "And then give you a full confession."

Which was exactly what he did.

With the plane cleared, including Hawthorn's aides and the pilot, the FBI swept in to search the entire craft. Symon and Mayher left, stepping down to the tarmac.

The Congressman had been read his rights, just as Symon had hoped, and had been placed in the back of a car, his hands cuffed behind him. Symon watched as the car carrying the Congressman pulled away, with several police cars in escort.

He turned, looking at the plane, and shook his head.

This was down to the wire. They'd gotten here just in time, but it was close. Hawthorn, always as slick as Teflon, had finally been brought down.

Thanks again to Alex Kayne.

He was still smiling as he slipped behind the wheel of the rental car, and he and Mayher left the scene. There would be paperwork for days, that was for sure. There would be inquiries and investigations and an endless number of interrogations.

This wasn't quite over, by a stretch.

But it was over, all the same.

They pulled away, driving into the Chicago night, leaving behind a carnival of flashing lights.

EPILOGUE

It was a media blitz, and things did not look good for Congressman Hawthorn.

Which, Alex figured, was almost the best part. It was high up there, anyway, following as a close second to the redemption of Kenneth Hebert.

The Congressman was facing charges and implications for everything from human trafficking to drug running, weapons dealing, and murder. It was absolutely scandalous. Which made it the biggest story for every media outlet in the country. Even the foreign press was having a field day with it all.

Kenneth Hebert—former detective, formerly disgraced, now revealed to have been framed in a web of corruption that went from Chicago's local government to the hallowed halls of Congress—the good man was now being credited with bringing down one of the most vile and corrupt political figures in history.

Alex smiled at every mention, every headline.

Jason Hawthorn's death was looked at with some scrutiny, but Natalia's story of abduction became the center of it all. And the tale that played out in the media was that Jason had been justifiably killed by one of his "toys." It was speculation, supported by leaked footage. But the media had spun things to appear as if Jason had been done in by one of the girls he had abducted.

Which, Alex admitted, was technically true.

It helped a great deal that women were now coming in out of the woodwork to tell their stories about Jason Hawthorn and the intimidation and bribery that had been used to keep them quiet. Many of them were able to identify Hawthorn's attorney as the man who had paid them off and implied that leaving was a better survival strategy than staying.

Things did not look good for anyone with any connection to Anthony Hawthorn. Even his formal political allies had distanced themselves the second the story hit the presses.

Alex's name was never mentioned in any of this, and that was just fine by her. It would only complicate things, and things were complicated enough as it was.

She'd already left Chicago. She wouldn't see Kenneth Hebert again, and she got the impression that was pretty alright with him, as well. Their final goodbye had been when an Uber had dropped him at his place before carrying her on to her next stop. They'd only said a few words to each other after leaving the port, and most of that was Alex, trying to assure him that things were about to be more than alright.

He'd know that now, at least. But it was clear he hadn't trusted her. And she understood why.

She had to admit, it stung a little to know that he distrusted her, even after everything she'd done. But that night, at the docks, he'd given her the benefit of the doubt, if only for a moment. Enough trust that she was able to help him and get him out of there. It meant successfully finishing the job—something she clung to as a personal rule. That would be thanks enough. It had to be.

For now, she was on to the next client, the next case. She would wind her way in the right direction, soon enough. She wasn't actually sure which direction that would be–there were a lot of clients to choose from. A lot of injustice to set right.

But for the moment she was in a cabin at a seasonal resort in Holland, Michigan—a hundred-and-sixty miles north-east of Chicago, with the whole of Lake Michigan between her and the city.

She would take a week or two here, to relax and recoup. It was an idyllic spot, with beaches to wander and groups of tourists to blend into. The resort had a strict rule against alcohol on the property—a rule she was flagrantly breaking as she sipped bourbon from a coffee cup, seated in the cool comfort of her front porch. She let the whiskey warm her and calm her.

It helped.

This was a lovely spot. Most of the people she encountered here were either retirees with small lake houses, or small families taking a last summer holiday before the school year kicked up again. Alex sat on the front porch of the cabin, coffee cup in hand, as a cool breeze blew the sun-dappled leaves of the tree in her little yard. There were sounds of life—kids laughing and playing, old-timers chatting, the distant sound of lawnmowers and leaf blowers.

Good sounds. Living sounds. Healing sounds.

She was reading through the headlines about Hawthorn and Hebert and then finished her bourbon and went back inside the cabin.

It was time for the call.

She had already set up a backdrop of blankets, both to mask her surroundings and to dampen sound from outside. The earbuds she was using had noise cancellation, and they did a fantastic job of filtering ambient noise. Between those and QuIEK, she felt confident she could keep any identifying sounds from being recorded. But for good measure, she played a track of sounds from Boston Harbor, just loud enough that someone with high-end equipment could filter them out and put pursuing agents on a really wrong trail.

That might give Symon and Mayher a nice side trip. A little FBI-funded vacay, courtesy of their top fugitive.

She had a smart tablet on a tripod in front of her chair, and she connected to Symon via video, down to the second for the time they'd agreed to.

His face appeared, and though he was making an effort to look serious and stern, she could tell he was in a good mood.

"Good morning, Eric."

"Good morning, Alex," he replied.

She smiled. "It looks like Hawthorn has been all wrapped up."

"Nice and tight," Symon said. "Thanks to you, of course. Though, officially, you had nothing to do with it, and you need to turn yourself in."

"I'll get right on that," Alex replied. "I know having me come in from the cold is a hot topic these days."

Symon laughed lightly. "It is, actually. Ludlum was in touch with me again."

Alex nodded. "I thought she might be."

"Have you made a decision?"

Alex paused. "I have some questions. But first, I wanted to make sure everything was good. With Hawthorn. With Hebert. With... us."

"Good is kind of a relative term," Symon replied. "But I think so. I do have a question of my own, though."

"Shoot," Alex smiled.

"When you leaked the trail of footage of you leaving Colorado Springs and coming to Chicago, did you have all of this in mind? Was taking down Hawthorn already a plan?"

Alex shook her head, smirking. "Now what makes you think I leaked that to you? Wasn't that just good investigative work on your part? Your crack team of tech guys traced me fair and square."

Symon shook his own head. frowning. "Yeah, we both know that's a lie, Alex. You put them on that trail, gave them the whole thing in a nice, easy package, to bring us here."

"Did I?"

"You did," he said. "I realized it when you met with me in the hotel bar. You said, 'footage doesn't just get out, when I'm involved. It becomes part of a strategy.' I remembered thinking at the time that it was weird, you letting your guard down enough to get caught on video. And worse, to be traced to Chicago with that video. Not like you at all. So when you said that in the bar, it clicked. This was your strategy all along. Get us here, so we would help bring some justice for Hebert. And then again, when you had to kill Jason Hawthorn, in self defense. You leaked the security cam footage. I had our team recheck it. The time stamp was for the next day. You went back and staged that so we'd find the warehouse."

"Sounds awfully elaborate," Alex replied.

"You're an elaborate kind of girl," Symon said.

She smiled and shook her head. "Well, whether I orchestrated anything or not, it all worked out. Hebert is getting compensated, and his name is being cleared. He's gotten a few offers from police forces across the nation. He doesn't really need the work, at this point. There's a very big settlement coming his way. But I think he'll take something. Far from Chicago."

"Good idea," Symon replied. There was a pause, then, "Ok... so what about you? Are *you* going to take the offer?"

She huffed. "Are you?"

He pursed his lips, then nodded. "I am. Both me and Mayher. We're in. Gave Ludlum our answer this morning."

Alex blew out a breath. "Ok," she said, nodding. "That makes a difference. But here's my question: Is QuIEK part of the deal?"

Symon nodded, as if he'd been expecting this. "It is," he said. "Ludlum made it clear that handing over access to QuIEK was the only deal her superiors would accept. You had to know that was going to be the way it would run."

She nodded again. "I knew. And... you know, too."

He was watching her, silent, then nodded. "I do."

"They can't have it, Eric. None of them. No one. Not after everything they've tried. They forget, I can see them. I can look at what they do, what they say, what they want. What they plan."

"And it isn't good?" Symon asked.

"Some of it is," she replied. "Despite all the legitimate conspiracies out there, not everyone in government is onboard with them, or planning some kind of world domination play. Some of them are actually good, decent people, with the best of intentions. And then there are guys like Hawthorn." She shook her head. "Can you imagine what a guy like that would do with QuIEK? This is too big. Too much power. It wouldn't take much for it to be misused, in some pretty horrible ways. I can't risk that, even if it means running forever."

Again Symon contemplated her and ultimately nodded. "I told Ludlum you'd say that. Or... well, something close to it."

"So I guess my answer is no," Alex said.

"You know this means you'll still be hunted. By the FBI. By... by me."

"You?" Alex asked. "Even from Historic Crimes?"

"I'll still be FBI," he shrugged. "Historic Crimes is inter-agency. And when I'm not working cases for them, I still have my regular caseload. You are my regular caseload."

She nodded. Then shrugged. "Well, that's good news, at least."

"I won't stop trying to arrest you, Alex," he said. "It's my job."

"Oh, I know," she replied. "I don't see this as a special favor or anything. I just... I know you. You're a good guy. A good agent. You'll take me in, the second you get the chance. But you aren't doing it blindly, and you aren't doing it for the wrong reasons. You're just out for justice. I get that."

"So you keep running," Symon said.

"I keep running," she replied.

"And you'll keep trying to help people who have fallen through the cracks?" he asked.

"That, too," she smiled.

"Good," he said. "Ludlum said that if you answered that way, I'm supposed to make the next offer."

Alex made a confused expression.

"You're still a fugitive. That won't change, unless you turn over QuIEK. The offer stays on the table, for now. Turn it over, and you're in from the cold. Until then, you're officially a fugitive. But Ludlum has also managed to get you classified as a Confidential Informant."

She blinked. "Oh... ok."

"That means that information you share with us can be used as evidence," Symon said. "There will still be trouble with information obtained illegally, without a warrant. But as long as I don't know exactly *how* you got the info..."

"Got it," Alex said, nodding. "You see nothing, you know nothing."

"Don't abuse this," Symon said. "Cases have fallen apart and bad guys have gone free on flimsier claims than illegal wiretapping or illegal search and seizure. But this means that certain documented evidence can now be on the table. It also means I can officially reach out to you and communicate with you, regarding cases."

She thought about this, then laughed. "So what you're telling me is, I'm basically working for Historic Crimes after all?"

"You can even get paid," he replied. "There's a stipend for CIs. No dental or health benefits, though."

She laughed again. "Fair enough. Donate my paychecks to Agape International Missions. They're working to end human trafficking. After all this... I think I'd like to help them."

He nodded. "I can arrange that."

She smiled. "Good. It sounds like we're going to have a chance to work together. I like that."

"I'll still have to arrest you, if I get to you," he said. "And I'm going to do my damndest to get to you. But... yes. We're sort of working together now."

They chatted for a few minutes more, getting some details straight, making arrangements for regular contact. It wouldn't be that difficult. Alex had essentially already set up the infrastructure for this. QuIEK made it easy to give Symon some contact information that could never be traced back to her. He'd essentially had it all along.

Not much had changed.

Everything had changed.

When she signed off from the call, she slipped back out to the porch. She had refilled her mug, this time with actual coffee, and as the morning started to shift toward noon, she sat and watched the leaves and listened to the sounds of children playing and retirees chatting, and thought about the next client, the next job.

And about Agent Eric Symon, and Director Liz Ludlum, and of course, Historic Crimes.

She had no idea where this would lead, or what would happen from here. She was still on the run, still in danger at all times.

Still hunted.

But for the first time in a very long time, she felt like she could breathe a bit easier. She felt like the purpose she'd chosen for her life—the pursuit of justice for the disenfranchised and helpless—finally that purpose had some official backing. It was like getting validation. She could live with the uncertainty of her life, knowing that someone in some official position knew and understood what she was really doing.

It would be better to be free. It would be better to come in out of the cold.

But she could live with this.

She took a deep breath now, letting it out slowly, and nestled in for a well-deserved rest.

The work would start again soon, and she'd be ready for it.

SYMON CALLED LUDLUM the second his call with Kayne was finished.

"Well?" Ludlum asked, the moment her face appeared on-screen.

"As predicted, QuIEK is off the table. But otherwise, she's in."

Ludlum nodded, smiling lightly. "Good. I wasn't comfortable handing that over."

"Neither was I," Symon said.

"So she's fine with still being a fugitive? Having to stay on the run, being hunted, even while we use her as an asset?"

Symon shrugged. "I think this isn't so different for her, from what she's been doing for the past two years."

Ludlum considered this, then nodded. "Ok. I can see that she's the real deal. She wants to help people, bring real, actual justice. I like that. I respect it." There was a pause, and she shook her head, peering out of the screen like she was viewing a bug close up. "What about you, Eric?"

Symon blinked, then shook his head. "I'm not following," he said.

Ludlum pursed her lips, then asked, "Why are you doing this? Why did you agree to it?"

Symon sighed, leaning back. He rubbed his eyes with one hand, then leaned forward again. "The truth? I'm doing this mostly because I believe her."

"Believe Alex Kayne?" Ludlum asked. "About what?"

"About being innocent," Symon replied. "I believe she was framed, and by some pretty powerful people in our government. I believe she was set up from the start, and I believe that if she's taken into custody, and they can somehow get her to release QuIEK, they'll use that software to do something truly nasty in the world."

"Agent Symon," Ludlum said, a note of caution in her voice, "this is sounding a little like a conflict of interest."

"It isn't," Symon said flatly. "It's self preservation. It's safeguarding my country."

Ludlum thought about this, nodded briefly, then said, "It's about vindicating Alex Kayne."

Symon said nothing.

"I understand," Ludlum said. "I really do. Believe me. There's someone in my life—someone who has more than his share of demons and skeletons."

"You're talking about Dr. Kotler," Symon said.

She nodded. "He's usually at the heart of all the trouble. It'll be interesting to see someone else in that spot, for a change."

They spoke for a few minutes longer, about logistics, about duties and responsibilities, about how Symon would and should handle Alex Kayne.

The conversation ended on a hopeful note, and Symon went away from it thinking he'd made—well, if not a *good* decision, at least it was a decision that shouldn't have any immediate dire repercussions, and not unforeseen complications.

That last bit was purely wishful thinking, he realized.

When it came to Alex Kayne, unforeseen complications would always be part of the deal.

A NOTE AT THE END

As I write this—and indeed as I wrote the final couple of chapters of this book—I am sitting in a pleasant, shaded spot just off of Lake Michigan, at a time of year when the air is cool, the energy is refreshing, and the people surrounding me are mellow and kind.

That last one may have nothing to do with the time of year —I've never been here before. They could always be like this.

In fact, the bulk of this book was written in places similar to this. It was started in the Texas Hill Country, at Buckhorn Lake in Kerrville, Texas. Some parts were written lakeside in Houston, and other parts were written in the shade of trees along the Mississippi, in a soy field in Indiana, and in various picturesque spots in between.

My wife and I live in a van.

It's probably nothing like you're thinking.

The short version of this story is that a few years ago we sold our home and bought an RV. We traveled a bit, but found ourselves tethered to Houston, thanks to Kara's job. Having to leave whatever beautiful spot we found out in the world and hotfoot it back to Houston at a grueling, drive-all-night pace was exhausting, and not at all what we'd had in mind when we'd decided to go full time in an RV. So, reluctantly, we came off of the road for about three years.

Then, about a year ago, we were in the process of buying a house. When the bank asked for a bigger deposit, we paused to consider whether it would be worth it—and to ask a few questions that we hadn't yet considered.

Were we settling? Could we find a better house in a better neighborhood? If we were going to be out-of-pocket even more cash, shouldn't we make triple sure we were getting what we wanted?

And then there was the question—*the* question—which I'll get to in just a second.

We found ourselves uncertain, for the first time since the house-buying process had begun. We went from being in love with the place to wondering if we were making a mistake.

We then did what we often do, when faced with big, scary, grown-up questions: We took a drive.

We call this "dream driving," and it's something we've done our whole marriage. Even before we could afford the kinds of houses we like to look at, we would drive through nice neighborhoods and dream of what it would be like to live there. We'd comment on all the wonderful things we saw, the parks and the quality of the streets, the well-groomed lawns, the shade of trees and the presence of local walking trails. And when we were done exploring one neighborhood, we'd drive to the next.

It was a way to inspire us.

We love road trips, so we would often hop in our vehicle and range out to some place distant, taking a look, thinking about life in this or that place. I like to think of it as "road therapy."

We were doing one of these dream drives, rethinking what

neighborhood we wanted to settle into, when Kara asked *the question.*

"Are we just checking boxes?"

See? I told you I'd get back to it.

"What do you mean?" I replied

"Here. This place. This life. Are we just buying a house because it's what we think we should do? Or do we really *want* to do it? We wanted to travel the country for a few months, live full-time on the road for a bit, while you wrote and published. What happened to that?"

And of course, as we talked it out, we determined that "what happened to that" was pretty simple: We couldn't have things exactly the way we wanted, at the time, so we walked away.

Our mistake was thinking that was the end.

The thing is, we (like everyone else) sometimes fall into the mental trap of believing that the way things are is the way they *are.* As if the life we're living at *this moment* is the only life possible.

Spoiler alert: It isn't.

There's an apocryphal story I hear from time to time, about cooking a roast.

It's usually told in first person—I first heard it from a preacher who was giving a sermon, and he presented it as something he'd learned from his mother, who learned it from his grandmother.

Basically, a child is watching his mother prepare a roast, and as she cooks, she cuts both ends from the roast before putting it in the pan, and cooks those ends separately (or in some stories, throws them away, but that just feels wasteful).

The child asks, "Momma, why do you cut the ends off of the roast before you cook it?"

The mother smiles patiently and says, "It's just the way you cook a roast, sweetie. It's how your grandma taught it to me. It's the way things are done."

This is the sort of answer that isn't quite an answer, and so the young boy saves his question for a time when he's staying with his grandmother. When the day comes, she, too, is preparing a roast, and, as the boy expected, she cuts the ends from it before cooking.

"Granny," the boy asks, "why do you cut the ends off of the roast before you cook it?"

Expecting to hear "That's just the way it's done," the boy was surprised by his Granny's answer.

"Well, my pan isn't wide enough for a whole roast, so I cut the ends off to make it fit."

Isn't that just jaw-dropping?

That's the sort of generational thinking that creates unthinking tradition, rote habits that are passed down throughout an entire lineage until they become unquestioned reality.

This is how lotteries to determined who gets stoned to death get started.

That's a literature joke.

This example of blind tradition, though, is kind of touching and heartwarming in its way, but this kind of thinking can actually be quite dangerous. And at the very least, it can be quite limiting.

The thing is, we do this to ourselves all the time, as a culture and as individuals.

In fact, this is exactly the sort of thing Kara and I were doing when it came to buying a house. We were checking boxes. We were doing what we thought was the next step, even though it was a step in a different direction than we had wanted to travel.

Worse, we were making a pretty big decision based on a bad assumption.

We'd fallen into the habit of thinking that the limitations that applied *before* were limitations *still*. And we were making a big life decision based on that thinking.

Never a good start.

The point here is pretty straightforward: You should occasionally question your thinking, and how you do things. It can open up all kinds of new ways of living.

So what does this have to do with Alex Kayne and *Triggered?*

Not a lot, really. Not directly. It's just that this book was written in that kind of headspace. It was the result of a shift in the dynamics of my thinking, and in my overall perspective. And the result of that shift has been new perspectives, on my life and only work.

I've traveled quite a bit. As an author and as an influencer in the self-publishing industry, I've moved around in the world often, visiting cities worldwide, speaking at conferences, in general getting a taste for different perspectives and local cultures. Sometimes these can be wildly different from what I'm used to. Often, there are usually some striking similarities.

Small town life, for example, is pretty much the same everywhere I go. Having grown up in a small town myself, it makes me feel kind of welcome and comfortable to realize that the people are the same from place to place.

Cities tend to have their own unique flavors, but they can be pretty similar as well. There's a definite undercurrent to life in a city, common from place to place. Multiculturalism, metropolitanism, a confluence of art and music and theater... these are almost universal in cities, and nearly always lacking to a high degree in small towns.

Or... they were.

We learned, while in Kerrville, Texas, that even small towns can have budding art and music scenes. They had their own high-end theater and concert hall, for example, where concerts and art shows and plays were a regular event. Famous musicians played that venue often. It was a scene.

We've been to hundreds of "small towns" now, and it's surprising how many of them have the same general setup. There's more going on in small-town America than would first appear.

And in fact, the closer you look at a place, the more you notice that there are common threads everywhere, a cultural awareness and growth you may not have expected.

But to bring this back around to Alex Kayne and the *Quake Runner* series, it simply comes down to *research*.

Van life (#vanlife if you prefer) is giving Kara and I a chance to see the US up close, from the perspective of "almost insiders." Unlike our huge RV, or the travel trailer we had after that, the van is kind of "urban camouflage" when we're in cities, and is ubiquitous enough that no one really notices it. It's the same in suburban areas. And in rural areas, it's enough of a novelty that people are curious, and ask questions.

Everyone loves the van.

And we love it, too. Because it gives us a chance to range out and explore without having to worry about going back.

We are road trip people. And the best kind of road trip is the one you don't have to cut short to go racing back to home base.

In terms of my fiction, that means that we're out exploring and researching the sorts of environments that my character would explore. We're exposed to the history of interesting places we may never have heard of before. We are in the thick of cultures that people may not even realize *are* cultures, connecting with people who think similar thoughts, but are still different.

Gaining new perspectives is good for everyone, but it's gold for writers.

In terms of Alex Kayne, this life of travel is fuel for more stories. Kayne spends her life on the run, and thus on the road. She moves from place to place trying to remain as invisible as possible. She uses whatever resources are available. She reinvents herself with every new city or town.

That's essentially what Kara and I are doing, too. We're just not as worried about the FBI tracking us down and throwing us in a cell for the rest of our lives.

I mean... not *as* worried.

As I sit under a beautiful oak tree, the sounds of birds and camp life all around me as the sun rises to my right, the cool air bringing with it the ionized energy of the lake, I sip my coffee and smile about where I am and what I'm doing.

I'm blessed. Some would say "privileged," but given that I worked my butt off to get us to this place, and to this way of life, I'll stick with "blessed."

Travel is fuel for storytelling. It is inspiration and energy. It is a window into the uniqueness of humanity, and a door to new ways of thinking and considering the world.

Alex Kayne travels because she must. She's running, trying to stay ahead of those who would take her work and use it for something dreadful and evil.

We travel because we must, as well. We're not running, not trying to stay ahead of anyone or anything. We're just out here looking, exploring, connecting.

We questioned how the roast was cooked, and the result is we get more roast to enjoy. And that includes more books and more stories to tell.

There will be more books. There will be more stories. It's

the end result of this life, to be fueled up and ready for more creativity, more growth.

And our journey includes you, as well.

Thank you for being a part of this journey with us. Kara, our little pup Mini, and I all welcome you and carry you with us.

Happy journey,
Kevin Tumlinson
Holland, Michigan
01 September 2020

KEEP THE ADVENTURE GOING!

GET MORE THRILLS FROM AWARD-WINNING AND BESTSELLING AUTHOR, KEVIN TUMLINSON!

"MOVE OVER, INDIANA JONES"
DAN KOTLER ARCHAEOLOGICAL THRILLERS
AVAILABLE AT KEVINTUMLINSON.COM/BOOKS

FIND YOUR NEXT FAVORITE BOOK AT
KevinTumlinson.com/books

★★★★★ "Half way through I was waiting for Harrison Ford to leap out of the pages!"

—Deanne, Review for *The Coelho Medallion*

★★★★★ "Kevin has crashed onto the action-thriller scene as only an action-thriller author can: with provocative plot lines, unforgettable characters, and enough adrenaline to keep you awake all night."
—Nick Thacker, author of *Mark for Blood*

★★★★★ "Move over Daniel Silva, James Patterson, and Dan Brown."
—Chip Polk, Review for *The Atlantis Riddle*

★★★★★ "Move Over Indiana Jones, there is a New Dr. in Town!"
—Cycletrash, Review for *The Coelho Medallion*

★★★★★ "[Kevin Tumlinson] is what every writer should be—entertaining and thought-provoking."
— Shana Tehan, Press Secretary, U.S. House of Representatives

★★★★★ "I discovered Kevin Tumlinson from The Creative Penn podcast and immediately got his novel, Evergreen. I read it in like 3 seconds. It's the most fast-paced story I've encountered."
—R.D. Holland, Independent Reviewer

★★★★★ "Comparison to Clive Cussler is a natural, though Tumlinson's 'Dan ' is more like Dan Brown's Robert Langdon than Dirk Pitt."
—Amazon Review for *The Coelho Medallion*

FIND YOUR NEXT FAVORITE BOOK AT
KevinTumlinson.com/books

HERE'S HOW TO HELP ME REACH MORE READERS

If you loved this book, you can help me reach more readers with just a few easy acts of kindness.

(1) REVIEW THIS BOOK

Leaving a review for this book is a great way to help other readers find it. Just go to the site where you bought the book, search for the title, and leave a review. It really helps, and I really appreciate it.

(2) SUBSCRIBE TO MY EMAIL LIST

I regularly write a special email to the people on my list, just keeping everyone up to date on what I'm working on. When I announce new book releases, giveaways, or anything else, the people on my list hear about it first. Sometimes, there are special deals I'll *only* give to my list, so it's worth being a part of the crowd.

Join the conversation and get a free ebook, just for signing up! Visit https://www.kevintumlinson.com/joinme.

(3) TELL YOUR FRIENDS

Word of mouth is still the best marketing there is, so I would greatly appreciate it if you'd tell your friends and family about this book, and the others I've written.

You can find a comprehensive list of all of my books at http://kevintumlinson.com/books.

Thanks so much for your help. And thanks for reading.

ABOUT THE AUTHOR

Kevin Tumlinson is an award-winning and bestselling novelist, living in Texas and working in random coffee shops, cafés, and hotel lobbies worldwide. His debut thriller, *The Coelho Medallion*, was a 2016 Shelf Notable Indie award winner.

Kevin grew up in Wild Peach, Texas, where he was raised by his grandparents and given a healthy respect for story telling. He often found himself in trouble in school for writing stories instead of doing his actual assignments.

Kevin's love for history, archaeology, and science has been a tremendous source of material for his writing, feeding his fiction and giving him just the excuse he needs to read the next article, biography, or research paper.

Connect with Kevin:
kevintumlinson.com
kevin@tumlinson.net

facebook.com/jkevintumlinson

twitter.com/kevintumlinson

instagram.com/kevintumlinson

bookbub.com/authors/kevin-tumlinson

ALSO BY KEVIN TUMLINSON

Dan Kotler

The Coelho Medallion

The Atlantis Riddle

The Devil's Interval

The Girl in the Mayan Tomb

The Antarctic Forgery

The Stepping Maze

The God Extinction

The Spanish Papers

The Hidden Persuaders

The Sleeper's War

The God Resurrection

Dan Kotler Short Fiction

The Brass Hall - A Dan Kotler Story

The Jani Sigil - FREE short story from BookHip.com/DBXDHP

Dan Kotler Box Sets

The Book of Lost Things: Dan Kotler, Books 1-3

The Book of Betrayals: Dan Kotler, Books 4-6

The Book of Gods and Kings: Dan Kotler, Books 7-9 (Forthcoming)

Quake Runner: Alex Kayne

Shaken

Triggered

Citadel

Citadel: First Colony

Citadel: Paths in Darkness

Citadel: Children of Light

Citadel: The Value of War

Colony Girl: A Citadel Universe Story

Sawyer Jackson

Sawyer Jackson and the Long Land

Sawyer Jackson and the Shadow Strait

Sawyer Jackson and the White Room

Think Tank

Karner Blue

Zero Tolerance

Nomad

The Lucid — Co-authored with Nick Thacker

Episode 1

Episode 2

Episode 3

Standalone

Evergreen

Shorts & Novellas

Getting Gone

Teresa's Monster

The Three Reasons to Avoid Being Punched in the Face

Tin Man

Two Blocks East

Edge

Zero

Collections & Anthologies

Citadel: Omnibus

Uncanny Divide — With Nick Thacker & Will Flora

Light Years — The Complete Science Fiction Library

Dead of Winter: A Christmas Anthology — With Nick Thacker, Jim Heskett, David Berens, M.P. MacDougall, R.A. McGee, Dusty Sharp & Steven Moore

YA & Middle Grade

Secret of the Diamond Sword — An Alex Kotler Mystery

Wordslinger (Non-Fiction)

30-Day Author: Develop a Daily Writing Habit and Write Your Book In 30 Days (Or Less)

Watch for more at kevintumlinson.com/books